i'm not her

janet gurtler

sourcebooks
fire

Sourcebooks and the colophon are registered trademarks of Sourcebooks, Inc.

Published by Sourcebooks Fire, an imprint of Sourcebooks, Inc.
P.O. Box 4410, Naperville, Illinois 60567-4410
(630) 961-3900
Fax: (630) 961-2168
teenfire.sourcebooks.com

Library of Congress Cataloging-in-Publication data is on file with the publisher.

Printed and bound in the United States of America.

VP 10 9 8 7 6 5

A crowd gathers for the funeral. The church walls seem to strain to accommodate the bodies, but there isn't enough space for everyone. People cram together, squished thigh to thigh in the pews, shoulder to shoulder in aisles. The back is standing room only.

Not surprisingly, I don't hear anyone complain. I hardly hear any sound at all except the occasional whisper, cough, or sniffle. Everyone wears dark colors, even kids who don't usually follow rules or social customs. I guess it's like that when someone young is snatched from the earth. It's wrong on so many levels that thinking about it makes my already sad heart ache even harder.

Dad says parents shouldn't have to bury their children. He says a lost child leaves a hole in the heart of the parents, a hole hacked out with a dull knife. The heart can function with the wound, but it never entirely heals.

chapter one

No matter how much I don't want to care, it's not easy being stranded all alone in the middle of a crowded room, like the ugliest dog at the animal shelter. Kristina shoved me into her shiny red Toyota like she's my fairy godmother, insisting I do the party "for my own good." But other than a few heys and disinterested stares, no one notices that I'm there. Before long, even Kristina forgets about me. Swept up by her friends and admirers, Kristina leaves me bathing in my own flop sweat.

I begin plotting my escape just as a drunk guy plunks down on the couch beside me and leans against me for support. Smoke and alcohol fumes waft off him and he blocks me, pinning me in place. Wrinkling my nose, I elbow him in the side, trying to move him. He hacks up the equivalent of a human fur ball, focuses his eyes on me, and then grins the carefree smile of the intoxicated. He leans closer, giving me an up-close view of the angry red pimples on his shiny skin.

"Hey, Freshie. You're Kristina's little sister aren't you?" He whistles through his teeth. "She's seriously hot."

He's implying that I'm not and, honestly, I'd be okay with his observation if he'd get out of my way. I take a deep breath, but no words form in my mouth. I glare at him but he doesn't notice. His long blondish hair curls up at the edges and in the middle of his face is a big crooked nose that looks like it's been broken or something, but the imperfection kind of works on him. His eyes look like they might have been a great shade of blue before the alcohol consumption hit, but they're pretty much pinkish now.

Folding my arms across my chest, I push hard with my shoulder, but he doesn't budge. Other than the brief pant over my sister, there's no indication he even notices I'm not part of the furniture. I wiggle and push and finally make progress, when he snaps his arm out and grabs mine, pulling me back down. The strength in his arm is deceptive for such a skinny guy.

"What's she like?" Drunk Pimple Guy stares at her, his voice dripping with the kind of reverence people save for the very famous or very beautiful. Far as I know, Kristina isn't famous outside of Great Heights, but even I can't deny she has the beauty part down.

Breathing deep, I try to shake him off but he doesn't let go. Propelled by growing humiliation, I decide to give him some truths. "She burps. Red meat gives her gas and she won't eat anything that contains a carbohydrate. Oh, and she takes medicine to control her acne." I consider recommending the brand to him but no. Not cool. "She also hogs the bathroom and is a slob who treats my mom like her personal maid."

I think it's the most I've ever said to a boy at one time. I don't add that Kristina cries at sad commercials, never mind the blubbering she does during movies, or that when I was nine, she punched a boy who called me ugly and gave him a bloody nose.

He stares at me as if I've grown three horns from my ever-so-ordinary, two-minutes-to-get-ready face. Well, if he didn't want the truth, he shouldn't have asked. After all, as the younger sister of Kristina Smith, I have an in on the lifestyle and personality of the Goddess.

I try to break free again, but he holds on like I'm his security blanket and he's five years old. He grins and his expression changes and he almost looks cute. If he weren't holding me hostage and all.

"You mean she doesn't have a real maid? I heard your old man is loaded."

Please. My mom would never share control of her home with hired help, but I don't tell him that.

He studies my face. "You don't look much like her."

My crooked nose matches Dad's and I also inherited his stupid red hair. Unlike my curvaceous sister, I'd never be mistaken for a pole dancer. People would be more likely to compare me to the pole. DNA is indeed a baffling concept. Thanks for pointing it out, dude.

"Whoa, she can dance," he says, without letting me go.

I'm forced to watch with him as Kristina performs as if she's on a stage, acting like she doesn't know almost every eye in the room is on her.

Kristina continues to grind and shake to the music in her skinny jeans and a tank top seriously helped along by a push-up bra. She gets off on crowd approval, like I get off on watching the guys on *MythBusters* blow up things.

Silence hangs between me and my captor. Well, not exactly silence since a new pop song is vibrating the speakers in the living

3

room, and all around us kids yak and laugh. But there's a definite lull on our couch.

"All righty then."

Just like that Drunk Pimple Guy lets me go and vaults himself off the couch.

"I have a name too," I say under my breath, because of course, he didn't ask. "It's Tess. Rhymes with mess." No one ever asks my name. No one knows that there are jokes trapped inside my head.

I push myself up, even more determined to sneak down the hallway, slip out the back entrance, and escape. I don't care that it's dark outside or even that going home alone will require walking over two miles. And that I hate walking. And the dark.

I start pushing past bodies crowded in the living room. People brush me away like I'm an annoying insect, or their eyes meet mine for a brief second before they look away. Just as the entrance to the kitchen is visible, a hand reaches out and grabs my shirt from behind and pulls. Hard. Kristina latches her free hand on my arm. Damn. She pushes me back into the living room where flocks of freshmen lurk awkwardly in twos and threes. She bops her head and keeps mouthing the words to the song playing, just as well since her voice is not as pretty as her face. I don't brag about it but I'm the one who can sing in our family. She's the one who looks good lip-synching.

Eyes follow us because, after all, she is Kristina. She doesn't loosen her grip on my arm, and shoves me past a group of seniors and the freshies stalking them. Great. Might as well stick a kick-me sign on my butt the way she's dragging me around. Kristina leans in close, making a wincing sound as she pushes us toward an open spot by the dining room table. From the corner of my eye, I catch the art of Robert Bateman and a teeny part of me notes that based on the textured look of the paper and the pigments collected in tiny hollows, it's an original, not a print.

Kristina lets go of me and leans down, rubbing at her knee. "Ouch. My stupid knee," she mumbles. "What are you doing?" she demands in her "I'm the big sister, now listen to me" voice.

"Going home." I stick out my bottom lip for courage. "This is humiliating."

She stops massaging her knee and straightens, glancing off in the direction Drunk Pimple Guy disappeared. "Did Nick make a pass at you or something? I'll kill him. He's such a man-whore."

I shake my head back and forth, mortified by the concept. As if he'd make a pass at me.

"There's lots of cute boys here your own age. You promised to at least try to make friends."

"I already have friends," I mumble, wishing she would try to understand how hard it is for me to talk to people.

"No. You have friend. One. And Melissa is a socially inept, religious freak. You can do better."

"Melissa is a better friend than you'll ever have." Melissa does have her religion thing but it doesn't come between us. Well, except for the time when she told me I wouldn't be going to heaven because I don't go to church.

Anyhow, I'm not about to argue quality versus quantity here, but all Kristina's friends do is giggle a lot and screech OHMYGOD and talk about boys. And take pictures of each other, usually in skimpy clothes. And then post the pictures online.

Kristina sighs. "This is an opportunity to meet *new* people. Not just art freaks or brainiacs from the Honor Society."

"Art is not freaky," I remind her for the millionth time, but it still hasn't registered in her head. She's exactly like our mom. She doesn't understand how important art is to me. Or even that I'm pretty good at it. "And neither are people from the Honor Society," I add, and ignore her huge eye roll.

"You can't leave," she whines. "Come on, Tess. Live it up a little. It's your first high school party. Have fun. I really want you to get something out of this."

I can't understand why she even cares. She checks me out from head to toe but then something catches her eye and she directs a full-watt Reese Witherspoon smile across the room.

Her eyes don't twinkle though, and she self-consciously fixes her tank top as she wiggles her fingers in the air. I see her ex, Devon Pierce. The male equivalent of Kristina. Prince Charming to her Cinderella. Except in this story they split up instead of living happily ever after.

"He broke my heart," she whispers in a sad voice, without wiping the mega-grin off her face. I can't tell if she's lying about the state of her heart. Sometimes I wonder if she has one.

"So why're you smiling at him like he's a bowl of sugar-free Jell-O?"

She leans forward and the force of her breath on the tiny hairs on my ear hurts. "I kind of have to. He's super A-list."

I almost feel sorry for her having to be nice to a boy who broke her heart. I want to go over and punch him in the stomach on her behalf.

She keeps smiling though, watching him from the corner of her eye. "He's not a bad guy. We mostly broke up because I wouldn't hook up with him."

I pretend to stick my finger down my throat, but I'm a little relieved to hear that she didn't give in to him just because he's a hot guy. From what I've heard, most of her friends don't have the same reservations.

Her expression tightens and her eye twitches slightly in the corner. "You have to be careful with guys."

No, *she* does. I don't. Boys don't notice me. For example, right then a boy approaches us, checking out my sister. He has a cute baby face but is wearing a dorky rap star T-shirt. He's carrying a digital camera and has a look of utter adoration on his face. I don't think he even sees me standing beside her.

"You were awesome in the game last night," he says. "You're captain this year, right?"

Kristina nods. "Yup. And as of last week, I'm the outside hitter too. If my knee holds out." She frowns for a second and then shakes her head once.

"Can I take your picture?" His lips tighten as if he's nervous.

"Sure," she gushes, and flashes her perfect teeth at him. She treats her admirers with equal deference, I'll give her that. No one can accuse my sister of being one of the mean girls; she's not like that.

She throws an arm around me. "Take one of me and my little

sister, Tess. She's a freshman, you know, just like you." She smiles and squeezes my shoulder harder. "And she's also available."

My face warms and she pinches me to warn me not to run in horror as she tries to pimp me out to some kid. I say nothing but can't stop blushing and refuse to smile at his camera.

"Say 'Facebook,'" the boy says.

Kristina squirms happily, hearing one of her favorite words. "Facebook," she says, smiling at his camera with her eyes, her arm tight around my shoulder so I can't escape. She manages to turn her body to expose her most flattering angle. I glare at the camera. "Make sure you friend me so I can see the pics after you post them. My last name is Smith," she chirps, as if he didn't already know.

"Cool. Thanks," the boy says. "I'm Jeremy. Jeremy Jones. I play volleyball too."

"Jones?" Kristina says. She taps her fingers on her chin, thinking.

I almost smile. His last name is as lame as ours. Jones. Smith. As common as celebrities in rehab.

"I made the junior team," he tells Kristina.

She smiles but she clearly hasn't heard of him.

He peeks at me but I duck my head.

"You're in my friend's homeroom and a few of his classes," he says to me.

Kristina nudges me out of my stupor.

"Oh," I say, only because of her prompting. I have to admit he's kind of cute in a lost-puppy-dog way, but he's obviously a member of the Kristina fan club and that deducts major points.

"What's your friend's name?" Kristina asks him sweetly, nudging me harder with her pointy, anorexic elbow.

"Clark."

Clark Trent. I know who he's talking about. The poor guy's parents obviously have a warped sense of humor. I mean, come on. Clark Trent? Superman much? He even wears glasses.

I know who he is because he's one of the top freshmen this year. Academically. Rumor has it he's after a spot in the Honor Society. Well, the rumor is between Melissa and me. She made a list of all the prospects. In our school, freshman members of the Honor Society aren't chosen until the end of the first semester, so it's imperative we get great marks until November.

Jeremy squirms, holding his camera tight as if he has something else to say, but Kristina's already been distracted. She only feels she owes her fans so much time, I guess.

She signals her hand at a boy leaning against the wall opposite ours. He appears at her side in a flash. Jeremy makes a quiet excuse and leaves. I lift my hand and wave good-bye, mostly sorry for him because Kristina doesn't even seem to notice his exodus from stage right.

"Sweetie, would you get a cup of punch for my sister? You know. The special punch," she says to the boy she's called over.

He grins, thrilled to be put to use for Kristina Smith, and hurries off to do her bidding. Seconds later he returns and hands a cup to me.

"Drink up, little sister," he says with a laugh.

I take a sip from the cup and sputter and cough. I stare at Kristina, shocked, while the boy laughs some more. I put it down on the table and cross my arms, glaring at Kristina.

"What?" Kristina says. "It has a little rum in it. Drink it fast. Maybe it'll loosen you up a little." She studies me for a second. "Tell Mom and I'll kill you. She's already freaking—"

I shake my head. "I'm not drinking alcohol to loosen myself up."

Kristina sighs. "You know, most little sisters would think I was pretty cool giving you a drink. I'm not trying to get you drunk. You need to chillax a bit. Take the edge off."

The boy wisely steps away from us and takes off toward the kitchen.

"I don't want to get drunk and throw up just to show people how cool I am," I say.

"I didn't say you had to get drunk. Or throw up. I just want you to be, you know, a little more relaxed." She lifts her chin. "Get you a little more connected. I only want what's best for you."

"So does Mom and she tries to make me eat porridge for breakfast every day."

As far as I can tell, Kristina's idea of connected is how many people text her each day.

"I won't always be around to try to help you out socially, Tess. You need to make an effort on your own too."

"Did you ever think I don't want your help?" I glance around to see if ears are tuned in to our conversation, but no one appears to be listening in. "Maybe I'm happy."

She crosses her arms. "Define happy."

"Happiness is going home," I tell her.

Kristina frowns and is about to continue to lecture me when a gaggle of volleyball girls burst into the room and squeal her name. The volleyball girls stick together like waterlogged book pages.

She has no choice but to go to them. She turns to me before she takes off.

"I just want to help," she says and then she walks off, limping toward her friends.

"I'm not the one who needs help, Kristina," I tell her. Pure bravado. Kristina doesn't know what I would give to be like her. So outgoing and likable. Not to mention beautiful.

• • •

"Is your sister still in bed?" Mom asks as she enters the kitchen from the sliding patio door. "We have to go to the doctor in a couple of hours."

I don't bother to ask why Kristina's going to the doctor this time, or which one. She's always getting tested and poked at and prodded and X-rayed by chiropractors, naturopaths, and sports therapists. My mom invests a lot of time and energy in Kristina's volleyball "career."

I glance up from the newspaper and then at the oversized clock. "Yup. A new record."

Mom pulls out her ear buds and chugs the bottle of water she'd taken on her run. Her blond hair is pulled into a high ponytail; her aqua running band matches the stripe on her running pants, and does double-duty keeping stray hair from her face. She puts her water down on the table and checks the Garmin GPS strapped to her wrist. "Five miles in forty-nine minutes, even without Kristina keeping up my pace."

I raise my eyebrows, pretending to be impressed, but really, I don't think there's a good reason to run unless someone's chasing me. Seriously. And that hasn't happened since Brad Myers came after me in fourth grade when my art was featured in the local paper instead of his.

"Kristina's knee's been bothering her," Mom says as if I've asked a question. "That's why I didn't wake her to run with me. We've been having a few things looked at. Trying to figure out the problem."

Her voice sounds off, higher than usual, enough that I look up and see that she's frowning, but then she glances at the clock.

"Good party last night?" she asks, and turns back to me, hope I've actually frolicked at a party lighting up her entire face.

My unease flees and I shrug and return to the comics. I don't have to look at her to see her disappointment.

"Honestly, Tess. You're just like your father. I swear, if he didn't have me and his golf partners, he'd be a hermit."

I flash my best good-daughter smile. "Well, you do give good parties."

If she hears contempt in my voice, she chooses to ignore it. She complains all the time but he gives her a purpose. She helps my dad, Mr. Introverted University Professor, with his networking by throwing parties for his colleagues. No one intimidates her, not even stuffy college professors.

Despite their opposite personalities, Mom clings to Dad in public and crawls on his lap to make out with him, which is completely gross and embarrassing. It might be kind of sweet if they were someone else's parents, but they're mine.

"You need to get ready," Mom says. "And a shower would be nice."

"Awww, Mom. Do I have to go?" After finishing with the newspaper I was looking forward to finishing an English assignment.

I know I'll ace it and pump up my GPA. Honor Society beckons. After that I planned to work on some sketches of Melissa's cat. A surprise for her birthday.

Mom turns her back on me and opens the refrigerator. She bends at her waist and peers inside as if something's calling her name. Like plain yogurt or fat-free cottage cheese.

"I promise I won't go on the Internet."

She's got this weird thing about the Internet and rarely lets me use the computer unsupervised, as if I'm going to search around the Web for hot muscle men or be lured into private chat rooms by creepy pedophiles. It's not like I'm the daughter with the social networking addiction.

Mom closes the refrigerator door without taking anything out. She walks over to my side, glancing down at the newspaper. "I'm a little nervous about this meeting," she tells me.

"Please?" I say, ignoring her. Kristina is her purebred pony. She's always worried about her.

She lets out a deep breath, seeming distracted. "Fine," she says, taking me completely by surprise. "You can do your homework on the computer and use your art program, but nothing else online."

I'm so shocked I don't know what to say, but I'm no idiot either and keep my mouth shut.

"I wonder if I should wake Kristina," Mom asks, glancing toward the stairs.

I flip a page in the newspaper but follow her gaze to the stairs, wondering if Kristina is suffering from drinking too much of the "special" punch at the party.

"She'll be up soon," I say. "I'm sure she's just tired from social-izing last night. You know. Like mother, like daughter."

Even though Kristina pretty much added to my total humiliation, it's still us vs. them when it comes to the units.

"Yeah, and like father, like daughter," Mom says.

I stick my tongue out, knowing she doesn't mean it as a compli-ment, but she's already leaving the kitchen and misses it. I reabsorb myself in the newspaper and a write-up in the Arts section catches my eye. My heart skips out an excited beat. An art contest for contemporary drawing. I read on. The Oswald Drawing Prize for emerging artists.

Me. I'm an emerging artist! I continue to read and see there's a Junior Division for grades nine to twelve. A winner from each state will be announced along with a Grand Champion. Winning pieces will be shown in universities and art galleries across the country.

My eyes scan the fine print. The winner from each state will be interviewed for a television documentary, plus an illustrated catalog will be published to accompany the exhibition. The catalog will include images of the winning drawings, biographical details of each artist, and a statement about the drawing.

The Grand Champion will receive a full scholarship and accept-ance into the Academy of Art University in San Francisco in their graduating year. *The* art school I've been salivating over since I studied the art school rankings over the summer. Gah! On top of all that, there's a free trip to San Francisco for the winner.

A rumble like the lava of a volcano surges through my body. There's a three-hundred-dollar entry fee, but I've got more than enough to cover that in my bank account. The entry deadline is November 1, so there's time. Not a lot, but enough if I get to work right away. I glance down. Winners will be announced the week of November 18 by email or phone.

There's kind of a destiny vibe, coming across the article like this. Feelings I didn't know I had stirred in my soul. True, serving killer volleyballs is not in my future, but I'm truly proud of my art skills. Something no one else in my family can claim. A recessive gene, probably.

Maybe, just maybe, winning would quiet the voice in my head. The voice that tells me drawing pictures is silly, unimportant. The voice that sounds a lot like my mom. As I try to visualize myself accepting the award and finding my voice in a room full of admirers, something brushes against my arm. I grab my throat and yelp. Kristina stands over me, looking unusually pale and drawn. Not nearly as radiant as last night.

"Did you have to sneak up on me?" My heartbeat sprints like a greyhound charging after a mechanical rabbit.

She takes a step back. "Sorry," she whispers. I look closer at her. Bags under her eyes. Washed-out skin.

"Whoa," I tell her. "You look terrible. Did you freebase a bottle of tequila or what?"

"Funny," she croaks. She heads to the fridge, pulls out bottled water, undoes the cap, and chugs it, much like Mom a few minutes before her. "I must have the flu or something."

"Flu?" I stare at her. "More like hangover-itis."

"I never have more than one drink. One hundred calories max."

Mom says the same thing. One glass of red wine is acceptable as an antioxidant. Dad teases her that she doesn't drink because it makes her mean, but I've never seen it and have no idea if it's true or not.

Kristina glares at me and then walks forward and leans right over me. "Here. Feel my forehead."

I stare at her and scrunch up my face to show my reluctance, but she doesn't leave, so I relent and reach up and put the back of my hand on her forehead.

"Hey." Her body definitely doesn't feel like it's running at 98 degrees. "You feel like you slept in polar fleece or something."

"I know, right? I'm hot. I feel like hell." She collapses into a chair opposite mine at the kitchen table. "It has to be the flu. I don't want to be sick. We have a big game coming up. Against Westwood High." She drinks more water and then plunks it on the table and stares at me. "You got home okay last night?"

I don't meet her eyes. "Yeah. Fine." I close the paper and slide it away from her. I don't want her to find out about the contest. Not yet. I have to do some thinking about the perfect entry. I want it to be my own thing.

She gulps more water and then gets up and walks to the stove. Standing on her tiptoes, she reaches to the cupboards above and pulls out a bottle of Tylenol. The only non-herbal medicine Mom allows in the house. She opens the cap, pops two pills in her mouth, and swallows them without water before returning the bottle to the shelf.

"Gross." I don't know how she swallows them like that.

"I hope it's nothing serious," she says as she stares off into space. "I can't afford to be sick in the next few weeks."

"Don't worry about it," I tell her. "You won't get sick. You're perfect. Just ask that drunk pimply guy from the party last night."

Kristina focuses and tries to hide a smile but she's pleased. She takes a sip from her water bottle. "Which one?" she asks.

I focus back on the paper, refusing to feed her unquenchable ego. I can't wait until she's gone so I can have the house to myself and start brainstorming ideas for the drawing contest.

• • •

A few hours later Mom and Kristina walk into the kitchen right while I'm in the middle of dunking Oreos into chocolate milk. I stop chewing, with cookie crumbs bunched up in my cheeks like a chipmunk. Busted. Dad came home early and brought the cookies with him as a peace offering for making me go to the party. He often provides me with stashes of sweets instead of heart-to-heart talks. I was supposed to hide the cookies before Kristina and Mom got home. I can hear him clattering away in his home office off the kitchen.

I'm scrambling, about to make up an excuse about why I'm gorging myself on cookies instead of something healthy like Mom's delicious yogurt with fruit or nuts, but neither of them even says a word about my snack. I chew as quickly and quietly as I can and wipe my mouth with the back of my hand, trying not to look guilty.

Mom takes one look at me, though, and bursts into tears. I blush, ashamed my gluttonous actions have caused her such anguish. On one hand I wonder why she's freaking, but I also can't help worrying if I've messed up my future shots at staying home alone?

"Mom. It's my first snack of the day. I swear. I finished my homework and I'm starving…" I don't want to tell on Dad for bringing the treats home.

Kristina plops hard onto the chair beside me. "Don't sweat it." She keeps her back straight, her posture perfect. "That's not why she's crying." Her face is pale and strangely devoid of emotion, a creepy contrast to my mom's tears.

Mom sniffles and struggles to get a hold of herself. "I'm sorry, Kristina. No tears. It's going to be fine. I'm just shocked, you know. That's all. You're going to be fine."

My heart skips a beat. Mom turns away from us, opens her mouth and hollers. "Dan!" she yells in a most unladylike way. "Dan, come in here. We need to have a family meeting. *Now!*"

I hear my dad mumble something from his office at the end of the hall. When he's working I think he forgets our names.

"Seriously, Daniel, I mean it. Come here this instant."

Uh-oh. She used his full name. I look back and forth from my mom to my sister. Mom rarely interrupts Dad when he's working. "What's going on?" I ask, too afraid to even try to imagine.

The cookies bungee-jump to the pit of my stomach. Mom pulls out a chair and sits gingerly, as if she's afraid someone might have put a tack or a whoopee cushion on it.

"What?" I repeat.

"I want to wait until your father joins us," she says to me. She avoids Kristina's eyes. "We'll discuss this as a family." She stands up and leaves the room to go and get him.

"What's going on?" I ask my sister. I haven't seen my mom this flustered, well, ever. It isn't easy to ruffle old Lisa Smith.

I wonder if my perfect sister lied about not doing it and got herself pregnant. I hope not. I know I'll be stuck changing diapers. And rubbing lotion on her fat belly to avoid stretch marks on her flawless skin.

"It's no big deal."

Kristina's top lip quivers a second but then she swallows and looks right into my eyes. A cold feeling runs up my spine and a chill settles on my arms. I realize I'm holding my breath.

"I have cancer," she says.

chapter two

Kristina stands up. Then she sits down again. Then she stands and wrings her hands in front of herself and then sits. I don't know what to say or do, so I push the bag of cookies I've been scarfing toward her. I watch in disbelief as she reaches into the bag and shoves an entire Oreo in her mouth.

"Cancer?" I say, not wanting to believe her. She's too healthy to be sick. I wonder for a moment if I've caused it with my mean thoughts about her. I stare at her, wanting to take back every bad thought I've had. "How can you have cancer?"

She doesn't look at me but slowly chews the whole cookie she's shoved in her mouth.

Mom steps around the corner then, dragging my dad by the arm. He's wearing his professor uniform. Cardigan sweater and a big pouf of gray hair standing north, south, east, and west on his head. Glasses that always slip down to the bridge of his nose are perched there now. The only thing that stops him from being a cliché is his physique. He walks a lot of golf courses.

The look on Dad's face mirrors my own. Bewilderment. I can tell he wants to slip away, back to his work, away from the sloppiness of real life. He sits down on the other side of me and reaches over inside the bag, his fingers rooting around for a cookie. Mom slaps his hand away though, so he pulls it out of the bag, empty.

We all wait for her to speak.

I stare at Kristina; Dad watches Mom. Kristina pretends to find the table fascinating but her face is pale, her lips pressed together. Angry. I want to cry. I swallow but it hurts as bad as the time I had strep throat. I focus on my chewed nails instead, studying them as if they have a cure for cancer hidden somewhere inside them.

My heart thuds. Cancer? I don't want to believe it, but my mom's mouth starts moving and I'm too upset to even put my hands over my ears to block out what she's going to say.

"The doctor confirmed that Kristina has osteosarcoma."

My dad looks like he wants to leave the room and hide in his office. "What?"

"Cancer," my mom whispers. "Bone cancer. She'll need a biopsy to see how…um, to see how she is. It's in the knee. They're testing to see if it has spread."

Spread? That does not sound good. I can't make myself look at my sister.

"That's impossible," my dad says. "You said it wasn't serious, that I didn't have to come to the appointment. You said there was no way it was cancer."

I look up at him. Horror is etched into his familiar features. Blame. Guilt. I watch emotions cross his mind and his face, just like my own. We exchange a look and then I drop my eyes to the table, afraid he can see inside me. Or that everyone knows that as the bitter person in the family, I should be the one who gets sick. Not sunny, happy, and healthy Kristina.

"I was wrong." Mom's trying hard to keep in control but her lip quivers and her eyes are watery. "I didn't think you needed to come. I thought it was just a sports injury. I didn't think it could really be cancer. I thought it would be okay."

Dad glances at Kristina and back at Mom. "You thought?" He shakes his head. His bangs fall across his forehead and he angrily brushes them back. "Kristina has cancer?"

"Surprise," Kristina says.

I stare at Kristina, my mouth open. Her cheeks are blotchy and her lips tight, as if she's seriously ticked off. She's still the most beautiful girl I've ever seen, but for the first time in my life when I study her features and wonder how they work so perfectly on her, I don't feel envy.

"When the doctor mentioned the possibility of osteosarcoma, we didn't want to focus on it," Mom says.

"Oops," Kristina says.

My insides tighten. I struggle to breathe properly. I want to yell that no one told me a thing. That I've been in the dark, jealous of my sister's perfect life.

"I told you we were having X-rays, Dan. And that we had a follow-up appointment with Dr. Turner today."

"But you said they would rule out cancer." His hand slams down on the table and he jumps to his feet. Mom and I wince but Kristina doesn't flinch. "We need a second opinion. Krissie is too healthy to be sick. You said sports injury."

"I hoped." Mom lowers her eyes.

The power of her denial astounds me.

"Well, I guess you thought wrong, huh? Looks like I won the prize. The big one," says Kristina.

"Oh, honey," Dad says. He slowly sits back down in his chair. His face turns a worrisome color of pink. "I want another opinion," he repeats.

"Dan, I got the best doctor money can buy. There is no one else to confer with. The doctors will handle this, she will be fine."

"Fine?" My dad hides his face under his hands.

"I know." Mom glares at Dad. "We know. We're not pointing fingers here. We're all upset." She wipes a tear from underneath her eye. "I just didn't think it could be possible...there's no cancer on my side of the family."

Dad looks around like a lab rat trapped in a corner, searching for an escape. "Well, don't look at me. My dad died from good old-fashioned alcoholism and my mom is physically healthy despite her Alzheimer's."

Kristina jumps up. "It's not my fault," she yells, as if she's been caught cheating on a test or something.

Mom frowns and pulls on Kristina's arm so she's sitting with us at the table again. "It's no one's fault. Anyhow, you're going to be fine. Fine. We're going to get you through this." She gets up and walks to the fridge and pulls out a pitcher of lemonade she probably squeezed herself.

I'm unable to say anything. Dad crumples further down in his chair and drops his head into his hands again. His shoulders shake and he wheezes and gasps, trying to control himself.

I stare at him. He's crying. Mom told us he sat through his own father's funeral without even blinking but now he's crying. Mom is getting ice from the freezer and filling up glasses. Dad covers his eyes with his big paw-like hands. Mom keeps talking.

"At least we can afford this," Mom is saying in her most pragmatic voice. As if we're discussing signing Kristina up for a spin class. "Thank God for your grandfather's money," she says to Kristina.

My mouth hangs open. She's talking about money. Now?

Mom shakes her head. "I can't even imagine how awful if would be if we didn't have money." She picks up a glass of lemonade and plunks it on the table in front of Kristina and then plops another glass in front of Dad. I shake my head frantically back and forth. Lemonade? Seriously?

"Mom, I don't want lemonade," Kristina echoes as her face squishes up in distaste, her eyes water, and her forehead wrinkles.

Mom takes a glass for herself and sits back at the table and sips it properly.

Kristina starts to laugh. Dad uncovers his hands. We all stare at her.

"Maybe we should arrange for a psychologist to help you cope," Mom says.

Kristina ignores her and waves her hand at me. "Come on, Tess. Let's go for a ride in my car."

I stare at her, confused. "What?"

"You can't go running off." Mom takes a sip of her drink and runs her hands over the smooth oak tabletop. The custom-made kitchen table she designed. She hates mass-produced furniture. She loves to be unique.

"Why not? I just want to go for a drive. I'm not dead yet. I've made it this far with cancer eating my body; I think I can manage a car ride. It's not like I'm going to collapse behind the wheel or anything." Kristina juts out her hip, a stubborn tilt to her head.

Mom presses her lips tight. "I think you should stay home."

"I don't want to. I want to go for a drive. As you pointed out, we can afford the gas."

Mom's eyes open wider. Kristina doesn't speak to her that way. I do. But not Kristina.

Mom makes a face at me, trying to send me a subliminal message of some sort, but I don't even try to pick up her attempt at mental telepathy. I'm not exactly thrilled about running off with my emotionally distraught sister, but Kristina's not in the right emotional state to be driving off alone. Even I know that. And taking off with her is better than being stuck in the house with my parents.

Kristina starts walking toward the door. I shrug and then follow her. I can hear my dad crying quietly behind us. I'd never thought I'd put crying and Dad in the same sentence. My mom's eyes bore into my back.

"Look after your sister," she calls, but I'm not even sure which one of us she's talking to.

chapter three

Kristina rushes down the driveway and is already climbing into her Toyota. She starts the car and waits while I climb in and do up my seat belt. She watches me and laughs. I can't help but notice it's still a little hysterical.

"What are you laughing about?" I ask.

She nods at the seat belt. "I guess they can't always protect us, can they?"

She doesn't put hers on as she pulls out of the driveway and roars down our street. I don't mention it even as the car bell rings over and over, reminding her to buckle up.

"Mom told me not to worry. And I believed her."

After a few blocks the warning bell stops. I'm gripping the dashboard because Kristina is driving much faster than normal. I don't know where she's taking me, but sense it's not to McDonald's for a cheeseburger.

I'm afraid this trip is not going to turn out well. I feel it in my bones.

• • •

We don't speak until Kristina pulls up to a street I've never been on before, close to downtown. She parks in front of a big white house. I note the color mainly because of parental brainwashing.

Mom hates white houses for reasons I don't even try to understand. Her voice rings with disgust and the leftovers of her Southern accent become more pronounced, as it does when she's angry. She came to Great Heights on a scholarship and never went back South. She works hard to cover up her accent, but she's so morally offended by white paint, her twang is easy to hear. Personally, I've got better things to worry about than house color, but I figure Mom's life is intellectually lacking and shrug it off as one of her Southern quirks.

I think we're somewhere close to the frat houses on University Avenue, which runs right through the university campus and all the way downtown, but we drove down a quieter street. The houses are old and the lots are a good size, not as huge as the houses in the south part of town where we live, but big. A cluster of houses in a row look like they've been renovated and Kristina's parked in front of the nicest one. She abruptly shuts off the engine.

"Uh, what are we doing here?" I ask.

"Shut up," she snaps, her giddy mood now gone.

Anger instantly slithers through my body, pumping in my veins, heating my face, but I stifle it. I want to show support as her only sister. A wave of sadness washes away the resentment and I blink fast, struggling not to cry.

"Sorry," she says. "I know I'm being a bitch."

I secretly agree but say nothing and listen as she inhales deep and fast. It's so quiet in the car, I try to think of something to say, something to make her feel better, but I have no idea what that is.

"If you thought you were going to die…I mean, if there was a good chance that you only had a little while to live, what would you do?" she asks, her voice quiet, serious.

"You're not going to die, Kristina." I wiggle around on my seat, afraid of saying the wrong thing. I know she needs someone to talk to but I don't know the words to give her.

She stares at me for a minute, and then shakes her head as if I'm letting her down and picks up her phone. She starts texting a message.

"Um," I start to say. "What are you doing?"

"Talking to someone who isn't afraid to say what's on their mind."

I clear my throat and try again. "I'd, uh…well, if I was going to die, I mean, I'd…" I try to answer her question but stop, not able to think of what I want to say.

"Seriously, Tess? You have no idea?" She rolls her eyes at me and then focuses back on the message she's texting, tapping her fingers on the keyboard like I'm not even there.

I bite my lip and stare out the window at the white house. There's a huge front lawn with two stone lion statues at the entrance to a triple-car garage. Mom would hate those statues too. Tacky, she'd say.

It's still light outside, but the street lights flicker and turn on. We're at the point where summer is behind us and fall is coming, but it's not quite here yet. The leaves on the big trees lining the street are changing from green to burnt orange, giving up, and dropping to the ground.

Kristina giggles and I look back at her. She's looking down at the message from whomever she's been texting. The pain in her eyes doesn't match the smile on her face.

"Will you wait here?" she asks and giggles again.

"What?"

She smiles, as if I'm precious or slow, and then reaches over and pats my arm. "Just for a little while." She pulls the keys out of the ignition and hands them to me. "There's a 7-11 a couple of blocks that way." She's talking in a singsong voice that sounds on the verge of hysteria. She points to the right. "You could walk over and get yourself something fattening to eat." She pulls a five-dollar bill from her pocket and hands it to me.

I stare at the money in my hand. "What?" I repeat.

"This is Devon's house." She runs her hand through her bangs.

I look over at the big house. "It's white."

"I'm not Mom, I don't care," Kristina snaps and then takes a deep breath and clears her throat. "I'm going to go inside, talk to him for a while." Her giggle-snort confuses me. "His parents are out, so would you mind, I mean, I'd like it if you'd stay and wait. I won't be long. I just want to talk to Devon."

Like I have a choice. We're miles from home and even though I'm holding the car keys, I'm not licensed to drive.

"Why him?" I ask. I wonder why she's not turning to Gee or one of the other volleyball girls, or if she's afraid to be less than perfect in front of them. Even now. With something this big.

"He's the one I always talk to about things. I mean, I did." She grabs the rearview mirror, points it to her face, and opens her mouth, checking out her teeth. "It won't take long. By the time you get back from the 7-11, I should be ready to go."

I want to tell her no. I have no desire to hang out and wait while she confides in her old boyfriend instead of me. It deepens my sense of sister fail. And kind of pisses me off.

"I can talk to you," I spit out, but I'm clearly out of my element.

"It's okay," she says, and actually pats my hand, like I'm a little kid.

I nod, because what else can I do? She steps out and closes the door, and I watch her walk up the long walkway, past the lions, to the front. She rings the doorbell and I wait with her, holding my breath until it opens. Devon's gelled hair is visible from where I sit. He smiles, puts an arm around her, and pulls her inside. She looks small and fragile next to him and then the door closes.

"Great," I mutter to myself.

I don't move, but it's so quiet the bark of dogs down the street is my background music. A few minutes pass and then boredom crushes my brain. I think about the 7-11, but surprisingly don't want to eat anything. Not even with my sister's five bucks.

I open the glove box and pull out the iPod she always leaves there, and then get out of the car, clicking the doors locked behind me.

I shove her ear buds in my ears and turn on music, wrinkling my nose at a blast of a top-forty pop song, and skip by her selection of crappy music until I reach a song by Hedley that I can stomach. I walk for a while, and I'm the only one on the street. No one passes me or is outside looking after their house or anything. It's almost creepy, and I imagine serial killers or zombies and hurry back to the car, climb inside, lock the doors, and sit with my eyes closed, listening to bad music. Eventually Kristina leaps into the car and my heart skips. I pull the headphones from my ears as she slams the door behind her.

"Hey," I say, and sit up straighter. "You okay?"

She nods and giggles, but her eyes fill with tears.

"What's wrong?"

"What do you think is wrong?"

Then, as if her neck breaks, her head flops down to the steering wheel and she grips the wheel with both hands. Her back starts to shake and her knuckles turn white. She heaves and gulps and tries to control herself. I pat her on the back but she doesn't respond to me so I take my hand away.

I look out the window at Devon's house. Her body shakes harder. I reach out my hand again and touch her hair. Her soft blond hair. Hair I've pretended not to envy since I was old enough to recognize how beautiful it was and how different my orangey hair was. I've always secretly loved her hair. Even with the new highlights.

I swallow hard and wonder if she'll lose her hair to cancer. I don't want her to. I don't want her to have cancer.

"It's okay," I say over and over, and I'm the one petting her now, stroking her hair as if she's my dog or cat. For a moment, she lets me, and it's yet another sign that our lives have done a one-eighty.

And then she starts to hiccup and snort and it's impossible to tell if she's laughing or crying. Her hand reaches over and grabs mine, and she grips so tightly it hurts, but I don't say a word or try to pull back. She lifts her head from the steering wheel.

"Keys," she says, and holds her palm up in the air.

I take a second to compose myself as she lets my hand go.

"Hurry, Tess. We have to leave now," she squeals, as if she's being chased by rabid demons. I yank them from my pocket and plop them in her palm.

She starts to giggle softly again and then, while I stare at her, concerned, she takes a few deep breaths, shoves the keys in the ignition, starts the car, puts it in drive, and peels out without looking back at Devon's house.

She speeds down the block and onto a main road.

"So," I finally ask, my voice a half-whisper. "What did he say when you told him?"

"Told him what?" she asks.

"Um, that you have cancer."

She gives me a sideways glance before she focuses back on the road. She's driving slower and I've stopped fearing for my life. But she chuckles again. Soon she's hiccupping and coughing. I look around the road outside us, glad there's hardly any traffic, because she snorts and wipes tears with one hand and drives with the other.

She clears her throat. "I didn't tell him, Tess," she says, breathing in and out like she's doing yoga from the classes she and Mom sometimes go to. "I'm not going to tell him. I don't want anyone to know. No one." She pauses, getting her control back. "I mean it."

I bite my lip hard and study her profile. "Uh, what did you talk about then?" She was gone for over an hour. Oh my God.

"We didn't talk much actually." She snorts softly as we pull up to a red light, but her laughter doesn't spiral out of control. "We had sex." Her voice is emotionless, detached. All traces of laughter are gone and she sticks her chin out. "I didn't want to die a virgin."

But then a sob slips out and her eyes glisten with tears. "I thought it would be nicer," she says. "But it felt wrong. It wasn't...what I expected."

My heart hurts with wanting her to have the fairy-tale romance.

"It felt like it was happening to someone else. I mean I didn't even feel like I was there, you know?"

But I don't know. The thought of her so vulnerable with her news and so naked in every way makes me want to throw up. I want to protect her from Devon as if he's the bad guy. As if he should have done better by her.

In front of the car, a group of college boys cross the street. They wear university jackets and are whooping, pushing each other around. They spot Kristina and me in the car and start whistling and making rude gestures at us.

The light changes and Kristina rolls down her window, gives them the finger, and speeds up, almost running into the slowest one, and he jumps on the sidewalk and yells at her.

I wipe away tears until we reach our house. As she pulls the car to the curb and shuts it off, I sniffle and try to get a hold of myself.

"You can't tell a soul," she tells me before she opens the door to climb out. "Not about me and Devon, and especially not about the cancer." She glares at me. "Promise?"

"I won't say a thing about Devon, but why not the…?" I don't want to say the word. "That you're sick. Your friends will want to know. They'll want to help…" My throat tightens and I can no longer talk.

She shakes her head and her blond hair billows around her face. She's so pretty, even with runny eyes and a red nose. It strikes me that she doesn't look different. Not from the sex or the cancer. Not yet.

She opens the car door and looks at me as she holds the door, ready to climb out. "You promise?"

I sniffle. I don't want to agree. But I nod.

She gazes right into my eyes and it feels like she sees more than I want her to. She gets out of the car. I call her name, wanting to say something more, but she doesn't hear me, or maybe she chooses not to. She slams her door and my heart breaks a little more.

When I walk in the house, Kristina is already upstairs. I hear Dad in his office, clanking on his keyboard, pretending he's not waiting up for us, knowing he won't come out.

Mom has left one of her scented candles burning in the kitchen. I blow it out. The smoke swirls up and disappears.

chapter four

Our house is party central for the academic university crowd. Mom loves throwing parties. She flings invitations around like confetti at a wedding. I thought Dad would convince her to cancel her planned Sunday brunch for his colleagues under the circumstances. Oldest daughter having cancer and all. But no. Apparently, in their little game of denial, they aren't planning to tell anyone about Kristina's cancer. Party on.

"It's the best way to handle it," I hear Mom tell Dad as I pass their bedroom on the way to the bathroom. "We don't want to change everything and upset Kristina."

Yeah, I think, except I guess Mom totally missed the memo that everything *has* changed. Whether she throws a party or not.

Dad lets her make these kinds of choices, so he can focus on his work or do eighteen holes uninterrupted. I peek around the corner. Mom has an outfit laid out for him on the bed, one she picked herself from the gigantic walk-in closet. It's embarrassing the way she treats him like she's a lovesick 1970s housewife.

Dad's upbringing was a lot different from hers but he doesn't talk about it much either. His dad made uncanny investments in early technology, almost as if old Gramps had a crystal ball. The Smith family will benefit for generations.

I've gathered, though, that Grandpa Smith liked his whiskey, so things weren't hunky-dory. Dad tells us money doesn't buy happiness, but I don't think Mom agrees, the way she fills space under the Christmas tree every year and has made shopping an aerobic sport.

I think Mom gives parties to celebrate her good fortune.

"We won't say a thing," Mom is telling Dad. "We have to show Kristina that life goes on..."

"What about my mom?" he asks.

"Her Alzheimer's is too far along to bother her with this," Mom mumbles.

"What about your parents?"

She doesn't answer him and glances toward the hall where I'm standing, so I slip around the corner toward my bedroom. I consider protesting the party, but it's way too late to cancel anything now.

"Kristina! Tess!" Mom yells, and I hurry inside my bedroom as quietly as I can.

"I want you girls dressed and down to greet our guests," she calls, but her voice lacks her usual resolve.

Kristina doesn't even bother to answer and stays locked in her bedroom. Before long, Mom's demands turn to pleas and she bangs on Kristina's door, but Kristina refuses to budge. She doesn't even bother with me. I'm not the one she usually shows off anyhow.

I stay in my own room, taking advantage of Kristina's rebellion and hiding upstairs, away from their friends. I'm grateful not to be forced to mingle with Mom's party guests, listening to university profs tell me how much I've grown and ask how my grades are and if I'm still playing around with art. It's like asking them if they're still breathing.

There's a light tap on the door. Dad opens it and sticks his head inside.

"You okay?" he asks.

I bite my lip and lift my shoulder. Does he actually think I'm going to go along with the pretending and say yes? Does he want my real answer? Why isn't he in Kristina's room, talking to her?

He clears his throat and runs his hand through his hair, then steps inside my room and closes the door behind him. "I heard you in the hallway."

I don't say anything.

"Your mom just wants to protect all of us," he says, his voice gruff and uncomfortable. He walks to my bed and stands in front of it as if he's perched on the high diving board at the swimming pool downtown. He has an extreme fear of heights. I wonder if it's worse than his fear of expressing his feelings. But he walked into my room. I have to give him that.

"So she's throwing a party to keep out the bad news? Pretending it's not happening is supposed to help?" I'm supposed to make things easier, be on his side. But I can't.

"You know your mom and the stiff upper lip. She didn't want to cancel this party, give Kristina the wrong idea. That life stops. She plugs along. It's how she copes with things." He reaches for my hand and then pulls back. "She didn't have it easy growing up."

Mom never talks about her childhood and I long to ask him more but it's too hard, and he's already standing up and heading for the door.

"We're going to need you to be strong, Tessie. Our rock."

My old nickname. He hasn't called me that in years. Rock, for my own stiff upper lip. Never letting people see the things that scare me, see inside at all. Just like him.

When the doorbell rings, announcing the first guest, I hear Mom clomp down the stairs, probably in a pair of her high boots. Her voice drifts up as she makes excuses for both of us. I grab my sketch pad and start some warm-up exercises to get my creative juices flowing and my fingers limbered up. My mind feels blocked though, and my attempts at shading are epic fails.

The living room and attached kitchen fill with noise as more guests arrive and swarm the lower level of the house. I plunk down on my bed and start flipping through a magazine for inspiration, when Kristina slips inside my room. I hide my surprise. Her face is pale, makeup-free. Her hair hangs in wet strings to her shoulders. She's wearing Hello Kitty pajamas. I expect her to look more mature or grown-up after hooking up with Devon but there's no visible change.

She tiptoes to my bed and sits on the edge of it like she used to do when we were kids. She was always the one who had nightmares, not me, but she pretended to sleep in my bed to keep me safe.

We stare at each other without speaking, and then a ghost of a smile turns up the corners of her mouth. "I screwed up," she says, and remorse crackles in her voice. "With Devon." She pauses and sighs. "I wish I hadn't done that. I mean, it didn't make me feel the way I thought it would. I guess I thought it would make me feel more alive, you know?"

I have no clue but nod. I want to ask what it did feel like. If it changed her.

"I don't even love him. And it was almost like...well, it wasn't like when we used to kiss for hours. I'm such an idiot." She laughs, but it's a strange sound that's far from happy.

Under the circumstances she could have done a lot of worse things. But I don't know how to say that to her. Words won't even form in my head. My mouth seems to have no connection to my thoughts or my brain. I don't have experience saying what's really on my mind. Especially to her.

Kristina sits up straighter, pushes her hair out of her eyes, and studies a photograph framed and sitting on my bookcase headboard. It's the two of us when we were six and nine, wearing inappropriate two-piece bathing suits Mom picked out. We're standing back to back, smiling at the camera.

I love the memory of that day. I'd thought she was the coolest girl in the world. She'd won a sand-castle-building contest and shared her ice cream prize with me even though I'd knocked her castle over accidentally after the judging. I thought she could do anything. When she became a teenager though, she stopped finding me cute and I didn't know how to talk to her anymore. My stomach pretzels with the anxiety of not knowing what to say to her. My own sister.

I reach my hand out as if to touch her, but pull back when she glares at me.

"Well, I guess you had to lose your virginity sometime?" I mutter and study the bright yellow walls as I speak, and I know even the dried paint can hear the lack of conviction in my words. It's not what I mean to say, not what I want to convey to her.

I wish she hadn't done that with Devon, but not for the reasons she might think. I believe she deserved her first time to be special. Not because she felt like she had to. "Yup. At least I won't die a virgin." Her voice is as rough as the first sketches of my art project.

"You won't die at all."

She shakes her head and pushes herself off my bed, her expression betraying her anger. "How do you know that, Tess? Did the doctor send you a guarantee? If so, I'd like a copy of it." She hurries out my door and slams it behind her. The sound of her feet storming down the hallway is like the rat-tat of a woodpecker pecking wood.

Click.

She locks her door behind her.

On the floor below, laughter and clinking cutlery and glasses float through the air. I imagine Mom raising a toast to everyone, the way she loves to do, forgetting for the moment the tragedy in her own home. A tear runs down my cheek. It drips into my mouth and the salty taste taints my tongue.

I want to go to Kristina and hold her hand. I want to hug her and stroke her hair like she used to do for me. When she used to put my hair in pigtails and add ribbons and pretend I was just as pretty as she was.

I want to reassure her that I would have done the same thing if I found out I had cancer, even though I don't have a guy I could even kiss, never mind lose my virginity to. I want to tell her that she will have sex with someone else and it will be beautiful and perfect, like the romance books she likes to read.

I want to tell her that she's brave and I love her. But I don't know how to say it. Talking about things is not what I do.

So I sit in silence. I close my sketchbook and toss the magazine on the floor. I close my eyes and imagine all the things I should have said.

chapter five

Kristina refuses to go to school on Monday. I don't really blame her. Far as I'm concerned, she deserves time to mope. Time to contemplate her abandoned virginity and the fact that a disease is eating away at her bones. She deserves whatever she wants right now.

And honestly, I don't really want to face her, and even though my lameness offends even me, I skedaddle out the door while she's arguing with Mom. Mom is blabbing on about keeping up appearances.

I should go back inside and yell at her to leave Kristina alone to chill and watch TV all day if that's what floats her boat. Instead I clutch my backpack, run to the garage, take out my hot pink bike, and hop on it, zipping off down the road, not wanting to pick sides or face my sister and everything that's happened.

My shame turns to anger and it propels me along, and for a while I forget how much I hate exercise as I pedal. Soon my butt is aching, but at least the wind dries my damp hair. I consider it a free blow-out without having to deal with Mom's annoying hairdresser in her clothes two sizes too small and two decades too young.

I finally reach the school just as my legs are telling me to stop pedaling already. I'm about to pull into the parking lot when a horn honks behind me. I almost fly off the seat of my bike. A car streaks by and through the rear window I see Bree, one of my sister's teammates, giggling in the passenger seat. I recognize the driver too. Drunk Pimple Guy from the party.

His car is a Pile, capital P. Rusting and dented, an ugly thing from the 1990s. I want to give them both the one-finger salute but I'm afraid to take my hand off the handlebar in case I wipe out.

I drop one foot to the ground, watching as they squeal into a parking spot. I could waste more energy being mad at them and their low IQs and thus low form of seeking entertainment, but my heart isn't in it. I don't even bother to watch them get out of the car.

Instead I picture my sister's face. Her bitter and broken laughter. The way she stepped on the gas pedal on the way to Devon's, drove like she was Thelma or Louise in the movie our mom made us watch on an imposed "Girl's Night."

In my daydreams I never get as far as having sex, but when I imagine kissing, it's like licking my favorite ice cream on the hottest day in summer, not dropping the entire scoop on the ground and watching it melt.

I hop back on my bike and head to the almost empty bike racks. Riding a bicycle to high school is apparently a faux pas. Especially a bike like mine. It's expensive of course; Mom picked it out—only the best for the Smiths—but who buys pink bikes after their ninth birthday besides my mom? I'm not crazy about my mode of transportation, but it beats the bus.

A lump clogs my throat. I won't cry. I won't. Not only would it be humiliating, but Kristina would kill me. I agreed to her cone of silence. Bawling in public wouldn't be a great way to keep her secret.

"Hey, Tess, right?"

I turn and the kid from the frosh party is standing behind me, an inquisitive look on his babyish face. I try to remember his name.

"Jeremy," he supplies.

"Oh yeah. Clark Trent's friend." My lips turn up as I think about his friend's name. "Are you going to be in the Honor Society too?"

Jeremy stares at me. "No, I'm not smart enough." He glances around. "Uh, where's your sister today? Don't you usually get a ride with her?"

Thunk. The mention of my sister sends spikes of pain through me.

I turn and concentrate on opening my bike lock and unraveling the chain from around the bike seat. When I peek up, his cheeks are practically smoking, they're so red. He looks guilty, like he's been caught browsing a girly website or something.

"Why are you so interested in my sister?" I ask, redirecting my anger at him for reasons not his fault.

"I just noticed her car is all." His cheeks stay red. "She always parks in the same spot. And you're usually with her."

I wind my bike lock through my bike wheels.

"No, seriously. Because of her red Toyota. My friend has the same one in black. I'm into cars. I noticed Kristina drove a red one."

Great. Kristina has a stalker. The car was Kristina's sweet sixteen present. At the time I didn't think she'd done anything to deserve it, except have rich grandparents, but Mom thought it was the best thing since leopard-skin spankies. And now, under the circumstances, spoiling Kristina doesn't seem so bad.

"I don't think I'd ever buy a red car, the cops tend to pull over more drivers who drive them. I can't remember where I heard it, but it makes sense, you know? Not that I think it's bad your sister has a red car. I mean, it suits her. She's doesn't seem like the type to speed or anything."

For some reason, Jeremy's still talking.

I stare at him, wondering why he's going on and on. I shrug. "I just decided to ride my bike today is all."

"Is Kristina sick?"

Man, I've been at school for less than five minutes and I'm already getting quizzed about her whereabouts and her health. It's not a good sign. I don't want to explain things all day. I want everyone to ignore me like they usually do.

"She's fine." The lie makes my insides percolate like Mom's morning coffee.

His cheeks recharge with color as if he feels my mood. "I just thought, you know…I wanted to ask Kristina if she saw the pictures I posted on Facebook. From the party. It's no big deal."

He's obviously nervous and it makes me a little less annoyed by his intrusion. The thing is, a few days ago she would have been all over his pictures. He would be the happiest guy on the planet right now, because Kristina would be giving him props for the cool pics of her. But even though he has no idea, it's all changed.

"She hasn't seen them." I start to walk away but he follows slightly behind me. I take a quick look over my shoulder and his whole body is deflated. He looks so sad that guilt nibbles at my crusty core. "I mean, I doubt she's had time to look them up. We had a really busy weekend." I want him to go away, to stop making me feel bad about being creepy to him, but most of all to quit reminding me why Kristina's at home.

I swallow another big lump, desperately wishing for my self-centered and carefree sister back but I'm afraid that girl is gone forever and I'm not sure what to do about it. When we reach the front doors of the school, Jeremy darts ahead of me, opens the door, and holds it while I pass by him. At least her stalker has nice manners.

"I have to get to class," I tell him, and practically run to get away. I keep my head down as I pass a group of kids in the hallway and wind my way past bodies until I'm almost at my locker.

Melissa leans against it, her eyes on the floor. Even though we don't have any classes together, she checks in at my locker almost every morning before we face our school day.

Her long hair hangs in front of her face and it almost looks like she's praying. She's wearing an oversized yellow T-shirt, probably her dad's. She's always raiding his closet instead of wearing the plus-size clothes her stepmother buys for her. A long blue skirt covers her flip-flopped feet like she's trying to hide.

"Hey," she whisper-calls in her soft voice when she spots me. Her eyes dart around as if to make sure no one is paying attention to us. As if anyone cares what she and I discuss before we rush off to class.

She pushes her long bangs behind her ear. "I tried calling and texting you all weekend but you didn't get back to me." I hear hurt in her voice. "What happened?"

Melissa's parents finally allowed her to get a cell phone for high school this year, though she has to pay for it with the money she earns helping out her church's secretary. Her social life is even worse than mine. Church both days on the weekend, Saturday for work, Sunday for services. And she has strict weeknight curfews.

"Oh, you know. My mom had all sorts of family stuff lined up and another one of her stupid parties on Sunday." I glance over my shoulder as if someone called my name or I heard something interesting. Avoiding her eyes, I add, "Anyhow, I didn't have my cell phone charged."

That much is true at least. I always forget to charge my phone.

When I look back at her, Melissa rolls her eyes ever so slightly. "I don't know why you even bother with a phone. Except you get it for free. Like everything else in life." She says it lightly and smiles, but I've heard it a million times before and barely register it. She's always teasing me about the things I have. It's not my fault my family can afford things and my mom loves to spend.

She pushes away from the lockers and I step forward to get my stuff.

"So…" she says, her voice soft but excited. "Tell me about the party. Did anything happen? How was it?"

The party. It seems so distant, like it happened or even mattered a lifetime ago. I grab the books I need for the morning from my backpack and blow out a deep breath of air, wishing I could confide the truth. The party is old news. My sister's cancer is new.

I'm torn by my promise to my sister and my friendship with Melissa. We've always shared things. Melissa narrows her eyes when I say nothing, a slightly resentful expression on her face. Her parents don't believe in parties and she's not allowed to go to any.

"It was lame," I finally say to throw her off the scent. I can't stir up the energy to tell her anything else. It strikes me how much time we spend discussing the lives of others. She's dying to find out if anything scandalous or exciting happened.

"I took off early." I shove my backpack into my locker and stand on my tiptoes to reach my sketchbook off the top shelf. My elbow knocks my blown-up picture of Randy McGovern, a wildlife artist I scanned off the Internet. I automatically straighten it out, taking care not to wrinkle his face.

"How early?" The way Melissa bobs her head around reminds me of an agitated burrowing owl.

Blushing, I close my locker door. "Early. I just had to get out, you know?"

Melissa glances around to make sure we're still alone. "Kristina must have been pissed off. She really wanted you to make an effort." She snarls her lip. "To *socialize*." She makes it sound like a curse word.

It's my cue to make snide remarks about Kristina, or boast about how we're too intellectually superior to care about stuff like that. Even I know we make fun of my overly gorgeous sister to burn off our own insecurities. I can't do it though. I can't play along today, no matter how much I know I should, to keep up appearances. It's too much work, so instead I shrug.

"What was she wearing?" Melissa demands, pushing back bangs that refuse to stay behind her ear.

For a moment I have an image of Kristina's low-cut tank top with the push-up bra, but it's replaced by the picture of her distraught face in the car on the way home from Devon's. Who cares? I lift a shoulder. "I don't know. I don't remember."

Melissa clucks her tongue on the roof of her mouth, sounding more like an old woman than a high-school freshman. An old woman disappointed in me.

"Well, were her and her friends all drunk?"

I shake my head.

"Was Kristina all over a guy trying to make Devon jealous?" Melissa won't stop and the mean streak in her voice makes her sound harsh. I wonder if it's always been there and I never bothered to notice before. I wonder if I sound the same way.

I shake my head again and press my lips tight.

"Were the volleyball girls doing the girl-kissing-girl thing?"

I regret telling Melissa about the time Kristina and her friends dared each other to kiss at a sleepover at our house. Mom and Dad went out to a university party and one of the girls brought wine coolers and they'd knocked them back and got silly. I'd spied the kissing when I'd gone to the kitchen for a snack.

"No." I snap and slide my lock in place and shut it. "It's not like she's a slut. And she doesn't get drunk. A waste of her precious calories."

Melissa sucks in a quick breath and stands straighter, tugging on the strap of the backpack slung over her shoulder. She carries it around all day instead of ditching it in her locker, mostly I think because she keeps stashes of chocolate bars and snacks in it. It doesn't seem fair the way our metabolisms work, but we don't really talk about it. Her stepmom is on her case about losing weight, even in front of me. She tells Melissa to ask God for help controlling her appetite. I haven't seen God giving out helpful diet advice though. Melissa also has a skinny little stepsister, which doesn't help. She can't stand her sister and I think weight is half the problem.

I glance away from Melissa. Of course the first thing I spot on the wall is a poster for a rally in the gym, featuring an action shot of Kristina. She's high off the ground, her arm high in the air, about to spike a volleyball over the net.

"The party was stupid," I say to end the conversation. For the first time in my life, I lie by omission to my best friend. I don't mention how Kristina dragged me around the party like a loser. I don't tell her about Jeremy taking our picture or how he kind of stalked me in the parking lot on Kristina's behalf. It seems trivial now.

Melissa stares at me, as if I've somehow betrayed her. But I can't play the game.

She finally says, "Oh," and glares at me as if trying to snap me out of my quiet mood. Then she frowns. "Well, I have to get to class." She spins away from me and marches off, getting caught up in the crowd of kids rushing around, without even checking in to make sure my homework is done. My stomach flutters with dread because, for the first time ever, the answer to Melissa's question would be no. I've actually come to school with an assignment only half-finished.

I wait for a break in the swarming bodies and then jump in, joining the flow toward my art class, and realize I didn't even tell her about the Oswald Drawing Prize, knowing she'd moan and groan about how with my family money, I shouldn't go after scholarships or awards. I imagine explaining it's not about the money, but that winning will change my life. But now, even without the Drawing Prize, that's already happened. It doesn't mean I should give up my dreams too, does it? I head down the hall contemplating it, and spot the gaggle of volleyball girls surrounding the water fountain outside my classroom.

All of the girls are tall and thin with identical low-riding jeans and long ponytails sprouting from their heads. I duck my head down quickly and try to get past unseen.

"Hey, Kristina's sister!"

Gee stares at me. Gee is her nickname, anyhow. The volleyball girls all have cute nicknames for each other, like Gee and Cee and Bree, but they can't be bothered to remember mine, even though they've been to my house a million times with Kristina.

"Where's Tee?" Gee says. "We have volleyball practice at noon."

Pretty, eager faces stare at me.

"Um, she's sick," I say, wishing they would ignore me and leave me alone like they're supposed to. It's only her first missed day of school and they're on me already?

"So?" Gee says and flips her hair back.

I try, but I can't remember her real name.

"Our big game is coming up. Tee should be tougher. It better be more than a little cold," she tells me, as if I'm responsible for Kristina's absence and/or health.

"Whatever," I manage to mumble. She has no idea how stupid

she's going to feel when she finds out the truth. I shrug and hurry past her, hoping she chokes on her own words later. Worse than a cold all right.

I zoom away and rush inside my class, even though I'd rather run to the bathroom and hide inside a toilet stall all day. Mr. Meekers is my art instructor, but he's also one of the faculty advisors for the Honor Society. He's everything I don't expect an art teacher to be. He wears dress pants and ties, and he's strict and has a bad disposition. I'd prayed to be in Miss Ingles's class. She's had listings at real art museums and wears long flowing dresses with scarves wrapped around her neck. She has jet-black hair like Cleopatra and speaks in a soft voice. She's much more of an inspiration and I imagine she'd be much easier to talk to, but I got Mr. Meekers. If I had her, I'd consult with her about the art award. But with him, I'm on my own. Still, staying in his good books is imperative to getting into the Honor Society, and Melissa wants that so badly. And me, I want it too.

I notice Clark Trent glaring at me through his Superman glasses. He's seated a few aisles from my desk, but instead of talking to his neighbors or texting people on his cell and ignoring my entrance like the rest of the class, he's staring at me. I'm tempted to stick my tongue out at him, but ignore him and plop down in my chair, wondering if it's possible to have a heart attack at the age of fifteen. I imagine cancer, black like an army of ants, eating away at Kristina's flesh from the inside, and lay my head on the desk and think about how it would feel being an only child. It makes my heartbeat fluctuate even more and the fear of heart failure makes me sit up. If I have to choose between Kristina never being born or being sick, I pick sick. Sick is better than not at all.

I swallow and swallow and stare at my desk until Mr. Meekers clears his throat, greets the class, and stands and pulls down the Smart Board screen, announcing we'll be watching a film on oil-painting techniques. He tells us to take notes for our exam and most kids groan. I wonder again why he is teaching art instead of science or biology.

He doesn't ask us to hand in our assignments that are supposed to be due today, an essay on sociopolitical issues in art. I pray none of the smart kids, like Clark, will remind him, and suddenly have a clear vision of how annoying I must be to regular people who aren't jonesing for Honor Society position.

Someone turns off the lights and the movie begins. I try to concentrate on the brush strokes but it's hard. When the movie mercifully ends, Mr. Meekers turns on the lights and babbles, but nothing soaks into my brain. Thankfully, the bell rings, releasing us from our seats.

I grab my books and stand and almost slam straight into Clark. His cheeks look splotchy.

I glare up at him. "What?"

His eyes get wrinkly in the corners as he squints down at me.

I try to step around him, but he moves in front of me and won't let me by. He smells like a bubble bath and I fight an urge to giggle, and work hard to avoid the visual of a naked Clark soaking in bubbles. I wonder if he wears his glasses in the bathtub.

"Why were you such a jerk to Jeremy this morning?" he asks, his voice stiff and his cheeks splotching even more.

The naked bubbles pop. "He's stalking my sister," I mumble.

His eyes narrow behind his black-framed glasses.

"She's not interested in younger boys," I say, wishing he'd go away and leave me alone and quit adding to the already too heavy bag of guilt and dark emotions weighing me down. God, I've talked to more boys this morning than the whole month and a half of school. And I'm not exactly doing a great job of it.

Clark pushes his glasses up on his nose. "He only wanted to know if your sister saw the pictures she *told* him to post."

He's right. "Sorry. He caught me at a bad time. I'm having a bad day. I had to ride my bike to school and I hate exercise."

Clark stares down at me for another second as if deciding whether I'm serious. And then he smiles. He has nice teeth. Really white and straight. He didn't go to elementary school with me but my guess is that he wore braces in grade school. "You know," he says. "You're in the pictures too. Maybe he's stalking *you*."

Laughter spills out from my lips and surprises me. It's a relief to find out he has a sense of humor. I like it better than confrontation.

"Yeah. Because I'm so stalkable."

He pushes his glasses up on his nose again and studies me. "Not really. You're not online very much. Do you even have an email address?"

"Of course I do." My cheeks warm and my insides flutter like hummingbird wings. I want to ask how he knows I'm not online. I contemplate supplying him with reasons. That social networking is stupid and for people with less stimulating things to do with their free time. But apparently he uses it. And maybe, just maybe, deep, deep down inside, I'm a little afraid that if I joined a bunch of these sites, no one would friend me and I'd be a social outcast online as well as off. People don't run up to me with their cameras and ask to take my picture with them. They run past me without seeing me and grab my sister and pose with her.

Or they did.

"You kids have a question?" Mr. Meekers asks from the front of the room.

Everyone else has cleared out of the class.

"No, sir." I start to walk and Clark falls in step beside me. He's taller than me and somehow walking beside him isn't so scary. It makes me feel almost…feminine. I imagine for a moment leaning up to kiss him and then hope like heck he can't read my mind.

"Have a good day, Mr. Meekers," he calls behind us, oblivious to my lechery. "So, is your sister sick or something?" he asks as we leave the classroom.

My legs suddenly are harder to move. When I missed a full week of class in middle school, no one even blinked an eye. Kristina is gone for a few hours and I'm already on inquiry number three. On top of the invasion of my privacy, I know it's messing with time and energy I should be devoting to being in the Honor Society. This is the crucial first semester when the selection is made. If I don't make Honor Society my freshman year, Melissa's dream of our becoming chapter leaders and attending the national conference will fade. I feel sorry for myself and a flash of resentment erupts toward Kristina.

It's quickly followed by a rush of shame. I'm worrying about losing my spot in a club for smart people. Kristina is fighting bone-eating cancer. She wins.

"It's no big deal." The words taste queasy as they leave my mouth. It is a big deal. A big freaking hairy deal.

No matter what my family wants, no matter how long they try to put it off, people are going to find out that Kristina has cancer. And maybe then they'll leave me alone. I hurry away from Clark, heading deep into the crowded hallway, and immediately get sucked up by a swarming locust cloud of kids all going in different directions. Noise and chatter fill my head. I imagine eyes staring at me from everywhere, curious, wanting answers, wondering where my sister is.

Instead of going to my locker I keep walking, moving against the crowd. I keep my head down and march on, until I'm going out the front doors of the school. I bolt down the steps and run to my bike. I'm even clumsier with the English books I'm still carrying, but manage to fumble with the lock, yank if off, and get on the bike, steering with one arm. I pedal as fast as my feeble legs will take me.

Tears blur my vision but I keep pedaling, zooming around a corner, almost home, when I cycle over a rock or something and, as if in slow-motion, flip over the top of the handlebars.

I do a graceless body plant on the pavement and my books go flying. My elbow instantly feels the burn from scraping concrete. Papers scatter into the air.

Car wheels screech behind me and I close my eyes and wait to be plowed over.

"You okay?" a voice calls out.

I open my eyes, relieved to find I haven't been flattened on the road, but humiliated nonetheless. I realize it's the same stupid car I saw at school earlier. The one that cut me off. The guy from the party is staring at me through the windshield, his eyes wide and gawky.

"I'm fine." I'm horrified. My eyes are filled with tears and I wince as I stand up. My leg is killing me but I don't need him to know that as I begin to fetch my books and papers.

The car engine shuts off and a car door slams. I turn and see he's pulled the car to the side of the road and jumped out. He walks over, picks up my bike, and rolls it off the road to the sidewalk.

"Better move out of the way or you'll be roadkill."

He smiles and his eyes twinkle with amusement, probably at my overwhelming clumsiness. He watches me as he puts my bike down on the sidewalk and walks back to me. "Hey, you're okay, aren't you?"

No, I want to scream. No, I'm not okay. And then, as if I'm a balloon filled with water, his kindness pokes a hole in my psyche and it starts to leak. Just like that, my nose gushes out gross liquids and tears stream down my face. I'm aware on some level that I should be embarrassed, but I collapse and sit in the middle of the road, crying like a little kid, while Drunk Pimple Guy stands there watching me crack up.

So much for the sturdy intellectual reputation I've been striving for.

He looks down at me and around at the empty road and then puts out his hand, grabs mine, and pulls me up. I let him help me to my feet, but drop his hand as if it burns as soon as I'm standing.

He motions with his head for me to follow him and I walk slowly to the safety of the sidewalk.

"I guess you're not okay?" he says, but his voice isn't judgmental.

I plunk down on the edge of the curb and put my head in my hands, but sense him sitting down beside me. Instead of saying anything, he sits quietly. My meltdown settles and with it my sense of normality returns. I realize what a complete and utter ass I'm making of myself. I snuffle, wipe my snotty nose on the back of my hand, and take a deep breath. A sigh escapes and drains the rest of my energy.

"I'm guessing this is about more than falling off your bike." He hugs his knees close and kind of rocks on his butt and doesn't look at me.

I start to giggle but it's kind of hysterical and completely inappropriate and reminds me of Kristina. I'm aware he must think I'm a freak maybe, or bipolar and in serious need of my meds. I don't want my sister to die. I don't want to lose her. I don't want her body eaten up by cancer.

"My name's Nick," he says. "And you're Kristina's little sister. I remember meeting you at the party but I was pretty wasted." He chuckles but it sounds self-conscious. "Sorry if I was a jerk or anything."

"You weren't a jerk. Just slobbering over my sister." I want to take my words back. I don't want to open up a conversation about her.

He lifts his shoulder in a shrug, but doesn't deny it or say anything more about Kristina.

"Your parents give you a first name?" he asks.

"Surprisingly, yes," I tell him. "Tess."

"Looks like Tess is having a pretty crappy day." The way he refers to me in third person makes me smile. "Does she want to talk about it?"

"She doesn't," I tell him.

"Well, maybe she should," he says. "Tell her it helps if you get things off your chest. That's what my therapist tells me."

I look at him and he's grinning. I wonder if he really does have a therapist.

"Nah," he says, as if I spoke the question out loud. "I don't have a therapist. Too rich for my blood."

Not mine but I don't tell him that. Part of me wants to tell him to go away, but in a strange way, I'm actually grateful for his company. He's not all in my face or flipping out, and honestly it seems to me having a breakdown with company is somehow slightly less terrifying than doing it alone.

So we sit on the curb. He rocks back and forth, kind of humming a song under his breath. I don't say anything, and for a moment I let myself feel what I'm feeling without trying to hide from it. Nick doesn't scream or run away from me, and it's the most emotionally exposed I've ever felt in front of a boy. But the thing is, I don't get struck by lightning. I don't turn to ashes. And he doesn't laugh at me.

I watch little ants crawl all over my sneakers, and sniffle, and wipe under my eyes. "Did you know ants can lift up to fifty times their own weight? That's like an eighty-pound kid lifting four thousand pounds."

Nick blinks, his features void of emotion. "And you're telling me this, because…?"

I shrug. "My head is full of useless facts." I glance sideways at him. "You really want to go to a therapist?" I ask him. "I could spot you a loan." I don't know what prompts me to say that. I sense he really does want to and it makes me like him a little better.

He laughs out loud and the sound gives me a tiny jolt of pleasure. "I don't take handouts." His voice is light but I sense some acidity under it. "Not even to improve my emotional health."

I nod. "You just get drunk instead?"

His lips straighten in a thin line and he looks away from me. My glow vanishes and I blush, wondering who I think I am, trying to act all mature and capable of witty repertoire. "Sorry," I mumble. "I didn't mean that."

"I probably deserved it." He smiles but it fades fast and its absence makes him look kind of sad. We're both quiet for a moment as we sit on the curb. It's surprisingly comfortable. I don't feel the need to get up or escape from him.

"So," he finally says. "Let me guess why you're so unhappy. You just got your first period?" His eyebrows wiggle up and down.

A laugh spurts from my mouth like water from an unclogging tap, and I quickly put my hand over my lips. "That's a totally jerky thing to say." I try to sound mad, but don't cut it.

"I know." He grins and his eyes light up and they're blue and much nicer when he's not drunk and smelly. "Okay then. Let me guess. You got an A minus on a test? Or worse, a B plus?"

I turn my head, trying to hide my smile, wondering how he knows I'm a brainiac. And then I look down at my loose jeans and hoodie and remember it's kind of obvious. Look at me. I ooze geek.

It's not like he's thought about it before this moment. A sigh slips out again.

He stands then and holds out his hand to pull me up. When we touch, a thrill races through me and my cheeks blaze. Man, what is wrong with me today? I would be a mess if boys talked to me all the time.

"Things aren't always as bad as they might seem." He checks his watch. "You are aware, Tess, that you skipped out of school in order to have this near-fatal collision? And that skipping is frowned upon by the faculty?"

Technically, I am skipping, but for once, rules don't matter. I'm entitled to an emotional health day. Like the days when Mom called in sick for Kristina so they could go to movies or to the spa. They asked me to join them, but I'd always said no. Afraid I'd somehow be caught. I sense those days are over now.

"What about you?" I say. "You're obviously skipping too."

He jumps off the curb to the road. "Sort of. I'm heading off for my tee time."

"Tea or tee?" I make the motions of drinking from a cup and then swinging a club.

He swings at the air. "I get free golf games once in a while, a perk of my job as grounds keeper at Largurt Country Club. I figure it's like a phys ed class, you know. I should get credit for it."

"My dad golfs there," I tell him. The only reason Dad has friends outside work is for golf.

He nods. "I know who your dad is. He's a gold member. He has killer clubs." He glances at his watch again. The strap is beat-up and its face looks scratched. It's funny, not many kids my age actually wear watches. "You want a ride to wherever you're going?" he asks.

"No." My voice drops. "I'm heading home. And I have my bike."

He dangles his car keys around his finger. "I could put your bike in my trunk and give you a lift if you want. I don't mind."

"No, it's okay." I don't want him near our stupidly big house. Or Kristina, which I know makes me a really bad sister, but for some reason I want to keep him for myself. I remember what Kristina said about him. That he's a boy-slut. But he seems pretty nice. And it's not like he's about to make any moves on me.

"You're the boss." We both walk to my bike on the sidewalk, with my books piled beside it, close to where he's parked.

In the sunlight his face doesn't look pimply. He's got normal teenage skin. He takes a step and bends down to pick up my bike, straightens, and holds it out to me. "You sure you're okay to ride this crazy pink thing?"

"Fine," I tell him, and take the bike. "I'm fine."

We both know I'm lying, but he holds out his hand and takes my books while I climb on my bike. When I'm on, he hands them to me and I tuck them under my arm and grab the handlebar with the other hand.

"See you around, Tess the freshman."

"Tess the Mess," I mumble and start to pedal away.

"Hey," he calls. I look around and he winks at me. "You're kinda cute when you get all flustered."

My insides smoosh around. The bike wobbles.

"Well, for a freshman," he calls.

"My sister told me you were a man-whore," I yell over my shoulder and then wonder if I've lost my mind.

I hear him snort. "See ya around," he calls. I hide a smile and concentrate on the road so I don't wipe out in front of him…again. He called me cute! Ha! Even though it's pretty clear he only said it because he feels sorry for me, it was nice. People surprise me. That much I know.

When I get home, Kristina is locked in her room. I tell Mom she needs to call in sick to the school for me. She gives me a funny look but goes ahead and calls the school.

I go to my room and pull out my sketchbook. Lines and textures flow from me. I'm inspired by images in my head. I've decided on a piece that is sort of a volcano landscape but suggests so much more, says something a little deeper. I sketch and know I'm not quite where I want to be, but getting closer. I lose myself in my work and slowly the realities of life disappear.

Escape is one of a million reasons I love art. I want to win this contest so badly I can taste it. The taste is better than warm pecan pie, my favorite dessert in the entire world. Winning would change my life. Change how people see me. How I see myself. It would show everyone who I am. Besides Kristina's little sister.

Through the walls, Kristina coughs. My concentration broken, I put my pencil down. My giddiness fades. I'm thinking about winning a stupid contest. Kristina is thinking about dying.

chapter six

My whole family is squeezed into one of a few cubicles in a row at the doctor's office. A thin curtain shields us from the hallway.

Mom insists we pile inside and wait with Kristina after she changes into a blue paper gown. Kristina is pale, but still looks as pretty as ever. Her hair is pulled up high in a ponytail. It's shiny and blond. She looks like she should be on a box of hair color.

Dad and I stand, but Mom sits with Kristina on the examining table, their legs pressed together. Kristina looks wrong in the papery gown, with her toned arm muscles, her square shoulders. Her trainer has worked her hard over the months and it shows. Her outfit and her expression don't suit the image of the high-jumping spiker who makes the opposition quiver on the volleyball court.

Kristina bows her head and closes her eyes. I wonder if she's praying. We're not a church family, not like Melissa's. Dad says he had religion forced down his throat when he was younger and he doesn't want to do it to us. Mom doesn't have a strong opinion one way or another. She doesn't talk about her childhood much, and the last time we saw her parents was over five years ago. Far as I know she hasn't even told them about Kristina.

We only go to church when someone dies. Not even at Christmas or Easter. Melissa told me once that she thought it would matter. As in after. It was the first time we had a real fight. Well, we're wimps so it was more that we didn't talk to each other for a few days. Then we pretended none of it happened. I never learned how to pray. I've thought about it and stuff, tried talking to God in my head sometimes, but mostly it makes me nervous and I wonder what he really thinks of me. Like does he think I'm a bad person because I don't go to church or read the Bible? I don't really feel like I have the right to ask for anything now. I mean, I really, really want to ask for God to fix Kristina, but I'm afraid it might make things worse. Like instead she might get punished because I'm only praying when I want something.

Dad stares at the wall, no expression on his features, but the blankness doesn't mask the fear he's hiding. I wonder if he's worried he won't be able to handle it. He's always been the kind of guy who prefers not to face things head-on. That's what Mom says anyhow. She says he inherited it from my grandpa, but he died before I was born so who knows if she's right.

Mom fusses with her purse, pretending to search for something, rooting through her worldly goods to keep her mind busy, focused away from what is happening. She appears to be planted firmly in the soil of denial. Kristina will be fine, just fine.

In the room next to us I hear a woman moving around, probably changing back into her street clothes. I saw her walk to her room alone in her blue gown, following a nurse.

I wish I could ask Kristina if she's okay, but I stand frozen, barely breathing, barely moving.

"Kristina Smith?" a deep feminine voice calls from the other side of the curtain. The raspy voice sounds like she should be on a morning show on the radio.

"Yes?" Kristina answers, her voice weak, frightened. She looks to Mom for courage.

A nurse pulls back the curtain and the four of us stare at her. She's short. Her uniform is red with Scottish Terriers on it and it makes her look boxy. She wears a name tag that says "Pamela."

"The doctor ordered a couple more X-rays, and when those are done, I'll take you to her office where she'd like to speak with all of you," she says. Her voice is rich with an accent. Scottish?

The nurse glances at the rest of us. "There's no one needing this room so you can stay here or wait out in the waiting room where it's more comfortable until the X-rays are done. You can join Kristina in the doctor's office afterward."

Her accent has a slight comforting effect on me.

"Can I go to the X-ray room with her?" Mom asks.

The nurse looks at Kristina for approval and then nods. Mom and Kristina disappear into the hallway, and Dad and I are left alone.

"I'd rather wait here than out there," he says, and his voice catches. "Jesus Christ, Tess. What am I supposed to do?"

I don't tell him that he's the parent, not me. I say nothing. We don't exchange another word until half an hour or so later when Kristina and Mom return.

"Okay, out," Mom tells us. "Kristina needs to change into her clothes and then we're to wait in Dr. Turner's office. Room 2. The nurse showed me where to go."

Dad and I stand awkwardly in the hallway. I pull my sketchbook from my backpack to see if I can get down some ideas or make a couple of rough thumbnails. If I'm going to get my entry in on time, I have to start getting inspired, but my brain won't allow me to work. Dad doesn't ask what I'm doing or even pretend to be interested. I still haven't mentioned the Oswald Drawing Prize to him.

Instead of working, I dream of taking Kristina with me to San Francisco. We'd attend the awards ceremony together and then she could go shopping or do something else she likes. Man, I need to get my piece going if that's going to happen.

Eventually, Kristina and Mom emerge from the changing room and I hurriedly put away my pad. Mom leads the way to the doctor's office. We follow, quiet and slow, like kids being shuffled off to the principal's office for doing something wrong.

The doctor's room is stark. White walls, no examining table. There's a big desk with a computer and monitor on top and a leather office chair pulled up to it. There are two cheap steel chairs opposite it. Kristina sits right away, her head bent. I lean against the wall close to the door and gnaw on my lip. Dad leans on the opposite wall, staring into space. Mom heads straight for the doctor's desk and opens a thick medical book sitting on top of it. She starts flipping pages. I think she's searching for something to tell that her daughter will be okay.

Minutes go by, painfully long quiet minutes. Finally the doctor walks in the room and all of us snap to attention. She looks young. She's pretty, with wavy brown hair. She's wearing makeup and jewelry and a blue dress under an open white lab coat. I think how unfair it is that she seems to have been dealt an overabundance of good genes. Brains. Beauty. She got it all.

She touches Kristina's shoulder as she passes. I have an urge to yell at the doctor, to demand she tell us it's all been a big mistake.

I glare at her, wanting her to fix my sister with her slender, pretty hands. Make the nightmare go away. Mom closes the book she's been snooping in and moves back, sitting in the chair beside Kristina. Dad doesn't budge, but follows the doctor with his eyes. The doctor walks around her desk, clicks a key on the keyboard, and checks the screen for a second before turning her attention to Kristina. My sister stares at her and her eyes fill with tears. When I look at Dr. Turner's face, I know immediately. The news isn't good. I feel sick to my stomach.

I blink rapidly, trying to keep my tears inside.

"Kristina," Dr. Turner says, and shifts her hip against the desk, not sitting yet. She nods at my parents. They've already met, formal introductions have been made. She smiles at me. "You must be Tess," she says, but doesn't seem to expect an answer, which is good because my throat is so tight, nothing, no sound is capable of coming out.

We all stare at her, holding our breath as a family. Waiting.

She sits in her chair, and leans back. "The tumor is directly above the knee. As expected with this type of cancer, we're looking at a Stage 2B. The mass is larger than I would like, but despite that, we're going to do what we can to help you keep your leg, Kristina. Many osteo patients can have limb-saving treatment and that's what we'll hope for you."

Bile boils around my stomach. I swallow a bitter taste, watching the doctor as if she's insane. Help her keep her leg?

"Stage 2B means it's a high-grade cancer, very aggressive," she says as if one of us asked the question.

No one says anything. The doctor waits. Tears stream down my mom's face. My dad's face is stony, blank. Kristina stares at her hands, twisting them around and around in her lap.

"I assume you and your family have talked about the possibility of amputation," the doctor says.

"Not really," Kristina whispers without looking up.

I have an image in my head of Kristina with a stump at the end of her leg and want to throw up.

The doctor's lips tighten. I wonder if she wants to give my parents a lecture. They certainly didn't have a discussion with me about Kristina losing a leg, but not even with her? I want to scream at them. Blame them for what is happening.

"Osteosarcoma can spread quickly to other bones or even to the lungs if we don't get it fast."

My mom gasps. "The lungs?"

It's obvious we've all been living in a state of denial. I've been busy trying to sketch and trying to study. I've even avoided googling osteosarcoma. God knows how my parents have managed to hide from it too, but here's reality poking its ugly head out and forcing us to deal. Kristina's cancer is serious. Very serious.

The doctor blinks slowly and stares at Mom. "Worst-case scenario is spreading. We have no way of knowing what will happen at this point, but spreading is, of course, a possibility. We'll start treatment immediately." The doctor smiles briefly, but it's not a happy smile. "Fortunately, we have a team of specialists in our hospital, and we'll be able to treat you here instead of shipping you off to another part of the country."

I feel like someone punched me in the stomach and pulled the breath out of my lungs, clamping long fingers around my windpipe. This is the fortunate scenario?

"We'll start the first round of chemotherapy right away," the doctor says in a soft but businesslike voice. "The initial MRI doesn't show any spread beyond the knee yet, but we took more X-rays today and we'll repeat tests throughout Kristina's treatment. I expect a few rounds of chemo."

Although it doesn't seem possible, my dad stiffens even more. I stare at him. He's so rigid I imagine if I pushed him with one finger he'd go down like a statue.

"How soon will she start?" my mom asks.

The doctor leans forward. "Like I said, osteosarcoma is aggressive. We'd like to get to it right away and since you've indicated that waiting for insurance is not an issue for your family, I had my secretary book her into the hospital…" She clicks the mouse and waits a moment while she reads the monitor. "In four days. September 30. First thing in the morning. Pamela, my nurse, will give you instructions on where to go and what to do before the treatment begins."

It feels like someone reaches inside with a long vacuum hose to suck out my insides.

"Four days?" my sister asks.

"It's fast, I know, but we want to go after it right away. It happens like this a lot with bone cancer. I'm sorry there's not more time to adjust," Dr. Turner tells her.

"Will her hair fall out?" Mom asks, her voice soft but machinelike.

"Most likely," the doctor answers and she turns to Kristina and studies her. "Not right away but usually after the first round."

Kristina makes a tiny sound, like a kitten's mew. Her face is as pale as the fresh snow that will soon be falling. Kristina stares at her hands, winding them around and around each other. "You should also know that chemo can be very damaging to fertility," the doctor says.

"I don't care about that," Kristina answers and shrinks into herself even more.

Mom makes a sound like a bird in distress.

"Well, it's a fact that has to be mentioned, but we want to get the chemo started right away." She pauses, but no one says a thing. "Do you have questions, Kristina?" the doctor asks in a softer, more sympathetic tone. "I want you to feel prepared for what lies ahead."

I wonder if the doctor has a sister. I wonder if her sister has ever been sick. Really sick. My heart thumps faster. It's not fair, I think. It's not fair. How can Kristina look so normal and be so seriously ill?

"How do I take it?" Kristina's voice cracks. She clears her throat. "I mean the chemo. Is it a pill or, um, a liquid or what?"

My dad opens his mouth to begin speaking but the doctor lifts her hand to cut him off. It's her specialty after all. His is university stuff. Not cancer treatment.

"Chemo has different forms and different ways of being ingested.

It depends on many factors—the type of cancer, and the stage, and so on. We have developed drug protocols for higher response rates." The doctor pauses and wipes a strand of hair from her eyes. Her eyes look tired. "Your type of cancer requires chemo to be given intravenously via a drip. It's a fluid. We'll put it in through a vein up your arm, or in your neck. Before you start chemo you'll have an intravenous catheter, or a line, inserted into your chest. It threads through to your heart. Scar tissue holds it in place."

I cringe and force myself to go numb, trying not to register what Kristina will have to go through. The thought of anyone inserting something inside me makes my limbs feel like jelly. I can't imagine what Kristina must be thinking.

"The insertion will be done under local anesthetic. It isn't terribly pleasant, to be honest, but once it's in we'll leave it there for the duration of chemo, which means you don't have to keep having needles and lines put in all the time."

"Great," Kristina says and drops her head down again. None of us other Smiths manage to say a word. We're not a chatty bunch today. The doctor glances at each of us as if she expects one of us to speak but when we don't she reaches a hand out and pats Kristina's hand. "I expect at least two rounds of chemo. We want to try to shrink your tumor. Save your limb if we can." Her voice is calm but detached.

If.

My head snaps up. I am so not ready to deal with this. Kristina has squeezed her eyes shut and her face is tighter than the fists I'm making.

"We hope to be able to cut out the diseased bone and replace it with an internal metal prosthesis. You have full access to all available treatments. Financially. You're lucky for that."

Thanks, Grandpa Smith. Boo for mean drinking habits but yay for financial wizardry.

Mom nods and draws in a sharp breath, and Dad shifts his weight back and forth, his eyes on the floor.

"Money is not an issue. We want the best for Kristina," Mom says.

Kristina doesn't move.

"Is that the expected outcome?" my mom asks. "Metal in her leg? What about her athletic career?"

My mouth drops open. No, she did *not* just say that. Dad continues his fascination with the tiles on the floor.

Dr. Turner lets out a quick breath. "In our opinion, an internal prosthesis probably wouldn't give Kristina back full mobility. I can't tell you for sure which will be feasible until we begin the process. We can hope for endo-prosthetic surgery, the internal prosthesis; however, often with limb salvage there are a bunch of activities that a patient will not be able to do, especially aggressive sports. We often recommend amputation if the patient wants to pursue aggressive sports. An external prosthesis is better for that." The doctor makes a note on her laptop and looks up.

"No," my mom shouts. "We save her leg. It's more important than volleyball."

The room starts to spin a little. Amputation. Prosthesis. In my head I see a chain saw revving up and being held over my sister's leg.

"No!" I echo out loud before my imagination carves off Kristina's bone. All eyes turn to me. "She can't lose her volleyball or her leg," I say, and my voice is louder than I want it to be. Angry. "She's the volleyball captain at school. The best player in the whole city. She's going to play in college next year."

"Tess," my dad says, and I hear the warning in his tone.

"No." I can't stop myself. It's unfair and I don't want to hear it. Kristina can't lose a leg or have a metal bone put inside her leg. She has plans. Plans that involve two legs.

"She needs her leg for a volleyball scholarship," I sputter.

My dad steps forward and puts a hand on my shoulder. "She doesn't need a scholarship. We can afford any university your sister wants to go to." He says it softly, but his hand squeezes harder and it feels like it's bruising my flesh.

I push his hand away. I don't want to be touched. I don't want people touching Kristina. I want to grab her hand and run from the room with her. Jump in her car and drive far away.

"But…" I sputter again, trying to put into words what I cannot say. "It's not the plan." I stop. She doesn't have the grades, I want to yell. I'm the smart one. She's the athletic one.

"Shut up, Tess," Kristina hisses. "This isn't about what you want." I deflate. She glares at me but her expression is unrecognizable. The life in her eyes is gone. They're dull. Even her posture is different. Her back is bent over, hunched, and the glow of perfection has faded. I close my eyes tight.

"I won't play volleyball if I keep my leg?" Kristina asks in a quiet voice.

The doctor clears her throat. "It's too soon to say what is going to happen. It depends how treatment goes. It will take time to find out. I do have patients who go on to do sports."

"No," my mom says again. "Kristina, you'll keep your leg."

Kristina doesn't even look at her. She's focusing on the doctor. "Like Paralympics, you mean?"

The doctor doesn't answer that question. "You need to be prepared for all the options."

My mom sniffles loudly and pulls Kristina in tight, as if she can keep out the big bad world with her embrace. Dad returns to his spot against the wall, stiff.

The doctor clears her throat, watching our family fall apart. "There is support available. Because Kristina is eighteen she's not considered a child, but we have resources for adults as well. Pamela, my nurse, will give you all the information you need."

Dr. Turner stands. She bows her head and then looks up. "Okay then. We'll be in touch. Please make sure you get all the information from Pamela." She leaves the room and with her, normality flies out the door.

Kristina starts to cry but it's soft and unbearable. "You can't tell anyone at school about this," she says to me. "I don't want anyone finding out I might lose my leg. Not a soul."

"But…"

"You listen to your sister, Tess," Mom says, cutting me off as I'm about to tell her how impossible that will even be. "We'll work out something. We'll worry about breaking the news later. Kristina needs her privacy right now."

She does? Or does she need friends who can back her emotionally and let her know she's still okay? I suspect Mom wants to keep it a secret for her own reasons and I want to yell that Kristina is a person who needs people around to help her deal, but I don't want to upset Kristina even more.

Dad says nothing. I stare at him and wait for him to tell them it's a bad idea, but he's mute. Anger flashes through me. How long do they expect they can pretend that everything is fine? And how can it be the right thing to encourage her to keep it quiet? Do they think people just won't notice her absence? She's not me. She doesn't fly under the radar.

Is she supposed to be ashamed of her bones?

chapter seven

When I turn the corner inside school, Melissa waits at my locker. Her hair is flat, and she tucks a strand behind her ear. When she sees me her eyes widen, almost as if she's frightened. I've been avoiding her and she knows it, but not why. I try to keep my expression neutral but it takes every ounce of control not to burst into tears and spill the whole thing. My sister's words echo in my ear.

"Not even Melissa."

Kristina slipped into my room after we got home from the doctor and sat on the edge of my bed. "You can't tell anyone. Not even her."

I looked her right in the eye. "But, Kristina," I said. "She's my best friend."

She shook her head. "She's not as nice as you think and she's no fan of mine."

I wanted to fight her on it, but under the circumstances, I let it go. Hiding her cancer seems like a stupid, stupid idea, but I'm the only one who thinks so, and for now it isn't my decision. If she wants me to keep it from everyone including my best friend, it's the least I can do.

"Hi, Tess," Melissa says, but her greeting is almost a question.

I wipe a dribble of sweat from my brow.

"You rode your bike again?" she asks.

I nod and shrug. "I need the exercise."

She stares at me. "You hate exercise."

"Kristina's, uh…sick. I think it's a bug or something."

Or cancer. Limb-stealing cancer. I close my eyes tight for a second and take a deep breath.

"She's kind of milking it, don't you think? Missing this much school for a cold." Melissa's bitter voice slices through my skin and leaves me covered in goose bumps. I never noticed how much it sounds like she really hates my sister. I mean real hate.

The two of us bitch about Kristina all the time, but it's not supposed to be vicious. It's supposed to makes us feel better about our own ineptness, slamming one of the chosen ones. To whom I just happen to be related.

"No. I mean, she's sick so she stays home. It's no big deal, right?"

"She's a drama queen," Melissa says.

"She is not."

My hands shake a little as I stare at her. The best friend I've ever had. She and I have been inseparable since she moved to Great Heights in fifth grade. Well, at school. Her parents don't let her socialize much outside of school.

We were thrown together, the last two girls picked for sports teams and the last two paired up in class. We bonded over brain power and challenge each other academically. Sometimes Melissa gets carried away with her gossiping but it's mostly harmless. I think it's because Melissa isn't good around people she's not comfortable with. And she's uncomfortable with almost everyone. It's our biggest weakness in the quest for Honor Society takeover.

Melissa stares at me. "Is everything okay?"

I nod and attempt a smile as if everything is peachy keen, jelly bean.

Melissa shuffles her feet in a mini box step. "Are you mad at me about something?" She peeks up from under her bangs.

I shake my head quickly but she just blinks. I'm about to try to convince her when movement and color catch my eye and I look to see Devon and Gee marching down the hallway. They're coming straight for us.

For me.

"Shoot," I mutter under my breath.

Melissa looks over and her eyes widen.

"Tess Smith," Gee calls.

They walk right up and stop. I avert my eyes before images of what Devon did with my sister burn into them.

"What's up with Tee?" Gee asks.

I focus on her. She's taller than me, with equally long limbs, but hers have been blessed with the gift of coordination. Instead of being gangly, the long legs and arms work on her.

"Uh…" I search my brain cells for something to say. "I don't know. She's got a bug or something." I long for the days when the two of them ignored my existence.

I don't tell Gee that Kristina and Mom met with the principal. Mom decided to tell him in person and asked for his discretion about sharing the news. I still don't understand why Kristina can't trust her friends to know the truth.

"A bug? You mean like a cold or something? Tee doesn't miss practice, games, and this much school for a cold." Devon's usually loud macho voice is kind of soft, dare I say almost worried. "She hasn't returned my calls or emails."

"I've been texting her every hour for the last few days and she hasn't answered me. This is not like Tee," Gee says.

Devon nods at Gee. "She hasn't called or texted anyone. It's like she's gone missing. It's totally bizarre."

He sounds upset and looks surprisingly unashamed of it. I wonder if he really does like her, if she means more to him than just hooking up. If so, I feel sorry for him. It wasn't really fair, what she did with him, for her own reasons. I'm on her side, but obviously she didn't think it out. I don't think she tried to hurt him, but either way, he's left with a memory too. A memory that he'll connect to her cancer when he finds out.

"She's fine." The word almost scalds my tongue and I bite down on my lower lip and study my shoes. "She's just tired and not up to going online or picking up any of her messages right now. Um, I have to go to class." I spin around and dart away as fast as I can, leaving Melissa alone with them. Probably scarring her for life.

Gee calls my name but I speed up and turn a corner. I slam into a body and groan a little from the impact. It's Mr. Meekers, my art teacher.

"Tess," he says. "Try to watch where you're going." I wait for him to give me hell.

"Sorry," I mumble when he says nothing.

He tilts his head for a second and then puts a hand on my arm to stop me from moving past him.

"How's your sister doing?" he asks.

"Fine." The rehearsed lie rolls off my tongue. I look him straight in the eyes. "She's doing okay." I shrug as if it's irrelevant to me.

He moves his hand to my shoulder and squeezes. It's awkward and it gives me the creeps, and even though he doesn't say anything, I'm certain that he knows. It's occurred to me that most of the staff knows despite what Mom and Kristina wanted. Gossip is a powerful drug.

• • •

I hate myself.

I do not want to walk into the hospital room. I do not want to see my own sister. Instead my impulse is to turn, sneak to the elevator, walk out the door, jump on a bus, and go home. I want to work on my art, or even just turn on the Discovery Channel and watch lions have sex. But as soon as I got home from school, Mom shuffled me to the car, not caring about my resistance in joining her.

"Your sister needs you," she says as she pushes me toward her car. "She's started her chemo and if you're not there for her, you'll regret it someday."

"What about Dad?"

"Your dad has to work late. He won't be around until later."

Nothing I say will change her mind. End of story. We drive to the hospital without saying one word. When we arrive and she finally finds an empty spot in the parking lot, she walks me all the way through the admitting floor. It smells like cleaning products. We pass a flow of people on our way to the elevator leading to Kristina's floor. Some look like patients, some like doctors. There are lots of people wearing different-colored scrubs. They could be nurses or janitors; it's impossible to tell. I wonder if there's some sort of code. Some sort of hierarchy that determines which color people wear. I see a lot of dark pink uniforms. A priest or reverend or whichever one it is that wears a black shirt and white collar passes by and smiles at me. I immediately wonder why he's smiling.

When we reach the elevator, Mom holds the door, tells me Kristina's room number, and then says she's going to pick up a coffee from the cafeteria and will join me in a minute.

"I never slept a wink last night worrying about your sister. I need caffeine," she says.

My guess is that she wants me and Kristina to have some alone time. As if Kristina's going to confide in me.

When the elevator opens there's new activity on the fourth floor. I pass a hand-sanitizing station and stop to clean my hands. People in scrubs walk past but no one stops me or asks what I'm doing or who I'm visiting. I wander up the hallway until I find her room and walk in slowly. Kristina doesn't hear or sense my presence right away. She's propped up against some pillows and her blond hair flows limply over them. She's staring out the window across from her bed. The only view I can see from where I stand is a brick wall. Great hospital scenery.

A nurse stands beside her, fiddling with tubes jutting out of Kristina's chest. Kristina started the drip a couple hours earlier, while I was in school avoiding her friends. She's hooked up to stuff inside a bag and it looks like bright orange Kool-Aid. Her chemo. It's awful stuff from what I've read on the Internet.

"Hi," I call, but my voice is weak. My feet feel clumsy and heavy as I walk toward her.

Kristina turns her head. I stop walking. Her skin tone is almost green, not helped by the ultraviolet lights in the room. She looks tired and so, so sad.

"Hi," I say to the nurse.

She smiles her greeting and walks over to a counter by the window where she grabs a pen from her pocket and starts jotting notes on a chart. She gives Kristina and me privacy without physically leaving the room.

My heart aches. I swallow and swallow but it's painful and dry. There's a big lump in my throat, a bump of trapped words and trapped tears. I force myself to move closer. There's a silver chair in the corner by the window, so I pull it out and move it beside her bed.

"So," I finally say, trying to sound normal. "Everyone at school is asking for you. Your popularity hasn't waned in your absence." I attempt a smile, but she doesn't respond in any way.

Slowly, I sit. I don't bother telling her how much grief her absence is causing me. Here in the hospital room, it seems stupid and petty how freaking hard I think my life is because of her. People talking to me, staring at me, is nothing compared to lying in a hospital bed being poisoned.

She closes her eyes and for once the quiet actually bothers me. I try to think of something to say. "Um, so, I found out about this really prestigious drawing contest. The winner gets a scholarship to the Academy of Art University and a trip to San Francisco. I'm actually going to enter, can you believe it? If I win, I get to take someone. I thought it would be really cool if you could come with me, you know, if you're done with your chemo and everything..."

Her face gets even paler and then Kristina opens her eyes as if she's alarmed and begins to cough. It takes energy she doesn't seem to have and then she groans and it's a horrible sound, more like an animal than my sister. The nurse who has been watching her closely darts to her side and then a spew of liquid shoots from Kristina's mouth and the nurse's blue uniform is splattered by foul-smelling stuff. I jump up from the chair and almost knock it over. The nurse mumbles as Kristina chokes and then throws up again.

Mom picks that moment to walk in, as Kristina projectile-vomits on the nurse again.

Mom runs straight back out the door and I stand frozen in place not quite believing what is happening. The nurse scrambles around as Kristina cries feebly. Seconds later, another nurse comes rushing in the room with towels in her arms and Mom right behind her. The nurse points at me and then the door as she rushes to Kristina.

I gratefully hurry out into the hallway and stand outside the room, shifting from foot to foot, listening to the retching sounds and then weak crying, barely audible beneath the reassuring words from the nurses.

Mom comes out of the room a minute later, still clutching a cup of coffee. "Jesus Christ, they need to give her better anti-sickness drugs on her next cycle."

I close my eyes, not wanting to think about my sister going through this again. Mom's hand brushes against my arm as she hurries past me toward a trash can and pitches out her coffee. We stand in the hallway awkwardly. Inside, we can hear Kristina retching and crying. Mom goes back inside but I'm frozen to the spot.

Eventually, one of the nurses comes out of Kristina's room with a handful of soiled towels.

"It happens like this sometimes," she tells me and gives me a sympathetic look before hurrying off, probably to the laundry chute. "We gave her antinausea meds, but we didn't get the dose right."

• • •

At school the next day, I duck down in my chair like I'm three years old. I can't see you, you can't see me. Kids wander into class and sit, draping bodies over chairs and desks, checking out their phones and texting. Despite trying to be invisible, I feel curious stares on me and hear my name and Kristina's whispered. Rumors circulate the air, invisible but always there, like tiny particles of dust.

I sit up a little straighter, wondering how I'm going to pull this off. It's nothing compared to what Kristina's going through, I know that, but my world doesn't seem the same anymore either. It's a lonely place pretending that everything is fine.

I pull books from my backpack and check over my unfinished homework as the classroom fills up. After the bell rings, Mr. Pepson stands, tells everyone to put away their phones, and begins speaking. He's the lead school faculty advisor for the Honor

Society chapter, so I've invested many hours demonstrating what a great student I am to him. By habit I pretend to be interested in his lecture about *A Midsummer Night's Dream*. I've worked hard over the first term to show him I'm quality HS material, but after a while suspect if he doesn't finish his lecture soon and I have to sit still another minute, my head will explode. As he assigns a thematic essay on Shakespeare, I gather my stuff and walk to the front of the class.

Clark Trent watches me with undisguised curiosity. I ignore him and lean forward and whisper. "I'm feeling sick," I tell Mr. Pepson. "I need to go see the nurse."

He stares at me for a second too long, and I'm about to resort to the female problem excuse that makes male teachers squirm, when his eyes flicker with sympathy.

"Fine, Tess. Go."

Mr. Pepson acts as if it's normal for me to get up before the bell and leave. An anal Honor Society wannabe. I head for the door, sensing curious, staring eyeballs on my back, but rush out. Instead of going to the nurse's office, I bolt down empty hallways, heading toward the front door of the school.

"Hey, Tess."

The voice startles me and I stop and freeze, grabbing at my chest to make sure my heart stays where it's supposed to. It's Jeremy. The stalker.

"Where're you going?" he asks.

"Home. Flu." I fake a cough to prove my point.

The look on his face convinces me he knows I'm lying.

"What?" I wish he'd go away and leave me alone. "What do you want?"

"I saw you running down the hall so I told Mrs. Sheppard I had to go to the bathroom. I wanted to make sure you're okay."

I wait for him to explain more but he says nothing.

I start walking again and he hurries along beside me. He's not as tall as me and has to rush a little to keep up. "Why wouldn't I be okay?"

"I saw Kristina," he says softly.

My entire body freezes as a cold rush of fear goes through me. "What?" I repeat, but my voice is hardly recognizable as my own. I look around but it's just the two of us. Everyone else is in class.

"At the hospital," he whispers.

I open my mouth to lie, to tell him he's wrong, but then I close it. If he's seen her, how can I lie about that?

Jeremy takes me by the arm and pulls me along with him. "Come on." We keep going until we reach the front door. He hurries to open the door and waits until I go first and then we're on the front steps and the heavy doors close behind us. It's cool outside and I'm not wearing a coat so I shiver a little, but nothing will make me go back inside the school.

"How did you know she was at the hospital? Are you seriously stalking her?"

Jeremy glares at me and his eyes shoot sparks of anger, but then he blinks and instantly they're gone. He drops his gaze to his feet. "I'm not stalking her." He looks in my eyes then. "I saw Kristina when I was visiting my mom. She's being treated for breast cancer."

I lower my gaze to the cement, and stare at initials someone etched into the top step years before. I wonder how that love affair turned out. If one of them got sick, or if they still remember the times they kissed. I hold my breath until my lungs shout for oxygen and then breathe out slowly and inhale again.

"I'm sorry," I say, and wonder why people always say that when they find out bad news. Sorry? It's not my fault, so exactly what am I actually sorry about? Am I sorry that his mom is sick, or sorry that I have to deal with the fact that he's told me?

I'm expected to show him compassion and understanding because he's suffering too. And I do. I feel bad, but I don't want to. I don't want to be forced to think of boobs as a source of disease and I don't want to think about cancer.

"Thanks." He lifts his shoulder and there's pain but also quiet dignity in the movement. I look away and feel ashamed.

"How's Kristina?" he asks.

"Terrible." I sigh, and speaking the truth drains me.

"That's about what I expected," he says. "Cancer is horrible."

His honesty has a surprising, calming effect on my anger. I realize if anyone is remotely close to understanding how I feel, it's him. I look at him, really look at him. He's a cute boy with his babyish face and his clean wrinkle-free clothes. Goes to show how deceiving appearances can be. He looks like he doesn't have a problem in the world.

"She doesn't want anyone to know about it," I tell him. "No one."

He smiles sadly and juts his chin down and then back up, in a sort of nod. "I'm not going to say anything, if you're worried."

"I'm not worried," I tell him. We stare at each other for another minute. "Should I be?"

He shakes his head and even I can see the weight of sadness in his shoulders. He won't say a word.

I start to walk down the steps and he follows.

"Aren't you supposed to get back to class?" I ask him.

"Aren't you?"

I gesture at my backpack. "I'm leaving."

He nods without pointing out the obvious. I'm skipping my next class too. I'm leaving school without permission. Again.

"I'm sorry about your mom." I mean it this time.

"I'm really sorry about your sister," he says. "It must be hard for you."

It's the first time someone says that. The first time someone recognizes that I have to deal with it too. I wipe away sudden tears. "Thanks. You better go back. See you around, Stalker." I give him a teeny smile.

He laughs. It warms my heart just a little to hear that people still laugh when the people they love have cancer.

I plow toward a group of kids across from the school yard, hanging out. I duck my head, hoping it's not volleyball players or friends of Kristina who in the last few days have constantly been seeking me out for updates. I'm no longer invisible and it annoys the heck out of me. The sudden surge in popularity has nothing to do with me.

The tears damned up behind my eyes press harder to get out. I hurry past them, hoping I can make it by without starting to cry, and then slam hard into another body. I catch my breath when a hand grabs me.

"Hey, Freshie. Take it easy. You almost knocked me over."

Nick.

He smiles like I'm amusing. My insides do the stomp from seeing him look at me like that. It pisses me off and I squirm to get away. I have an irrational urge to belt him in the stomach for making me crush on him and for looking happy when my world is falling apart. Fortunately, I'm sane enough to know that punching him in the stomach won't solve anything, and might get me expelled or thrown into intensive mental therapy. So I just stare and round up the butterflies in my belly with an internal net.

"Whoa." He stops smiling. "You okay? You look like your dog just died."

"What if my dog did just die?" I snap.

His face reddens and his eyes dart around nervously. "Seriously? Your dog died?"

I bite my lip and shift from foot to foot. "Um, no. I don't actually have a dog."

He focuses back on me. Then his eyes flash. Guilt rattles me.

"Sorry," I mutter. I seem to say that to him a lot. From the corner of my eye I see the group of kids moving away toward the front doors of the school.

He blinks, but then his expression relaxes and he holds a hand up to his ear. "What's that? Did Surly Girl just say sorry? Apologize to me?" He grins.

"A miracle," I say dryly.

"I'm glad your dog didn't die. I'm partial to four-legged creatures." He smoothes back his hair. "So you're skipping classes again?"

I automatically look around to see if anyone heard him but no one is around. Everyone's scattered off. I turn back to him and he's grinning even wider.

"I see you're becoming quite the delinquent. Must be bad for your academic record." He actually tsks me.

"I have no strikes. My mom has covered all my ditching." I glance around again in case anyone from the Honor Society is lurking around corners taking notes. For a moment a flash of fear rattles me, that they sent him to test my character.

"Must be nice to be so perfect," Nick says. "You and your sister."

His choice of words takes away my breath. I've never been called perfect in my life. Kristina's always been the perfect one.

"I am so far from perfect it's not even funny." I think of Kristina and my heart pounds. She's not so perfect anymore either.

"No? Well, what about your perfect grades? I heard you're going to rule the world one day. Or at least try to change it."

I breathe out slowly. "You heard wrong," I say, and my voice is shaky. My perfect grades are slipping. I've handed in substandard work in three classes, including Mr. Pepson's. I've not done home-work. I've missed classes.

"Your sister okay?" he asks in a softer voice, as if somehow I've blown her cover. "She must be pretty sick to be missing all this school," Nick adds.

God, can't she miss school like other normal people, without search warrants being issued? This conversation is officially not any fun at all. I don't care what Nick wants. I want him to leave me alone.

"Kristina's fine." I eye the parking lot and my horrible pink bike, the lone bike at the bike stand at the end. "Fine. Fine. Fine. As fine as the print on the bottom of a contract. Fine."

"A contract?" he asks. He studies me as if I'm behind glass at a zoo, picking bugs from my fur or something. "You know you're kind of weird, right, Freshie?"

I glare at him, daring him to say more, but he just grins. "In a good way. Listen, while I've got you here, being so friendly to me and all, I wanted to ask you a question."

It's just the two of us now. No cars pass on the street, no kids on the schoolyard. Nothing. People I associate with, the brainiacs and the art freaks, are all in class. Sitting at the front. Mouths closed, ears open, waiting to learn something new or show off what they already know.

I'm all alone. I want to run, but something about Nick keeps my feet planted on the spot, listening to him instead of taking off like I always seem to do lately. In the back of my mind I wonder how it's possible I'm talking to a cute boy when the bell's going to ring for the next class any minute and I'm outside the school instead of in it. My ears warm. When did Nick become cute in my mind?

"You're a tough one to figure out, Freshie. What makes a girl like you start skipping school?" he asks as if he cares. I hear other unasked questions hanging in the air.

I try to think of something to say, a story that will throw him off the truth, keep him from finding out about Kristina's sickness, but I got nothing.

He smiles again. But it's a different smile. It's warmer and I hate to admit it, but it makes my stomach swoop a little. I am crushing. I'm a stupid girl. Stupid, stupid, stupid.

Crushing on juvie D's is so not my style. Especially juvie D's who are man-whores.

"Never mind," he says when he sees my expression. "It's not my business." My heart skips. "I've seen your dad golfing a lot lately," he says conversationally. "He's taken a couple strokes off his game."

I struggle to contain my reaction to him and snap, "Good for my dad."

"Another touchy subject?" He holds up his hands in mock defense. "I'd better quit while I'm ahead. Okay, back to my real question. What are you doing after school?"

I picture myself that morning, promising Mom I'll hop the bus after school and meet her at the hospital to keep her company with Kristina. I tried to get out of it, telling Mom how much homework I have, how I need my quiet time to study properly and keep my grades up. I explained that the Honor Society is watching closely and these are crucial times for me.

"Clubs are not everything, Tess. Priorities," she said.

I wonder if I were the one sick if she would make Kristina miss volleyball practice. I'm glad I haven't told her about the contest, afraid she'd try to take that away from me too. Trying to sketch my ideas and get the right feel is the one thing that's helping me stay sane.

She doesn't care about homework or my grades. How important the whole semester is. Or that I'm being judged on more than just my academic proficiency. She doesn't know I'm avoiding my best friend. Or that I've found an art contest that could change my life, but can't connect with my muse.

She doesn't know any of it. She never asks.

I want to ask her why Dad isn't missing work. Why he's spending more time at the office and more time on the golf course instead of less. Why I'm the one who has to deal.

I drop that line of thinking and focus on Nick. He's much nicer to think about than my mom.

Focus. What am I doing after school?

Oh. My. God.

I lose my breath, imagining for a brief second that he's going to ask me for a date. My cheeks get hotter. As if, my brain tells me. As. If.

"Um," I fumble my words around. "Uh, family stuff. Why?"

"What about Friday?" he asks.

I stare at him. "What about it?"

"You doing anything after school Friday?"

I don't move. Me? He *is* going to ask me out? I tell my stupid fluttering heart to quit it. No way. I don't *want* him to ask me out. I don't care what my body is saying.

He needs something. He's probably trying to find out more about Kristina. He is in the fan club after all. Even though he doesn't know the group is about to disperse due to problems with the leader.

My lips press tight and I swallow. "Why?"

He flashes another smile. "Man, you're not exactly an easy person to ask a question."

My heart continues tapping out a fast tango. My cheeks are like a forest fire blazing out of control. "What question? Access to my sister or maybe a loan?" My mouth snaps out the insults without my permission.

His eyes narrow and he frowns.

I curse my brain for not stopping my mouth from spewing out words, and then he surprises me by throwing back his head and laughing.

"Your sister or a loan, huh?" he says. "Tess, why won't you just answer my question?"

"I got to go." I turn and run, heading for my bike as fast as my sneakers will take me.

I'm relieved yet bummed when his footsteps don't follow. Deep down, a part of me is developing an unhealthy crush on that boy, and that's so not a good thing. I don't want to have a crush on a senior who gets drunk at parties, drives around volleyball girls, and thinks my sister is hot. Even I have enough sense to predict the outcome of that one.

My crushes are not usually so ridiculous. I tend to covet boys who don't actually talk to me. Like celebrities. Or famous artists. My pheromones tend to hone in on unattainable intellectual types. Not that Nick is attainable. God! My face breaks out into a fresh flush of fire.

I run to my bike, longing for the days before cancer. The days when boys ignored me and I ignored them. I wonder what Nick was going to ask, but pretend it doesn't matter. Pretend that I don't hope he really planned to ask me for a date. Cause it sounded like it.

But no. How could that be?

chapter eight

A couple of days later, the deadline for the Oswald contest is looming and I'm no closer to finding my flash of artistic brilliance. Never has my ability to create been obstructed before. It's like the cancer slithered over to poison me with some of its evil.

Because Mom is out at some important charity luncheon with the professors' wives, she asks me to leave school early to be with Kristina, so I take a cab to the hospital. When I walk into Kristina's hospital room, she's alone. Not even a nurse around. She's lying on her bed and when I get closer my breath catches. Her eyes are closed, she's motionless, and I'm compelled to check her chest to make sure she's breathing. It's rising and falling slightly but she doesn't wake, so I pull a chair up beside the bed. I sit down and study her. Her cheek bones look more angular and her collarbones jut out from her blue hospital gown. I'd have to use different techniques to sketch her now. Her essence has changed. She's less charcoal and more shading.

She's thinner than me now. It kills me because just a few weeks ago it would have made her so happy.

After a while Kristina must sense me, because her eyelids start to flutter and then she opens her eyes. Her mouth morphs into a small smile but it disappears quickly.

"Hey, Tess." It almost sounds like she's glad to see me.

"Hi," I say shyly.

"I feel like crap," she says.

"I know." It's the best I can manage. "I'm sorry."

She makes a tiny mewing sound, but it's just a sigh. "I know you are."

We don't speak for a minute. "Do you want to see some sketches? I'm nowhere near where I need to be for the competition, but I've done some rough stuff."

"What competition?"

She doesn't remember.

"The Oswald. The winner gets showings of their winning piece and a scholarship to the Academy of Art University." I don't tell her my inspiration has dulled since she got sick.

"Really? Sure. Let me see."

She doesn't sound enthusiastic but I paw through my backpack and pull out the book and open it to some of the sketches I want her to see.

I've been working on volcano scenes. They're raw with rippling lava and harsh lines. I hand her the pad and she holds it as if it weighs a hundred pounds. She is quiet as she flips through the pages.

"These aren't exactly what I want," I tell her as she studies the sketch that is closest to what I want to portray. "I'm trying to get across the unique unstable ground. Volcano ridges. Explosions. I'm not there yet."

"I thought you just did portraits and animals, but this is amazing," she says, and lays the book down on her chest like it's too exhausting for her to look at it. "You're really talented."

My cheeks warm and I take the sketchbook off her. "Thanks." I close it and slide it back into the backpack. "That's nice of you to say."

"Well, it's true. You're artistic and smart." Her lips turn up at the corners, but she closes her eyes as she talks. "Being smart works for you. You're so much stronger than me in some ways."

"I am?" I ask.

"Yeah. You never worry what other people think. I know you think I care too much. But I can't help it. I'm more like Mom that way."

I snort softly. "I worry more than you know, Krissie. I mean, you, you're so good with people. Everyone likes you and you know how to talk to them. I'd love to be able to do what you do with people. People think I'm weird."

Kristina shakes her head but it's a weak movement. "They don't think you're weird. They think that you're judgmental. Or intimi-dating. With me, they only love who they think I am. Not who I really am. Or who I was." She opens her eyes and turns her head to the wall. "I'm afraid, Tess," she says, and a lone tear slides down her cheek. And then she closes her eyes again, her breathing slows, and she seems to drift to sleep.

"Krissie?" I whisper, but she doesn't respond.

The conversation bothers me. I did think Kristina's friends were shallow, but didn't know it showed. Besides, it seemed kind of cool having a group to belong to like that. It surprises me that she has so little faith in them. Was being popular for Kristina just as lonely as not being popular for me?

"I'm afraid too," I whisper, and vow to let her be whoever it is she wants to be. If she even knows anymore.

My thoughts whirl around my head, so I decide to get out of the room for a breather and head down to the cafeteria. As I ride the elevator to the main floor, I make deals in my head. Deals with God or whoever is in charge up there. Deals to help Kristina get better. I promise I won't eat crappy food if Kristina's cancer will go away. I won't make fun of her friends. I add the Honor Society to my list. I won't mind not making the Honor Society if Kristina gets better.

Guilt nibbles at me as I know Melissa would be upset if she knew I'd sacrifice it, but truthfully, since Kristina got sick, Melissa's been negative and nasty and it's like I'm seeing her through new lenses.

I don't want to deal with that idea, and hurry through the cafeteria lines, ignoring the apple pie and sweet squares I want and picking out healthier choices. Salad. A whole wheat bun. A glass of skim milk. At the cash register, I glance back and spot Jeremy. Shoot. He's in line with a tray of his own. I wave my hand, but turn back to the woman perched on the stool at the cash register. She gives me the total for my food, takes my money, and hands me change without expression.

"Share a table?" Jeremy calls.

I fake a smile. "Sure."

To offset all the healthy stuff, I slather butter on my bread as he sits opposite me, clutching his tray. I look at his selection of food. A triangle-shaped sandwich wrapped in plastic cling wrap, a glass of white milk, and a bowl of mixed fruit for dessert. Mom would approve.

He sits and begins unwrapping plastic from the sandwich.

"You here visiting your Mom?" I ask, stating the obvious.

He nods, a serious expression on his face. "Yeah. She's having a nap. How's Kristina?"

"Sleeping."

He nods again. "Chemo is really hard on the body."

I stop chewing and stare at the table. "Yeah," I manage to say.

"How're things with you?" he asks. "You hear anything about the Honor Society yet?"

I glare at him.

"Clark said the selections will come in soon," he says.

I resume chewing. "I guess. I don't know, I've missed more classes lately then I did my entire junior high career. And I haven't exactly been a model student." My stomach gurgles and I put down my bread.

He chews slowly, watching me. "The school must be pretty good about it though. Under the circumstances."

"Maybe. In theory they're not supposed to know. Outside of the principal. I think they do. But no one is talking." At tables around us, different colored scrubs gather for lunch. I see two women wearing hot pink. One is holding a clipped-out obituary from the newspaper and showing it to her lunch mate. I wonder if it's a patient they lost. If they care or it's just gossip.

"Yeah," Jeremy says. "People don't like to talk about cancer."

I see real sympathy in his eyes and then he turns the conversation over to less emotional ground. We talk about reality TV shows and I'm intrigued to find out he's also a huge fan of *MythBusters*. When we finish eating, I tell him I should get back to Kristina's room. Jeremy puts away his tray and heads out with me. I don't prevent him from walking with me to her room, but he stops in the hallway.

"I should get back to my mom," he says.

"Jeremy?" Kristina's hoarse voice calls.

He glances inside the room and the eagerness in his expression makes my insides flutter with a weird mix of happy and sad for my sister and him.

I hold out my hand for him to go in ahead of me.

"Hey," he says, and the sparkle in his simple greeting lightens the heaviness in the room.

I see Kristina struggling to sit up. He hurries to her side to help, but it's not awkward or patronizing. Her face glows with more happiness than I've seen in days.

"Beauty sleep seems to be working," he tells her. He doesn't let her hand go right away.

"Shut up," she tells him, but her lips curl up at the corners.

"Think it would work for me?" I ask, trying to be funny.

They both stare at me and then Kristina lets go of Jeremy's hand. "She wants you to tell her she's beautiful," Kristina says, but she smiles at him.

My cheeks turn red. "No, I don't." I'm horrified. Was I really looking for a compliment in the middle of all this?

"You're beautiful. Just like your big sister," Jeremy says.

"He's a smooth talker," Kristina says to me. "Watch out for him."

My mouth remains shut. I avoid looking at either of them.

"Nah. I am most decidedly not a smooth talker," Jeremy says with a shrug. "Mostly I'm a dork."

The thing is, he doesn't sound unhappy or apologetic about. Just accepting.

"You are not. You're sweet." Kristina points at the MP3 player on the end table by the window. "He burned me an entire disk of Neil Diamond songs and loaded them on my iPod." She looks back at Jeremy. "I think he made a copy for himself."

She's teasing and my insides relax a little, enjoying their easy sparring.

"Maybe." Jeremy glances at me. "I stop by and see Kristina whenever I'm here. Last time, we were talking about the music our parents made us listen to growing up. She professed an undying love for Neil. Instead of mocking her, I had my own confession." He seems to be trying to involve me in the conversation.

I pretend to gag as the two of them riff off of each other, but it's nice. I'm surprised I'm actually envious. Kristina eventually gets quieter and more tired and Jeremy notices too and excuses himself.

Kristina goes to sleep almost as soon as he's gone and I move my chair up beside her bed until Mom arrives from her late lunch. Kristina is still asleep so we make hand signals over her sleeping body and get up to leave.

We drive home in silence until Mom pulls the car to a stop at a red light. My head rests against the passenger window and I'm thinking about Kristina. And about how nice Jeremy is. Easy to talk to.

"Tess?" she says, as if my name is a question.

I consider pretending to be asleep but she knows me well enough to know I can't sleep in cars. I wish she'd leave me alone to think. Or not think. Just alone.

"Gee's mom called me today. She told me the girls are really worried about your sister. Apparently, the team had a meeting about it. They wanted to come by the house as a group with some magazines and books and stuff for Kristina." Her voice drops off. "She wanted to know if I wanted to come to the next game with her. She said they miss me in the stands. My cheering."

"What'd you tell her?" I ask, still looking out the window.

"I said it was a nice gesture but that Kristina wasn't up for visitors and I didn't feel comfortable going to the games until Kristina is well enough to come with me. But I miss them too. I miss the other moms and I miss the games."

Her answer makes my stomach hurt and I turn to look at her. She's gripping the steering wheel, staring straight ahead.

"Then she asked if she could bring over food or something. The girls want to do something for her. To show they miss her. That they care."

"Well, you can't expect Kristina to just drop off the planet without her friends noticing. It's a major source of gossip."

"I know. I just want to respect your sister's privacy right now. I want to do what's best for her."

I don't answer that. I have my doubts about her motives.

"I need a favor," she says.

I want to tell her no before I even hear what it is. On principle.

She's making me do enough things I don't want to do already. Missing school. Sitting with my sister, trying to think of things to talk about. Keeping her cancer a big friggin' secret.

"What?" I ask with a deep sigh, bracing myself.

She reaches across the console separating us and takes my hand and holds it. I have an urge to pull away. It makes my skin scratchy but I don't move.

"You think I'm silly," she says and her voice is sad. "You think my life is silly."

"No, I don't," I say, but it doesn't sound convincing, even to me.

She smoothes her fingers over my skin, patting me. I'm dying to break the contact.

"I'd like to take you shopping," she says, and her voice catches.

I pull my hand away. "What?"

The light changes to green and a car behind us honks but she doesn't move yet. "I don't know what to do, Tess. I don't know how to handle this. I'm lying to people. I don't know how to help my own child." She starts to cry. "When I'm upset, I shop. And I know it's silly and I know you think it's stupid, I'm stupid. But I'd really like it if you would go shopping with me."

The car behind us honks again and she starts driving.

"I don't think you're stupid. I mean, don't cry. Kristina's going to be all right. I'll go shopping with you. Don't cry."

It feels surreal. My sister is in the hospital getting chemo and not one of her friends is aware of it. My dad seems to have disappeared, and now my mom is crying and wants to take me shopping?

Mom's foot presses hard on the accelerator and she speeds up and drives to the mall. When we're inside, she drags me into her favorite stores.

"Try on a pair of these jeans," she says, and holds up an expensive pair of low-riding jeans that I would never in a million years wear.

"Those are Kristina jeans, not me."

Her eyes are lit up like patio lanterns at midnight and she ignores my comment. "Oh, come on, Tess, live a little. You're so skinny—you can wear these. They'll show off your long legs…"

I shake my head, but she's already grabbed one pair and then she grabs a few others and pushes me toward a changing room. A salesgirl sensing a woman with a wallet and a purpose runs toward us and Mom sends her off in search of cute shirts to go with the jeans.

Mom drapes the jeans over my arm. "Go," she says, and pushes me inside the dressing room.

Mumbling and grumbling and ignoring my pasty white skin that looks even sicklier in the fluorescent lights, I turn from the full-size mirror and pull on the first set of jeans. I can't even do up the zipper. I suck in my stomach, but the zipper won't budge. I check the size and shake my head as I pull them off. Good thing I don't have a complex, because they are my size but they definitely are too small. The next pair is too baggy around my nonexistent hips. Sighing, I toss them to the ground, remembering with vivid clarity why I hate shopping so much.

I pick up the third pair and they're softer than they look. I pull them on and they snuggle down below my belly button in a way that's surprisingly comfortable. I turn my head and peer over my shoulder, and a tiny thrill courses through me. My butt looks friggin' amazing in these jeans. I'm not supposed to care, but it looks…friggin' amazing.

I stare and suppress a giggle. Instead of being as flat as my chest, my butt looks rounder and, well, for lack of a better word…bootylicious. The bottom half of my body actually looks attractive.

Mom rattles on the other side of the door. "Let me see!"

I allow her access and she squeals with delight as she makes me do a pirouette. The salesgirl joins us and demands that I come out of the room and they practically shout with excitement. The salesgirl holds an armful of tank tops and offers them to me, but I shake my head.

Mom looks at my face and must sense my brain is about to go into overload. "Okay, no tops. Well, maybe just this one." She pulls a turquoise top off the salesgirl's arm and checks the size. "And a black one. They're your colors. You don't even have to try them on. Just these and those jeans." She smiles at the clerk. "Maybe another pair of the same style in black? Okay? Please, Tess."

I'm the weirdest teen in the world if my mom is begging to buy me cool clothes.

"Okay, okay," I say, like I'm being forced, but I close the door to the changing room and turn to admire the reflection of my butt and then the front view. The cut of the jeans makes my legs look long but the color and texture add muscle tone to my thighs. I'm rocking these jeans like a friggin' Sister of the Traveling Pants. It shouldn't matter. I'm above needing clothes to make me feel good. But I love them. And I want them. I imagine Nick checking out my butt and then freak out inside and pull them off and put my old comfy pair back on.

At the cash register, Mom pulls out her credit card and, as the clerk slides it through the reader, she smiles, seemingly having reached the shopping high she was looking for. While she's signing the receipt I wonder if I'll have the nerve to ever wear them to school. I don't want to look like I'm trying to be one of the cool kids, do I? I'm not sure I can pull it off or if I even want to risk it.

She puts an arm around my shoulders as we head to the parking lot. "I know it doesn't change anything, but believe it or not that helped." I wiggle out from under her. "Thanks," she says. "For doing that for me."

It's hard to say "You're welcome," to something so self-serving. Coping is so stupid.

• • •

The next day I bike to school but I don't stop at my locker before class. Melissa is acting snarly and I'd rather not face her questions or snarky comments about Kristina.

She finally catches up with me at lunch when she finds me outside. I'm taking advantage of the warm fall weather before the snow arrives. "Where've you been?" she asks.

I lift a shoulder and bite into my sandwich. She makes a face as she unwraps hers and plops down on the grass beside me. "How's your homework?" she asks, but there's much more in her voice.

"Fine."

"You getting good grades?"

I shrug again.

She takes a big bite of her sandwich. "I heard rumors about your sister." She's speaking with food in her mouth, and it turns my stomach almost as much as her words.

My head snaps up. "What rumors?"

"She's sick. I heard brain tumor." Chomp, chomp, chomp. She bites off another hunk of bread, watching me.

I swallow. "She does not have a brain tumor," I tell her, my voice tight and uppity.

"Pregnant?"

"What do you think, Melissa?" My hands shake a little and I lower my sandwich to my lap.

"Hospitalized for anorexia?" Melissa's eyes bore into mine for a second and I think she's going to say something else, but then she looks down at the grass. She eats in silence, but my appetite is gone. When she's done, she mumbles an excuse about studying in the library, packs up her stuff, and leaves me.

I head back inside to my own class, and when it's finally over I head out the door and stop. Devon is leaning against the wall, watching me. He stands straighter, as if he's waiting for me. "Hey," he says and I realize he was. He shuffles around and I actually feel a bit sorry for him, even as I'm wishing him away. I try not to remember that he's obsessed with sex. With my sister.

Other kids walk by, glancing at us. The hot senior boy and the freshman nobody. Of course, ever since my sister, the wonderful and mysteriously absent Kristina Smith, disappeared, I've become the freshman nobody with the missing hot sister. Less nobody only because people think I have the inside scoop on my sister.

Devon steps beside me so we're both facing the same way and I'm forced to walk with him. "So," he says.

I wait.

"Uh…" He puts out his hand and stops me. I don't want to talk to him. I don't want to see the confused expression in his eyes. "When's Kristina going to be back?"

I bite my lip and lift my shoulders, looking around at people passing by us, anywhere but at him. "I'm not sure," I manage to say.

"She okay?"

I try. I really do try. But I can't think of anything to say, so I shrug again.

"Is she, uh, mad at me or something?" He has no idea my sister is sick.

"I don't know," I say. "But I really doubt it." It's about as honest as I can be.

"Um, because…" He looks over his shoulder and checks to make sure no one is listening. He lowers his voice. "I've been texting and emailing and calling and she hasn't answered. She hasn't even signed onto Facebook."

I nod and wonder why Kristina didn't come up with a more elaborate explanation for her absence. Saying she's home with the flu isn't going to buy many more absent days. The flu wouldn't cause Kristina's total abandonment of her social connections on top of missing school. Rumors are flying if Melissa heard about a possible brain tumor. Or eating disorder.

Devon stares at me as if he's waiting for me to say something more. I chew my lip and squirm. "Uh, she, uh…she's just not up to it. She hasn't been on the computer at all."

"So she's really sick?"

I nod. "She doesn't have a brain tumor, if that's what you heard." At least this much is true. God! She lost her *virginity* to this guy and he has no idea why. I wonder if he thinks she's pregnant.

"Can I stop by to see her?" he asks.

"No!" I almost yell. "She doesn't want to see you."

His cheeks go pink and he throws his shoulders back and stands straighter. "Well, whatever then," he mumbles and then starts to hurry off. I almost see the steam coming out of his ears. Smooth, Tess.

"Devon."

He turns immediately as if he'd been waiting for me to stop him.

I walk forward so I can speak to him in a quiet voice. "She won't see anyone. It's not you. She really isn't feeling well."

He stares at me. I can tell by his eyes that he cares. "Is she okay?" he asks again. "I mean. Is it something bad? Or is she pissed at me for…something?"

My eyes burn with tears but I can't let myself cry. I bite my lip hard. "No. She's not mad at you. She's just…sick," I tell him.

He takes a deep breath. "You're sure?"

"No," I say softly. "She just won't see anyone. Not even you."

He lets out a breath of air and reaches out and takes my arm. "Okay. Well, will you at least tell her I said hey?"

A gaggle of freshman jock girls walk by then, openly ogling us.

Their eyes are wide and their ears are practically wagging, trying to pick up what we're talking about. I try not to be bothered by the girls but there I am again, totally visible, in a place I never wanted to be.

"Sure," I tell Devon. "No problem."

"Thanks." Devon touches my arm again and I step back, but he just spins around and leaves me while the girls whisper-squeal about the physical contact between us. Me, the invisible girl, and Devon.

"That is so skanky. She's totally hitting on her sister's ex," I hear one of them squeak as Devon saunters away from me down the hallway. "Sonya said she pushed Kristina off a ladder and broke her leg, and that's why Kristina's been away from school so long—she has to get one of those metal things put in it."

"I know. I also heard she's hooking up with Nick Evonic," another answers. "Someone saw them outside the school making out. Man, going after him and Devon."

A wave of fury rattles my head. "That's a lie, get a freakin' life," I yell at them.

They stop in unison and spin to stare at me, their mouths open.

I hear the sound of a voice clearing and look over my shoulder. Faculty Advisor Extraordinaire, Mr. Meekers.

And me. Not exactly performing a show of extreme student leadership.

"We didn't say a word to her, Mr. Meekers," one of the girls whines. "I have no idea why she yelled at us."

"That's not the kind of attitude or behavior we encourage around here, Miss Smith," he says, and his nose turns up as if he's smelled something foul. I'm doomed.

The girls scurry down the hallway, leaving me alone to face the lion. I hear their giggles as they hurry off, hyenas who escaped the predator.

"I expect more from you." He taps his finger against his cheek, staring at me. "You know that a measure of a man's worth is how he handles adversity."

"I'm not a man," I remind him, and groan inwardly. Way to assert my growing verbal powers and defend my gender to my obviously frustrated art teacher, whose only pleasure is the miniscule power control he holds over students like me.

I step into the human-body freeway rushing by and disappear in the opposite direction. He calls my name with an abrupt tone, but I keep moving, knowing I've just added another paragraph or two to my Honor Society obituary. Melissa would be so pissed off, but I'm definitely not going to be the one to tell her.

Truthfully, the drawing contest needs my attention now. I want to win it so badly. It means more to me than a club. It means redemption. I have to get myself in the proper mind frame to do it right.

• • •

The dinner table is quiet. For the first time in as long as I can remember, Mom hasn't cooked us a well-balanced, healthy meal. She ordered in pizza. Normally this would make me delirious, but now it is just another sign of how much things have changed around the house.

I gaze across the table at Dad. He's stuffing pizza in his mouth, chewing with gusto. The picture of health. Mom is nibbling on the crust of the one piece she'll allow herself. Her teeth nibble and nibble. My stomach hurts watching the two of them, so focused on their food.

"I can't keep this secret any longer," I blurt out.

Dad glances at me and then at Mom, and then takes another slice of pizza from the box and bites off a huge chunk.

"Why not?" Mom asks, putting down her single piece of pizza and reaching for her napkin to wipe her fingers.

I stare at her. "You're joking, right?"

"Well, it's not as if…I mean…you and Kristina don't have a lot of friends in common, so how hard can it be?"

"Are you freaking kidding me?" I shout.

"Hey," Dad says. "Calm down."

I shoot him a death ray. He's been burying himself so deeply I wonder if he even remembers my name. He's ignoring everything going on right in front of his eyes and we're letting him get away with it. A family pattern I'd never let bother me before.

"I'm being stalked by the entire girls' volleyball team. And half the boys' team. People are bugging me every single day. I'm supposed to be focused on school…making the Honor Society, not sabotaging myself by missing classes and hiding from people. I should be working for my leadership and service obligations, but instead the freakin' Prom Committee is chasing me down between classes and at lunch, looking for my sister and her witty quip contributions. They asked *me* for ideas. People are making things up. Brain tumors. Pregnancy. Worse, Kristina's boyfriend is hunting me down with big puppy-dog eyes, wondering why she won't return his phone calls or text messages. It. Is. Very. Hard."

"Her boyfriend?" my mom says. "Kristina has a boyfriend?"

"Give me a break!" I shout and throw my napkin on the table. "Do you really think that's what's important right now? Whether or not she has a boyfriend?"

My mom mumbles something under her breath but, for the sanity of both of us, I choose to ignore her.

"We can't keep the cancer a secret anymore. It's not doing anyone any good and what exactly is the freaking point? Are you ashamed of Kristina because she has cancer? Because to me, you're giving her the message that she should be ashamed, or maybe that *you* are ashamed that your perfect daughter is no longer perfect."

My mom clamps her mouth shut and stares at me with wide, shocked eyes. My dad looks guilty and uncertain.

"But what will people say?" Mom finally asks.

"Who cares what they say! They're already talking, and anyhow it's *not her fault!*" I yell at the top of my lungs. "And don't you think she wants to hear what people have to say? I mean, the people who care about her? She might get some support from her friends. Her entire volleyball team is freaking out."

When exactly did my parents turn into children?

"We need to respect Kristina's wishes—" my dad starts to say.

"Do you know what her wishes are, Dad? Have you sat down and asked her?" He harrumphs me, but has the decency to look embarrassed. He's come to me, but has he gone to her?

I don't want to hear excuses from my parents and their misbe-having, stubborn-little-kid act. I'm fifteen, for God's sake! I don't want to be the one to start having the power of veto in my family, but they both seem content to pretend we're living in a TV sitcom and our life is an episode that will miraculously be solved by a team of writers.

"What's wrong with you people?" I yell.

My mom lifts her finger and starts biting her nail. The only bad habit she allows herself. "Do you really think we should tell everyone?" she asks.

Dad runs his hands through his messy hair. "It might be best," he mumbles, then looks at me with watery eyes.

"Yes," I say. "It is." I'm so exasperated I want to shake both of them.

Suddenly, I am the voice. And it scares the hell out of me.

"Does she really have a boyfriend?" Mom asks.

I push away from the table and leave the room.

• • •

Mom decides we'll go to the hospital together and discuss it as a family. However, on the drive to the hospital, she announces her brilliant idea that I should talk to Kristina alone first. Sister to sister. As if Mom even knows what it's like to have a sister relation-ship, or how far off Kristina and I are from exchanging secrets like Mary-Kate and Ashley Olsen. As soon as we get to the hospital, Mom and Dad sneak off with an excuse about grabbing coffees to give the sisters a chance to talk.

"Tell her that it's probably for the best," Mom says. "To involve her friends."

As if fifteen-year-old me can do a better job talking to Kristina than they can. Great. Suddenly I'm the responsible one. How do you spell dysfunctional? S-M-I-T-H.

"So," I say, when Kristina and I are done with small talk. Like, hello.

She's laying on her side, curled up in a fetal position. I pull my chair up so we're at eye level. She looks so tired and pale I almost want to put off the conversation, but if I hold it in too long, I'll explode or chicken out.

"Mom and Dad and I think we should tell people. You know. That you have cancer," I blurt with all the tact of a mating elephant.

Kristina blinks and stares and then glimpses at the doorway. "Let me guess. They made you be the one to tell me?"

I nod once. "I guess they're afraid you'll be mad at them. Maybe they think you'll only hate the messenger. You can yell at me if you want, get it off your chest."

Without meaning to, my eyes go to the tubes poking out of her gown. Right from her chest.

Kristina sighs. She doesn't seem to have the energy to get mad. I kind of wish she would yell at me. Bully me and intimidate me with stupid threats.

"You're okay with it?" I ask. "I mean, everyone at school is going crazy worrying about you. I can't keep it quiet anymore. There are rumors."

"What are they saying?" she asks, but she's looking at the wall, not at me.

I lift my finger to my mouth and chew the hangnail. "You know. That you're pregnant, on drugs, being treated for an eating disorder."

For the first time in a long while, a real smile tugs at her lips. "I'd like to go with pregnant. It makes me sound kind of like *Juno*."

She's more *Clueless* than *Juno*.

She spurts out a single giggle. "Oh my God! Can you imagine if I really was pregnant with Devon's baby?"

I gag. "No, thank you." I stick out my tongue with disgust. "Anyhow. Seriously. I think that we should tell people the truth. I mean, for your sake too. There are a lot of people who care about you and stuff."

Her head dangles down and then up again, as if it's a huge effort. "Fine. What's the point in trying to hide it anyhow?" she says. "The doctor said I'm going to be as bald as a cue ball before long." She lets out a long, loud breath of air.

I'm not sure what to say. "If anyone can pull it off, you can," I mumble.

Kristina doesn't say anything for a minute, then looks out the window. "This chemo cycle ends tomorrow. I'm coming home for a couple weeks until the next cycle starts."

I'm not surprised no one bothered to tell me. Kristina doesn't seem excited to be coming home, but I guess it's hard to feel happy about much in her condition.

"I don't care who you tell," she says softly. But then she looks me directly in the eye and I see a flash of her old stubbornness. "But no visitors. Not at home either," she tells me. "I don't want to see anyone. No one."

"You don't have anything to be ashamed of," I tell her in an equally quiet voice.

"You have no idea how I feel." She snorts, but it's feeble. "And don't tell anyone I might lose my leg. Please, Tess?"

"Your friends will stand by you. Whatever happens."

"No. People are going to feel *sorry* for me. They'll be relieved it's not them and then they'll pretend we're still friends but we won't even know what to say to each other. If I lose my leg…well, then they'll just be grossed out. Who would want to be my friend then? I might as well just die."

Fear plummets my heart down to my knees. I suck in a deep breath. "Don't say that. You don't want to die. You'll still be you."

"You have no idea what I want."

"Oh my God, Kristina." I wish my parents would get their asses back this second.

My cheeks burn and I struggle not to cry, but she keeps speaking, her voice monotone.

"I won't be the same person. I'm already not the same person even if I do keep my leg. You know? I won't ever play volleyball like I used to. I'm not Kristina Smith anymore. I'm flawed."

"I always thought flaws made people more interesting," I say, trying to sound braver than I feel.

"I know, because you don't care what other people think."

I open my mouth to tell her she's wrong, but she keeps talking.

"I got a rose," she says. "A really pretty red one." She lifts her thin hand in the air as if waving away dust particles. "Well, I didn't actually get it. There's no flowers allowed on this ward or in the room, but Tracey, the nurse, described it to me. She said it hadn't bloomed fully yet, but was beautiful. I told Tracey to take it home

123

to her little girl, Carly. She told me Carly has an ear infection, so it'll make her feel better."

I smile. My sister loves little kids so it doesn't surprise me she'd do that.

"She gave me the card. It just said, 'Thinking of You.' No signature."

"Jeremy," we both say at the same time.

She smiles. "At first I thought he had a crush on you."

An image of him lighting up at the mention of her pops in my head. "On me? Are you kidding?" A laugh escapes me and Kristina smiles. I realize with surprise that Kristina says things like that to me, trying to make me feel good, when in fact it was pretty obvious Jeremy was falling all over himself to get to her.

"He's your fan, not mine." I pause. "Do you like him?"

"He's young but, yeah, I like him. He stops by my room a lot and we chat. He's always doing nice things for me. He doesn't treat me like I'm different than I was."

I nod.

"His mom has cancer," she says.

"Yeah, I know."

"How do you know?" she asks.

"Well, he is at the hospital all the time." I decide to stick to the truth. "I've talked to him at school too. He told me a while ago that she has breast cancer." I avoid looking Kristina in the eye. "He hasn't told anyone about you. At school, I mean. But anyway, I guess people will know soon enough."

"I don't want anyone coming to the house when I get home," she says. "No one is allowed to come and see me."

"What about Devon?" I ask. "He's super worried."

"Especially not Devon."

"That kind of defeats the purpose of letting people know, don't you think?"

"No," she says, "I don't. I can't deal with anyone. I feel terrible and I look worse. I don't want to see anyone." She clears her throat. "Will you do me a favor?" she asks.

"Of course."

"Tell Devon first. Before anyone else. I want him to hear it from you. First."

She blinks fast. Open. Shut. Open. Shut. "I feel kind of bad about, you know…I kind of used him."

"I think he'll survive. He got to have sex with you, right?" I keep my voice light.

Kristina turns her head and stares out the window. "Do you think he brought me a rose because he thinks I'm going to die?"

"Jeremy? No. God, no," I say. "He bought you a rose because he has the hots for you."

Kristina spits out a weak giggle and then reaches up and strokes her hair. "He doesn't have the hots for me. He knows I have cancer."

"So? That means he can't have the hots for you?"

"Pretty much," she says.

"Sorry. He wants you bad. Cancer or not. I can see it in his eyes—Kristina trance."

Her hand smoothes over her face and then her fingers linger for a moment on her lips. "Do you like being smart?" she asks.

I nod slowly.

"I liked being pretty. You know? That's so vain, right?" She closes her eyes again. "I'm really tired," she mumbles and almost instantly her breathing slows down and she slips away into sleep. I lean closer to make sure her chest is still moving and watch as she breathes.

A few minutes later Mom and Dad walk into the room, clinging to Styrofoam cups of coffee like life preservers, their faces betraying their guilt. Mom walks over and stands beside my chair, staring down at Kristina.

"Did you get a chance to talk to her?"

I nod.

"She took it okay?" Mom asks.

I want to be mad at them for leaving things to me, but I just nod, not missing the irony that I'm the one sitting in the middle.

chapter nine

In the morning I open my eyes, and for one wonderful moment my mind clings to a dream I had about Nick. With kissing. I sigh, but my brain refuses to go back to the dream, the only place I'll ever get any action. Gah! I sit up and peer at the clock. I'm later than usual. I'll have to skip the shower and dress quickly to make it to school on time.

I slide my feet to the floor and head to my dresser to pull out clean underwear. Yanking off my pajamas, I toss them in a heap by my bed. My parents' voices buzz in the kitchen. I can't make out what they're saying but it's obvious they're arguing. My warm and fuzzy feelings from the dream completely disappear. All too clearly, I remember the days when Kristina would be downstairs already, fully dressed and made-up. Mom would be too busy asking Kristina questions and living vicariously through her to argue with Dad.

"Tess has her own life to live too!" My dad's voice travels up. "She has goals. She wants to make the Honor Society and that means volunteering and getting involved with school functions and learning to show leadership qualities. It's about more than marks."

Hmm. *Thanks for noticing*, I feel like calling down, but my mom says something nasty about both of our snobby intellectual sides. His reply is lost in the walls.

I hear the door slam as I pull on comfy jeans and an old T-shirt. I grab a pair of striped toe socks from my drawer. The big toe has a hole but they're wearable, so I pull them on.

When I go downstairs, Mom is sitting at the kitchen table, cradling her coffee mug and staring into space.

"Hey," I say, when she doesn't seem to hear me entering the kitchen. "It's me. The smart one."

She looks at me and her eyebrows press together. "You're wearing that to school?" she asks, ignoring my dig.

I shrug. "Apparently."

Her face contorts, but she doesn't seem to have the energy to fight me. "Did you at least brush your teeth and hair?"

I nod as I head for the pantry. I may be a bit of a slob but I'm not gross. When I reach up to the cereal shelf, my hand stops midair. Instead of Bran Flakes or Raisin Bran, there's an unopened box of Cap'n Crunch. My all-time favorite, banned from our house years ago. I wonder how on earth it got there, but decide to go with my good fortune and reach to pull it out.

I pour a heaping serving in the bowl, glancing sideways and waiting for Mom to have an emotional breakdown at my breakfast choice. Nothing. I grab milk and a spoon and then dig in. Nothing.

"Dad bought it for you," she says as I crunch the cereal, not enjoying it as much as I usually would. "It's a treat, so don't get used to it."

Then she drops her cup on the floor and swears as it shatters. I jump and knock the bowl of cereal in my lap. Milk covers my jeans and shirt.

"Great," I say.

Mom stands and goes to the pantry to grab a broom. "Sorry. Listen, I'll drive you to school today."

I don't answer as I go back upstairs. The only clean things are the jeans Mom bought. I still haven't taken them out of the bag. I hesitate and then pull them on, embarrassed to be wearing such a trendy pair of pants. I pull on the shirt she bought for me too. When I go back downstairs, Mom has a fresh cup of coffee. She looks up and smiles but is wise enough not to say a word about my outfit.

"Do you have a busy day at school today?" she asks.

"I have a couple of tests. One this morning, one this afternoon," I say as I pour myself a new bowl of cereal. "I stayed up past midnight studying."

"Can you miss your afternoon test?" she asks.

My spoon stops in the air. It's completely obvious I am eating a bribe. She's allowing me sugary cereal so she can make me do what she wants.

"Uh, it's a test, Mom. In science. My mark goes toward my GPA. It's kind of important."

"I'll call the school and explain it's an emergency. You can do a rewrite another day and your mark will still count."

"Uh…" I stick another mouthful of crunchy cereal in my mouth, buying time. I want to tell her no. I want to go to school. I don't want to miss the test. I studied hard for it.

"I'd really like you to come with me to the hospital this afternoon to bring Kristina home."

I want to take the test. I want to ace it. I want to lose myself in the adrenaline-rushing place I disappear to when I take exams.

"Please, Tess. Your sister does so much better when you're around, and she's coming home today. I could use your help. It might be a tough day for her. I'd like you to be there."

"Um…" I chew another big mouthful of cereal. Methinks Mom doesn't want to deal with it alone. Doesn't want to be in the house alone. The rest is just an excuse. But how do I say no to that?

"Thanks," Mom says as I think. As if my silence is a big resounding yes. She stands up and goes to the sink, pouring the last of her coffee down the drain.

I clear my throat. "I'd really like to take my test today. I studied all night and I'll lose some of that momentum if I do it later. I need this mark for the Honor Society. I'm not a sure thing." Especially with my attendance lately and my other grades not being as good as they should be. I need to hold onto it. Some normalcy of my own.

"Oh, come on. You? You'll be fine. I'll call your school and arrange it. Since you're going to let people know today, I can tell them you're needed at the hospital. I'll talk to your principal. They'll be fine with it. I'll drop you off and then pick you up at noon."

She opens the dishwasher and places Dad's coffee cup neatly on the top row. She likes her dishes stacked just so. I rarely bother putting dishes away since she restacks them anyway.

"Finish your breakfast and brush your hair and teeth properly and I'll drive you."

I fume silently as she goes to the phone and dials the school number from memory. I sigh and stare at my cereal, which is getting soggy and is no longer appetizing. I push it away, leaving it on the table for her to clean up.

Instead of going to my room, I walk into the living room and log on to the laptop, blatantly disobeying her rules. I log on and click onto the Internet.

I type Nick Evonic's name into Google search and find his Facebook page. I can't see his profile without a Facebook page of my own. Without thinking about what I'm doing, I start typing. I put in my personal information and open up my own account. I stare at the screen. I'm officially on Facebook.

Quickly, I read through Nick's profile and then send him a friend request. I scour his wall posts and begin to officially cyberstalk him.

When Mom calls for me, I log off the computer. On the short car ride to school, I don't speak to her. When she pulls up to the front of the school, I grab my backpack from the floor by my feet and yank off my seat belt.

"You're going to talk to Kristina's friends today?"

I nod and my stomach flutters. I have to find Devon. And then Gee. Once I tell Gee, the entire school will know and my work will be done.

"Thanks." Mom smiles. "I appreciate you, you know."

"I know." I open the door, climb out, slam the door behind me, and start walking down the sidewalk toward the school entrance. "You appreciate that I have a purpose now. Dealing with the stuff you don't want to," I mutter under my breath. Mom sits idling in the car and I feel her eyes on me even though she's oblivious to my words.

"Dude. You realize you're talking to yourself."

My cheeks heat to butter-melting degrees. No wonder Mom hasn't moved. She's amazed that a boy has approached and is talking to me.

Nick.

He's staring at me with an amused look on his face. I grin like an idiot, trying to convince both of us that I am, in fact, sane. I don't need him to spread the word I'm having one-sided conversations. Last thing I need is for the entire student body to know I've been caught talking to myself. Like I need help committing social suicide. I turn around to see if anyone saw me and then turn back to Nick.

"Hey." He stops and whistles softly through his teeth. "I like those jeans." His eyes are on my butt. My entire body feels infused with pleasure and horror.

"My sister has osteosarcoma," I blurt out. "Bone cancer."

The smile disappears from his face like an Etch a Sketch shaken clear. "Are you serious?"

Great. Both a diplomatic and caring way to deliver the news. I want to go back to elementary school and stick my head in the sandbox. I start walking quickly and he catches up to me.

Mom toots the horn as she drives off, no doubt thrilled to see me talking to a real live boy. I don't wave or turn around to acknowledge her. Instead, I try to convince myself it's okay I told Nick first, instead of Devon. It's like pulling off a Band-Aid this way, fast and painful and done. Kristina will never know the order. "Um, would you mind telling Devon first?" I ask Nick. "And Gee? Kristina wanted to keep it quiet, but…well…I'm supposed to tell people now. But I hate talking to seniors."

"I'm a senior," he reminds me, but his voice is softer than usual. "And the Honor Society you so worship is full of seniors too."

"That's different. This is different." The air between us is heavy with the information I've given him. He runs a hand through his hair.

"She seriously has cancer?" he asks.

I lift my shoulder. "It's not exactly something I'd make up, right?"

He whistles softly under his breath. We walk up the front stairs of the school and he surprises me by stepping forward to hold the door.

"How's she doing?" he asks as I slip past, getting a whiff of his boy smell. He's wearing cologne, but not too much that it's gross. He smells older than me. Kind of yummy. My cheeks warm.

I look around to see if anyone is within earshot, but we're far enough away from clumps of kids that no one can hear me. "Terrible," I tell him. I bite down on my lip. "She's finishing her first round of chemo. She's sick and…well…kind of depressed. She doesn't want to see or talk to anyone." I glance around guiltily. "Don't tell anyone that part, okay?" I quickly add. "That she's not doing so great. She'd hate that."

He shakes his head. "I won't."

The way he says it, I believe him.

I sigh heavily again.

"Holy shit," he says.

"Yeah," I agree. "Holy shit."

We walk together and, as we pass a group of junior boys hanging out in front of a row of lockers, I'm sure I hear my name. This, I think, is a good example of why I prefer staying under the radar. This is one of the reasons popularity scares me. When people know who you are, they talk about you and make up stories. And it doesn't always matter whether they're true.

I spot Clark Trent with the group and he catches my eyes, shifts his body awkwardly, and then looks away, as if he's embarrassed. I imagine throwing kryptonite into the circle to see if he weakens, and a giggle escapes me.

Nick stares at me and frowns. His expression brings me back to the moment and away from the boys and what they might or might not be saying about me. A senior girl I've seen around walks by us, batting her eyes at Nick. He completely ignores her or doesn't even see her. To me, her expression says jealous. I remember his reputation.

"So, Kristina doesn't know? That you're telling people?" he asks, and my attention goes back to him.

"No, she knows. She just doesn't want the details."

I halt. I have to turn left, go down the hallway to my locker. I know he doesn't go in that direction. He stops beside me.

"At first, she didn't want people to know and my parents went along with it. They don't seem capable of rational thought these days."

"Kind of understandable, I guess," he says, his voice concerned.

I shake my head and start walking and he stays beside me, heading toward the freshman lockers. I'm both thrilled and horrified that he's being seen with me. In public.

"Kristina wants to tell Devon first?" he asks.

I wonder if he's jealous and then tell myself to quit being stupid and it doesn't matter even if he does.

"They have kind of a thing," I say.

"Had. They broke up right after school started."

I give him a sideways look and stop at my locker. I note the freshmen kids taking in the senior standing with me. I wonder what Melissa will say. I twirl my lock and try to keep my cool. "Um, I think they might have gotten back together." I swallow. Actually I have no idea what Devon and Kristina are, and neither does Devon. I shove my backpack inside the locker. "I mean, they've stayed friends and he's worried about her. And she does want him to know first. Can you talk to him? Before Gee."

"Really?" He sounds surprised and maybe a little disappointed.

I remember the way he watched Kristina at the freshie party. Like he wanted her for a snack. I slam the locker door shut.

"Yeah, they definitely got back together." I wince even as I say it. I'm not sure what they did except have sex and I'm acting like a jealous girlfriend. Which is insanely stupid.

"Sure," Nicks says. "I'll let him know."

"Thanks." My cheeks burn. Kristina made it clear she has no desire to see Devon. What if I've caused even more problems for her with my insinuations to Nick?

Nick keeps walking with me until we're a few feet from my classroom. I slow down as we approach, dragging my feet.

"Actually I'm not sure what Devon and Kristina are, so don't mention that part," I blurt.

He smiles and his cheeks dimple in a cute way. "No big deal, Tess. I won't say anything."

I sigh with more relief than necessary and wait for him to leave. I don't really want to be seen outside the class with Nick. People are talking already. As funny as it should be, me worrying about my reputation, I know it's hard to get rid of rumors. I read *Story of a Girl*.

I look longingly toward my classroom but am too chicken to tell Nick to go. He grins as if he's read my mind, not in the least concerned.

"Listen, I know it's not a good time for you…" He licks his lips and for a moment looks nervous. "But I have a favor to ask," he says.

I hold my breath and have a tiny out-of-body experience.

He stares at me and then he blinks quickly and shakes his head. "Nah. Never mind. It's not a good time. I'll catch up with you later."

He lifts his hand in a wave and turns and walks off. I watch as he leaves, all, *what?* Um, what did you want to ask me?

He glances back over his shoulder and lifts his hand and makes a peace sign. My heart swoons for a second, forgetting and then remembering with a jolt. My sister. Cancer. The school is about to find out.

I spin and run into my classroom.

Clark Trent gives me a boy nod as I hurry to my desk. His chin dips just once. He looks serious, as if he's focused on kicking my butt on the exam. I lift my hand and wave an acknowledgment and sit down, bending my head and focusing on my hands folded on my lap.

A throat clears. Surprised, I look up.

Clark stands in front of my desk, looking down on me. I feel like an ant on the sidewalk the way he looms over me. "You okay?" he asks softly.

I frown. "Fine. Why?"

He lifts his shoulder. "Just wondered. You look…sad."

There's an awkward pause then, and I feel obligated to try and fill it. "Uh, how's Jeremy?"

"He's at the hospital," Clark says.

I nod and look around but we're being ignored by everyone in the classroom. "Yeah. He told me, uh, about his mom."

I wait for him to say something more, but he just stands there.

"Is everything okay?" I prompt. "With Jeremy's mom?"

He shrugs. "I don't know. He doesn't say much about it. He's been at the hospital a lot lately."

"What about his dad?" I ask.

"His dad died a long time ago. When Jeremy was six. His mom's best friend is staying with him while his mom is at the hospital."

The bell rings then and I let out a deep breath as Clark walks to his desk and sits. Test papers are handed out from the front row. Mr. Pepson chants directions at the front of the class. Soon everyone settles and the class quietly works on the test.

The exam turns out to be easy, thank God. I rush through it and finish with fifteen minutes left. Instead of using the time to go over my answers for accuracy, like I usually do, I take my test paper to the front of the class and put it down on Mr. Pepson's desk. He nods toward the door to let me know I can leave. I feel Clark's eyes on the back of my head as I slip into the hallway but I ignore him.

I hurry down the hall to the girls washroom and rush inside a stall. Fully clothed, I sit on the toilet seat while my body twitches with nerves. People must know now. They'll be talking. They'll be coming after me.

I don't move even as the bell rings and the washroom fills with voices and flushes and high heels clacking on the floor. Minutes before the bell for the next class will ring, I stand.

When I hurry out of the washroom, I run straight into Clark Trent.

"Hey," he says, like it's perfectly normal for him to wait for me outside the girls bathroom.

"Hey. You're going to be late for class," I say.

He lifts his shoulder. "I have art with you. I'll walk you." Him. The Honor Society guy. Late to a class, because of me.

The bell rings and we both run inside the class, but he follows me to my seat and waits until I sit down before heading to his own. Around us, kids whisper. The buzz is in the air. I know word about Kristina has gotten out. Fresh gossip travels faster than a jackal running through the forest. I feel eyes inspecting me. I'm different to them now. I'm the girl whose sister has cancer. Fortunately, Mr. Meekers yells for silence. Everyone quiets down for the grouchy old fart who doesn't put up with classroom chatter.

I'm relieved when he announces we'll have a freestyle class to work with clay. I get my hands dirty and put my head down, concentrating on creating a sculpture of an ugly gargoyle. No one says a word to me. Just before the bell, Mr. Meekers yells for us to line up to wash our hands at the sink. I pretend to be preoccupied in my work and wait until the last person is done at the sink before sneaking over to wash up. As I finish, the bell rings and I head back to my desk slowly, wiping my wet hands on my pants.

Clark walks over. "You okay?" he asks, and blocks people from gawking at me.

I catch a reflection of us in the windows. He actually looks kind of hot, so tall and broad-shouldered. Beside him I look almost helpless and waifish, all folded into myself. My face burns. "Fine."

Thank God I'm not popular. I'm hormonally imbalanced or something, lusting after every boy who talks to me.

"We have science. Come on," Clark says. "I'll walk with you."

I can't look at Clark. I never even noticed how many classes we have together. I certainly don't know why he's appointed himself my personal guardian, but for now I'll take it. I just have to get through one more class. One more and then Mom will be outside waiting for me. I'm glad now she called in an excuse for the afternoon. I'm almost afraid to leave the classroom.

Outside, Melissa is waiting for me. She steps inside and gives Clark a dirty look, but he doesn't budge.

"Where'd you get those jeans?" she asks, pretending he's not even there.

"My mom got them for me." I refuse to elaborate or make excuses. I hold my chin high, waiting for her snarky remarks about me trying to be a cool kid.

"They're expensive," she says, but there's much more in her voice. We both know they're kickass jeans, but they're not something I normally would strut around in. I don't tell her I got them to make my mom happy. I know she knows about Kristina and I wait for her to say something, but she doesn't. As we move to the door the buzz outside gets louder.

"Oh my *God*," Emma Hart cries from the hallway. She's the youngest girl on the junior volleyball team, one of Kristina's biggest groupies. And she's staring right at me.

"Is it true about Kristina?" she yells at full pitch. "She has *cancer?*"

I open my mouth. Everyone's eyes are on me. I close my mouth, unable to get words out.

"Leave her alone," Clark says, and scowls at Emma. He puts his hand on my back and pushes me forward. "Come on," he says. He walks beside me, guarding me with his overgrown body, like a shield. He shoots daggers at Emma and everyone else gaping at us. Melissa is lost somewhere behind us.

"OhmyGodisKristinagoingtobeallright?" Emma hurries behind us, shrieking in my direction. "Ican'tbelieveitshelookedsohealthy lasttimeIsawher!"

"I said leave her alone," Clark growls, and everyone around us goes quiet, surprised by his snarly outburst. He pushes his glasses up on his nose and continues to shield me. It feels like every pair of eyes is on me. Probably because they are.

"Come on," he says, and I follow, happily hiding behind him as he leads me away.

When we turn a corner to the hallway where our next class is, we both stop. There's a new swarm heading toward us. A big swarm. Seniors. Led by Devon. Gee. The rest of the volleyball elite. They're heading straight for us. I hear the questions before they open their mouths. Like the seniors are Pied Pipers, more kids flock behind them, eager for information. They're focused on me like paparazzi without cameras.

This is so not how I envisioned my life at high school.

Clark stands straighter and puts a hand on my arm, but he's no match for the seniors and we both know it.

I brace myself.

Devon steps forward so he's right in front of me. I'm forced to look into his eyes, and see shock and pain reflected back at me.

"Is it true?" he asks. His voice is soft.

I wince and then slowly nod.

The volleyball girls gasp and all start asking questions at the same time. Devon turns to glare at them and they all shut up.

"I want to see her," he says.

My stomach feels like a snake is slithering around inside, tying itself into knots. Man, I should have prepared an answer for this. I should have prepared for the onslaught. While I was studying last night, I should have prepared a speech.

"She doesn't want to see anyone," I mumble.

Thinking I could pass the buck to Nick was not only naïve but stupid.

"Is she still at the hospital?" Devon asks.

"She's been in the hospital but she's coming home." The effort of speaking makes me queasy. "She's, uh, tired."

I look at her friends' faces. Concern. Fear. Horror. They want answers. I take a deep breath, dig deep, and decide to give them the truth. "She's done her first round of chemo."

I don't mention the side effects. I won't. No matter how much they try to press me.

Everyone starts to talk at once again, firing questions at me, and my brain goes into sensory overload. Clark puts his arm around my shoulder and I lean into him.

"Why didn't she tell us, Tess?" Gee pleads.

I look at her but questions keep coming at me from all around.

"Is she going to be okay?" someone demands, and I stumble. Dizzy. Clark grabs me tighter and straightens me.

I glance around, desperate to escape, and see Melissa blending into the crowd behind us. Grateful for more support, relief floods me and I wait for her to come closer and stand by me. Help to protect me from the questions being fired at me.

But she doesn't move.

Under her oversized T-shirt, her body remains stiff, her mouth tight. Her eyes squint in the corners. I don't recognize the expression. I've never seen it on her before. No, that's wrong. I have. But never directed at me. Her eyes travel down, sneering at my new jeans.

A kernel of anger pops inside me.

"So?" Melissa says, her voice hard and bitter.

It's the first time I've heard her speak in a crowd.

"Is she, Tess?" she asks. "I thought you said she was fine. Is Kristina going to die?"

My heart almost stops, because for a second I sense that Melissa wants her to. That she wants my sister to die. Kernels pop. Pop.

Clark makes a groan of disgust and starts moving, his arm still protecting me. I stumble, as if I've forgotten how to walk, but he helps me.

"Don't be an ass, of course she's not going to die," he tells Melissa.

I dig my feet into the ground to stop Clark. "How could you say that?" I glare at Melissa.

She stares back at me, barely blinking. Shameless. Then her cheeks redden and her mouth makes the *O* shape of a doughnut hole.

I can't stop staring at her, horrified. My best friend is someone I don't even know.

"Of course she won't die," Melissa snarls. "She's too *perfect* to die." Her voice spits out the word like it's dirty and her face betrays the extent of her hate. It's the worst expression I've ever seen. She might as well have lifted a pistol and shot a silver bullet right in the heart of our friendship.

I freeze. I want to smack her. Redden her cheek with my hand imprint. I turn my head around to see if anyone agrees with her venomous implication. My sister has cancer. There's nothing perfect about that. But the few people who heard Melissa are staring at her, confused.

"I can't believe you just said that! That's the most insensitive thing I've ever heard." Gee steps up to my other side. She and Clark guard me together.

How. Dare. She. I lean forward so we're almost nose to nose.

"You're fat and mean and no one likes you," I hiss. I know what to say to hurt her most.

"Kristina Smith is an amazing person," Devon says, addressing Melissa.

"Some friend," another boy says.

It's Nick. He's standing beside Devon. I didn't even see him in the crowd. But he's defending me. Melissa and I eye each other. I'm ashamed I've called her names in front of everyone but I want her to feel as hurt as I do. Our years of looking on together from the outside vanish. The people we used to mock are defending me now. I'm in the circle so she hates me too. No matter what my reason is for being there.

We've both gone too far to take the words back. She can never take back her hatred for my sister. And I can never take back what I've called her. Not that.

The taste of her bitterness and betrayal is rancid on my tongue. I think about how we used to gossip together. I thought we were being silly. Melissa hurries away from the crowd, her head down, her stance awkward. She'll go back to being invisible, but I remain completely exposed.

Her words have torn off the scab holding in my wounds. Is Kristina going to die?

No.

I won't let her.

I shrug off Clark and begin to run. My legs carry me, fast, faster. Away. No one follows. I hear Clark and Nick, two boys in my life because of my sister, both telling people to leave me alone. I run on. My name passes from one person to another. Tess. Tess Smith.

They know who I am now.

chapter ten

Dad is at work, apparently too tied up with his classes and paperwork to meet us at the hospital to take Kristina home. He called my cell earlier to deliver his apology to Kristina. I held in my anger about being asked to pass along his message. Mom is still mad at him for whatever they were fighting about and refuses to talk to him. Before I hang up, I asked him if he'd told his friends at work about her cancer. He pauses and then tells me he has.

Kristina has on her favorite yoga pants, an expensive brand she got on eBay for more than they're worth. They're baggy on her where they used to be tight. Her head is hidden under a baseball cap and she's got on a loose-fitting volleyball sweatshirt. She looks like a poster child for a refugee camp, slouched on the hospital bed, waiting, her feet dangling in the air above the ground with a pair of pink flip-flops on her unpainted toes.

Mom and I are stumbling around like *Dumb and Dumber*, gathering up belongings and going over the talk with the discharging doctor. We look like poster children for awkward when Jeremy walks into the room, and with him seems to come a breath of fresh air. Kristina looks less waifish and sits up straighter on the bed.

He's wearing his dorky rap shirt again but I'm more than willing to forgive him as he smiles at all of us and sucks some of the tension from the room.

"So, big day. Going home," he says and walks closer to Kristina. "You'll sleep in your own bed tonight." His voice isn't charged with false bravado the way mine sounds whenever I speak to Kristina today. It's natural.

I stare at him. He's so much more confident than I gave him credit for at school. Clearly he's a boy who does well in stressful situations. Either that or he just really likes my sister.

Kristina lowers her eyes but doesn't answer him. He steps closer and leans in and whispers something in her ear. She smiles ever so slightly but it disappears quickly.

"Remember what I dared you," he says, and then he steps back and lifts her arm. With a closed fist, he passes something into the palm of her hand and she holds it tight. I'm dying to know what it is. And what he said to her.

"Do you need help, Mrs. Smith?" he asks Mom. "Taking things to your car?"

Mom smiles at him, but shakes her head as she tosses Kristina's gym bag over her shoulder. "I think we've got it."

"I'll walk you down to the parking lot, if that's okay."

Mom, Kristina, and I practically shout yes.

"Let's go," Mom says.

Jeremy holds out the crook of his arm and Kristina takes it and gets off the bed. Her free hand is still tight around whatever Jeremy handed her.

Mom leads the way out of the room and they follow. I walk behind them and watch the nurses on the ward as they wave and call good-bye and greet Jeremy like he's an old friend.

He walks with us to the car and tucks Kristina in the back and then stands in the parking lot waving as we head home.

Mom drives about twenty miles an hour, gripping the steering wheel with ghostly white knuckles and annoying the hell out of me. Kristina is tired and withdrawn, and I almost wish Jeremy had come with us.

At home, Mom heads for the kitchen, chattering about whipping up a healthy meal as Kristina slowly climbs the stairs, holding the railing. She only answers questions in monotone one-word sentences. I follow her to her room, feeling like someone should fluff her pillows or get her some juice, mad at Mom for hiding in the kitchen.

"So, your friends really miss you. Especially Devon," I say.

She raises her hand and shakes her head. "I don't want to talk about it. Can I have some privacy please?"

Fine by me. I don't want to have to admit I screwed up her request and told Nick first and that he passed the message on to Devon and Gee. Her detachment is creepy though. A total contrast to life before cancer. It's like she's buried herself so deeply inside her head she's disappearing. I know that feeling, because I've done it too, but never for such a serious reason. Besides, on me, it's natural. The only thing that seems to bring her back to the real world is Jeremy, but he can't exactly move into our house.

"You want me to get you the laptop?" I call. "I have it in my room. I was going to do homework, but you can use it to catch up on stuff you've missed out on."

"Tess, leave me alone," she says. "I don't care about that stuff."

I don't move away. "You're sure? I don't mind."

I want Kristina back. I miss her. A memory flashes in my head. The summer, only a couple of months before. Kristina standing in the hallway in her tiny purple and white bikini, yelling at me for hogging the computer. I'd only had it for a few minutes and was using it to google art supplies.

She doesn't answer but hobbles further inside her room like a little old lady. "Where'd you get those jeans?" she says without looking back.

I'd forgotten I was wearing them and certainly hadn't realized she noticed.

"Mom got them for me. She wanted to shop. You know. Her personal brand of therapy."

"They look good." She turns to face me. "You look good. Different. They suit you. You're so skinny."

"You're the one who's skinny," I tell her, doing my best to make it sound like a compliment, hoping to cheer her up, but she hums with unhappiness, a cross between a sigh and a groan. "You're going to have to use dental floss for toilet paper," I try.

She doesn't even crack a smile. "I'm going to take a nap," she says.

I step away and shut the door quietly behind me. Alone in the hallway, the emptiness inside me threatens to eat me alive. I head downstairs to see Mom frantically racing around the living room, straightening things. She's a bundle of nervous energy. I sit down on the leather couch in the living room and watch.

"Can I do something?" I ask when she breezes by me with a duster in her hand.

She shakes her head. "How's Kristina?" she asks.

"Tired."

She nods and runs back to the kitchen and I hear her chopping vegetables. She whips up her healthy supper while I sit in the living room staring at the walls. Finally I turn on the TV and flick channels instead of studying or working on my sketches.

The doorbell rings, and when no one else appears to get it, I stand and walk over to the door. A delivery man with a bored expression stands in the doorway. He's holding the biggest, most colorful bouquet of flowers I've ever seen in my life.

"Kristina Smith?" he asks.

I shake my head. "She's here but not available."

He thrusts the flowers in my arms. "Well, if she's here, take them. I have another vase in the car. She's popular. What'd she do? Have a baby?"

I give him a dirty look and slam the door in his face. I take the flowers into the kitchen and Mom grabs her chest with one hand and then rushes forward. She takes the flowers and puts them on the counter and opens the card.

"It's from the volleyball team," she says.

The doorbell rings again. "There's more," I say.

Mom presses her lips tight but doesn't say anything or move to get the door, so I walk slowly back to the door and collect the next vase of flowers without saying a word to Delivery Dude. Mom takes the flowers and reads the card again. They're from Devon.

"Her boyfriend?" Mom asks.

I shake my head. "Ex," I tell her. "You know Devon. You've met him."

She nods absently. "Yeah. Kristina didn't bring him around much though." She returns to her cooking without another word. The fragrance of the fresh flowers makes me want to sneeze so I leave and go back to the living room.

A short while later, Mom hollers that supper is ready. "Wash up," she calls.

Dad still isn't home from work.

I go to the bathroom to wash my hands. She's chattering about Dad being late and saying we'll go ahead and eat without him.

"What else is new?" I mumble as I walk back to the kitchen. She's setting the table and I offer to help but she waves me away as if I'm causing her grief.

"Can you get Kristina for dinner?" she says without looking at me. "I'd like her to come down. She should see the flowers too. It was a nice gesture from her friends."

I head upstairs and knock on Kristina's door.

"I'm not hungry," she calls out.

"Mom'll freak out if you don't come down and at least have something."

Kristina doesn't answer, so I turn her knob and push the door open. She's lying on her bed, on top of the covers staring at the ceiling. She looks breakable. "You got a couple of bouquets of flowers. From the volleyball team and Devon," I tell her.

She doesn't even blink.

"Do you think I'm going to die?" she asks the ceiling in a flat voice. Unfortunately, I know she's talking to me.

"No!" I'm surprised by the ferociousness of my voice. A surge of anger sweeps through me. She's not allowed to give up.

"But what if I do?" she says.

"Then I'll get the bigger room," I tell her. "And your Toyota. But you can't die because I want a Volkswagen Beetle and you love this room."

She glances over at me then and sits up slowly. "My sickness is bringing out a sense of humor I didn't even know you had."

"Neither did I," I tell her honestly. "You're not going to die," I add.

She lifts her hand in the air and studies her fingers, kind of waving them about. The veins popping out on the back of her hands are clearly visible. They look like old woman hands. I try not to picture the poison that was running through them. Chemo to kill the cancer.

"What did Jeremy give you at the hospital?" I ask.

"A charm," she tells me. She holds up her wrist again and this time, instead of her veins, I notice the old silver bracelet she used to sleep and shower with when she was little.

I walk toward her bed and she holds it up for me to see.

"It's a dancer," she says, and points out a charm.

I study it. A silver girl with a long dress and a bun striking a ballroom pose. "A dancer?" I ask.

"Private joke," she says. I sit on the end of her bed. "I told him about my charm bracelet and how I kept it over the years. We were talking about things we loved when we were kids. He remembers stuff like that."

"He sounds like a good friend," I say.

She nods, pulling her wrist back and studying the dancer.

"He's a really strong person. And so easy to talk to. Probably because of his mom. He's so, I don't know, hopeful, I guess."

"Yeah." I can't think of anything to say so I improvise. "I didn't see him at school today."

"No. His mom wanted him at the hospital." She pauses. "He said she never asked him to do that before."

"He must be worried," I say softly, and hope it's the right thing to say. I'm so new at this. I need instructions. I need to download something off the Internet. How to talk to people who have cancer and not sound like an insensitive jerk.

"Yeah," Kristina pauses. "He's a nice kid. I mean, he's not that young. I like him. He's easy to talk to about stuff."

Shame creeps through me for not being easier to talk to.

"Your friends at school are so worried." I tell her.

She closes her eyes. "Of course they are. I have cancer. They're supposed to be. It's expected."

I wonder about her choice of words. "No, they really are. They don't know what to do. They want to do something to help. Gee wants to collect money to buy you the newest iPhone. She thinks it might make you better." I snort but she gives me nothing. "I told her not to. That you didn't want one. Maybe you should talk to them. You know, call Gee or someone. It might help. She's kind of your best friend, isn't she?"

"No."

It's funny that Kristina never had one person. A BFF. I guess it's Jeremy now.

"Gee wouldn't be able to handle seeing me sick. Anyhow, I don't want to talk to anyone from school. I don't want anyone to see me like this."

"How do you know what she can handle? Having friends around is important to you. She wants to see you. It doesn't matter how you look."

"It always matters, Tess. They don't know me. Not really. No one does." She opens her eyes. "Well, except Jeremy. He sees more than the volleyball star. The hair and the makeup and clothes. He even sees more than the cancer now, you know? He talks to me. He takes the time to ask questions, to understand who I am. He's the best friend I've ever had."

"Wow. I didn't know you were that close." I smile but it hurts a little. Jeremy can be something for her that I can't.

"Did you talk to him? About, you know, your leg."

A tiny smile turns up her lips and then disappears. "That I might lose it? Yeah. A little." She giggles but it's weak and she covers her mouth with her hand. "He said if I do, I'll be on *Dancing with the Stars*. You know. Like that lady who was married to Paul McCartney and only had one leg." She holds up her wrist again. "That's what this is for. To show me what I can do, no matter what."

I smile. It makes me feel better, thinking about that. Kristina dancing on TV.

"He made me a bet."

I nod, remembering what he said at the hospital. "What?"

She doesn't answer. I hear Mom shouting from the kitchen but we both ignore her. I wait for Kristina to tell me more about the bet but she doesn't. "He said I'll be the oldest one in the nursing home and all the old men will be secretly in love with me."

"He totally has a crush on you," I tell her.

She lifts her shoulder but it's barely perceptible. "Maybe. A little. But it's not really like that. He's a good guy. It's sweet. We're friends." She slides over her covers until she's flat out on her back again, staring up at the ceiling. "Really good friends."

I have an urge to tell her about Melissa. About how my best friend turned out to be someone I don't even know. That maybe she was right about her. But it's not the time or the place. This isn't about me.

Kristina looks at me and her lips turn up. "He told me he has a friend who thinks you're pretty."

I blush and then laugh, but warmth settles in my stomach. I guess that it's Clark and I want to ask, but don't.

I lower my eyes. "His friend obviously needs glasses." I hope she'll tell me he already has them.

"No. It's true, Tess. You are pretty. You look great in that outfit. You should explore this side of you a little more. Try a little makeup. You could be even prettier if you tried a little."

Familiar resentment crawls into my bones and I suddenly feel gawky. Pretty is her territory. Not mine. I don't want to listen to it and long to flee but then she smiles, though her eyes have the saddest expression I've ever seen.

"Remember when I was pretty?" she says.

My anger disappears. I prod inside for strength. I pretend to contemplate her question.

"No," I finally answer. "I can't say that I do remember when you were pretty." And then I grin at her and she gives me a fake death stare.

"Don't be stupid. You're still pretty," I tell her. "Just more hard core. Like a punk rocker on crack except without rad clothes or good taste in music."

She narrows her eyes. "You're the one who listens to bad music."

I point at the posters on her wall and roll my eyes with exaggeration.

"You ever notice no one ever says I'm smart?" she asks.

"Totally."

She sticks out her tongue and then runs her hand through her hair. Long strands of it come out. Bigger clumps than is normal. We both stare at it.

I reach out and take it from her hand. "It's only hair," I say. "It'll grow back."

I stand up, gripping her hair in my fist. It feels weird and my eyes fill with tears. I hurry for the wastebasket and throw it inside, and blink hard and fast before I turn around to head back to her bed.

I sit down again. "People like labels. You're pretty, I'm smart. It doesn't mean you aren't smart too. Dad thinks you're smart. I heard him." I grin. "He told me you're too lazy to use your brains, but smarter than you let on."

She snorts. "Thanks a lot." And then looks serious. "You're okay, you know that. We're just different."

"Yeah," I say. "I'm mute and you have verbal diarrhea."

"Aren't you supposed to be nicer to me when I'm sick?"

"Is that what you want?" I ask her.

She smiles again. "Not really, but yes. Besides, you're not so mute anymore."

I take a deep breath, trying to find courage. "I'm here for you," I blurt out and then duck my head as shyness overcomes me.

She closes her eyes then and her breathing slows, as if our conversation exhausted her. "I know," she says. Then she rolls over away from me, onto her side. Our conversation is obviously over. "Can you tell Mom I'm sleeping and I'll eat something later?"

"Yeah, sure." I push myself up from her bed and stare at her back. My heart aches but I stand straighter.

"Can you tell her Jeremy is coming over later?"

"Sure," I say.

After I scarf back food with Mom, I head to my room. I pull out my sketch pad and my favorite pencil and examine my work in progress. I've shaded in explosions from the volcano but they're not vivid enough. I've used shadows to show the lava running but the perspective isn't working. My feelings aren't spilling onto the page. I add a few lines and squint, trying to make the lava flowing from the image run right off the page.

It's not working.

Nothing seems to be working. I feel completely and utterly useless and put my sketch pad down.

chapter eleven

A few days later, clumps of Kristina's hair continue to fall out. Huge clumps. Soon, there are only a few strands on her head. It would be almost comical if it weren't so heartbreaking. Finally, one day I hear her in the bathroom. There's buzzing. The razor. When Kristina comes out, her head is round and shiny and bare. She looks smaller. Mom follows behind her, wringing her hands in front of her, tears streaming down her cheeks.

Kristina doesn't smile anymore when I go to her room to see her. She doesn't get out of bed unless she has to. Her energy is low and her mood lower. She sleeps or stares at the wall, her back to the door. Sometimes I hear the TV that Mom went out and bought for her room, breaking her rule that TVs should never be allowed in bedrooms. There are exceptions.

She won't answer the phone or talk to anyone who calls, yet it seems like the phone is constantly ringing for her. Mom talks to the mothers who call for their worried daughters and soon the daughters start calling for Mom to hear how Kristina is doing. Mom lies.

Jeremy pops over every day after school though and he's pretty much the only person Kristina talks to.

When he leaves, she locks her bedroom door and only comes

out when Mom forces her to eat. She refuses the laptop and all her friends at school keep telling me she hasn't been online since she's been home.

Mom is becoming more and more freaked, which makes for a very clean house and lots of running miles on her newest sneakers. The house overflows with freshly made healthy snacks but Kristina isn't interested in food. Only enough to keep Mom off her back.

I don't know how Dad feels about the dark cloud hanging over our house, because he's usually gone to work when I get up in the morning and isn't home until after supper or even later if he's golfing. He's avoiding Kristina, which makes me furious, but I don't have an outlet for my anger.

Hiding in my own room pretending to be busy with studying, it's all about trying to draw, fiddling with the volcano, trying to complete the image that is trapped in my brain. It's like there's a fly buzzing in my head. I reach for it, flail at it, try to trap it, but can't quite capture it. When I'm not failing at sketching, I'm book binging. I've read a full fantasy trilogy since Kristina came home and Melissa stopped being my best friend.

Strangely, I'm also the one becoming a computer addict now. I have more friends on Facebook than Kristina does. Almost every person at school has added me. My notoriety has more to do with Kristina than me, but it still blows me away how everyone is writing things on my wall, asking me questions, and sending me virtual flowers and funny questionnaires.

It's a weird mix of intimacy and anonymity, having virtual

friends. I finally get the whole attraction to the Internet thing. Having conversations online is easier; so is hiding behind a mouse and the keys on my keyboard.

One morning when I'm online, my chat window opens and pings. NICK E wants to chat. I hold in a scream and turn the computer off, my heart racing as if I've been caught unwrapping all the gifts under the Christmas tree on December 24.

When I get to school, I keep my head down in real time, but people I hardly recognize call my name and say hi, like I'm a friggin' celebrity because my sister has cancer. Kristina's friends hunt me down for daily updates and I grit my teeth and lie. Tell them she's fine.

I'm standing at my locker feeling all alone and missing the idea of Melissa being there waiting for me like she used to, wishing for a real live friend, when Clark walks up to my side.

"Hey," he says.

My hero.

"Superman." I greet him with a smile.

He grins and pushes his glasses up on his nose. "At your service, Lois Lane."

He waits for me and then we walk down the hallway together as if it's the most natural thing in the world. Melissa is nowhere in sight, but the ghost of her presence weighs on my mind. I wonder if she's watching from a distance. What she thinks about me and Clark hanging out. If she knows that some guys aren't scary. Some guys make really good friends.

I wonder if she hates me.

We pass Nick in the hall and I wave, determined to pretend it wasn't me who shut off the computer when his name came up on chat. Nick lifts his hand, but turns and leans down and says something into the ear of a blond standing beside him. Bree Silver.

When Clark and I enter Mr. Meekers's room, he eyeballs me and calls me to his desk where he's sitting, reading a book. He stands and speaks down to me in a quiet voice, presumably so the other kids rolling into class or already seated can't hear our conversation.

"We need to have a serious talk, Miss Smith. I heard you've been skipping classes?" He gives me an evil stare but doesn't crack me. "I've been pulling for you to become an esteemed member of the Honor Society, but the selection committee is very strict. We can't make exceptions for you if you're not meeting the requirements." He clears his throat and stands taller. "And I haven't seen you up on any of the volunteer lists."

My heart skips a beat. I want to defend myself. I want to give him the full, lengthy explanation. Bullet-point my excuses. It's not my fault. It's Kristina's fault. Her and her stupid cancer. My parents don't care. No one is worried about me. Or what I want. It's all *her*. I want to tell him I'd join the committees and volunteer, but between trying to cram in school work, dealing with my sister, my Mom, and my absentee father, I don't have time.

I open my mouth to defend myself but close it.

Images play in my head. Kristina throwing up on the first day of chemo. Her heartbreaking face, trying to be brave, but so afraid. I see her bald head and hear her tell me how she liked being pretty. As if pretty is forever a past tense for her. I hear her ask if I think she's smart. I've always had smart. I own it. Even if Mr. Meekers won't see it.

I stand tall and almost look him directly in the eye. He's only got an inch or two on me. I still have smarts. I know that. Even if the Honor Society faculty advisor doesn't. I take a deep breath and make a final deal with God.

I give up the Honor Society. Just please let my sister be okay.

I guess my priorities decided to shift without my even wanting them too.

"I'm sorry you feel that way, Mr. Meekers," I tell him. "But my sister is sick. And right now, that's the most important thing."

Well, that and the Oswald Drawing Prize, but I can't even talk to him about it or consult him about my problems with the sketch because he sucks as an art teacher. And a faculty advisor.

I take my seat as he glares at me, but eventually his eyes glaze over. He ignores me and instructs the entire class to get to work on our clay projects. He doesn't leave his seat once to offer anyone advice or assistance on their work. He ignores the buzz of conversation as long as it stays at a reasonable volume. Mr. Meekers doesn't bother with dirty details like involvement with his students. He's an ass. An ass who is not on my side.

I wonder if the lines are dividing everywhere.

chapter twelve

After school when I walk in the house, Mom runs straight for me at the front door. Babbling.

"I got back from my run a few minutes ago. She's in her bedroom. Burning up. I called Dr. Turner but she hasn't called me back."

We both run to Kristina's room. Kristina has a washcloth draped over her forehead. She's lying still and she's so pale and thin, she looks almost dead.

"Kristina," I shout, but she doesn't respond.

I rush to her bed and put my hand on her forehead. She's hotter than desert sand at high noon. "Did you give her Tylenol? What's her temperature?"

Mom's face blanks and then she turns and runs for her bathroom, rattling around in the medicine cabinet.

"Kristina?" I say. My heart beats triple time.

She opens her eyes slowly, but they're glassy and her pupils roll around as if her eyeballs might slide right out of the sockets.

Mom returns holding a thermometer and sticks it under Kristina's tongue. When it beeps, she pulls it out.

"105," she says.

Kristina groans. "My mouth hurts," she croaks. "It's full of little lumps."

"It's got to be neutropenia," I say.

Mom stares at me.

"Low white blood cell count," I tell her. "I read about it in the brochure the doctor gave us. A possible complication of chemo."

"Shit," Mom says. "Why didn't I read that? I'm a horrible mother."

I want to agree with her but refrain. I don't point out she's been too busy living in a pretend land where Kristina is fine, and her marriage is fine, and her life is still perfect to read about the cancer.

"I looked it up on the Internet." I don't mention how much time I've been spending online. My new computer addiction will only add to her newly emerging bad parenting guilt.

Mom stands and steps back from the bed. "We have to get her back to the hospital. I have no idea what else to do."

I nod my agreement. Kristina doesn't say anything. Her eyes are closed and she looks like a deflating balloon losing all its air.

"Help her up. I'll go get my purse and keys," Mom commands.

I rush to Kristina's closet and grab her fuzzy pink robe and run back to her side. I slide my arm under hers and help her to sit up as she groans about her headache.

She weighs almost nothing, but it takes a moment before I can get her in a standing position.

Mom rushes back and each of us takes an arm and we walk Kristina out to the car, tuck her in the back seat, and fasten her seat belt. I climb in beside her and Mom drives us to the hospital, taxi-style and in record time. On the way, she calls Kristina's doctor and as soon as we walk into Emergency, one of the nurses from the oncology unit meets us and expedites Kristina's re-entrance to the hospital.

In what seems like one big flash, Kristina is back in a hospital room, wearing her gown and sleeping on the uncomfortable-looking bed with steel guards, but no one complains. Doctors and nurses run in and out of the room, sticking her with needles and stuffing her with meds. They're fast to see her, and before we know it, she's been seen by a specialty team and she's hooked up to IVs. Mom and I do what we're told. We leave the room and go to waiting rooms and to the cafeteria and back and forth, until hours later, they've got her stabilized and we're all alone in the room with Kristina.

She sleeps while Mom slumps over in a chair beside the bed, looking like she's about to collapse. I close my eyes and lean back in my own hard chair, finally able to take a moment to breathe.

"Jesus Christ," a voice calls and my eyes pop open. Dad charges into the room, wearing his golf clothes—beige slacks and a white golf shirt. His eyes are bloodshot and frantic.

Mom jumps to her feet, looking a little frightened, and then her features harden and she looks more frightening than afraid. "Glad you could join us," she says, her voice edgy and raw.

"Why the hell didn't you call me?" he demands in a harsh whisper. "I got home from golf and no one was home."

"We were a little occupied. Kristina was suffering from neutropenia."

"For God's sake, Lisa. I thought she was dead. I thought she was dead." He rushes to Kristina's side and picks up her limp hand. She murmurs and stirs but doesn't wake.

Mom sits down and slides her chair closer to Kristina, her lips pressed tight.

I stare at both of them and then I can't take it anymore. The stupid games they've been playing. Accusation ignites and burns inside me. "You thought she was dead? Try being the ones who have to haul her body out of bed when she is on the brink of it. She's very, very sick."

His shoulders slump and his face crumples but it doesn't stop me.

"And where the hell were you? Golfing? Because God only knows how important those rounds of golf are."

"Tess," my mom warns. She strokes Kristina's bare head and closes her eyes. Her breathing is slow, steady, as if she doesn't have energy for my dad and his brand of coping.

"What? He has the nerve to yell at *us* because he doesn't know where she is, but, meanwhile, he can't be bothered to come home on time and find out? Get your ass home and start dealing with what is going on in our house. Mom is freaking out trying to cope with it, and all you're doing is avoiding being around and avoiding that it's happening to all of us."

He stares at me. My mom stares at me.

Their eyes are mirrors of each other. Wide. Confused. They look like they're waiting for me to tell them what to do.

"I'm not going to make the Honor Society. I lost my best friend. I'm also only freaking fifteen years old, but somehow I'm the one dealing with Kristina?"

Disgusted with both of them, I stomp past them out of the hospital room.

I take the elevator downstairs, too mad to even cry, and stomp out on the main floor and almost collide with another body. Jeremy. His face changes from a polite look of apology to panic when he realizes it's me.

"What are you doing here? I thought Kristina was at home. Is everything okay? Is Kristina okay?" he asks.

Tears spill down my face and, just like that, my anger vanishes. I shake my head, trying not to hyperventilate, trying to stay in control. I nod and then shake my head and then just stare at Jeremy, silently pleading for help. He grabs me by the shoulder. Hard.

"What happened?" he demands.

"No. No. She's okay. She had neutropenia. She's back in the hospital again. They got her stabilized. They said she's going to be fine."

I snort out a laugh and a stream of snot escapes my nose. Horrified, I wipe it off with my hand, and start walking away from Jeremy, not sure where I'm heading but needing to escape. "Relatively speaking."

"Hey, Tess, wait up."

I keep my legs moving to get away but he catches up and walks beside me.

"It's okay to be upset," he says. "Mad, afraid, whatever. I get it, you know. I've felt all those things about my mom too."

I glare at him. "Don't you know boys are supposed to keep their feelings bottled up inside of them?"

He gives me a dirty look but it quickly disappears, and then he shakes his head and laughs. "You really are funny."

It loosens up the knots in my stomach somehow. I slow down a little, stop racing to get away. My legs ache anyway. I'm still a wimp.

"Cancer kind of has a way of stripping away pretenses," he says.

I glance sideways at him and ask the question I've been dying to ask him. "Is that why you and Kristina have become such good friends? No pretenses?"

He shrugs his shoulders up and then they fall. "I don't know, Tess. I really like her. Is it bothering you?"

"Not really." My jealousy is stupid. We walk in silence for a minute. Around us, people rush about.

"I was terrified," he says in a quiet voice. "I thought my mom was going to die when we found out about her cancer. But I was mad too, for her getting cancer. She smoked when she was younger; I thought maybe that's why she got sick. I blamed her for her body getting sick."

I don't respond.

"Want to go outside for a walk?" he asks.

I wonder if my parents will worry about where I've gone, but right then I don't care, so I nod and he pushes the front door of the hospital open and we step outside into the crisp fall air. I shiver and wish I had brought my coat, but I'm not going to complain about the cold.

"You like my sister, don't you?" I say.

His cheeks turn red.

"No. It's okay. I'm not calling you a stalker or anything. But you do, right?"

He doesn't answer.

"She needs you as a friend," I tell him. "You're the only person she can talk to."

He smiles and it changes his face. He looks more grown-up and mature and something else shines in his eyes. A secret, maybe. "I know."

"I'm glad you're her friend," I tell him.

"Me too," he says. "She's a great person, you know. Cancer isn't going to take that away from her. I think she just needs to find out who she is. She's going to have to adjust to a new life. But she will, I think. She just doesn't believe it yet."

My turn for my cheeks to warm. "I don't think I've been a very good sister."

"I think both of you maybe have let other people decide who you are. She's struggling, Tess, but you can help. She'll come up with new goals and dreams; she's just mourning her old ones. You know? She has to. It's normal. Anyhow, she said you're handling her cancer better than your parents."

"Really?" I ask. Because I don't feel like I'm doing a good job either.

"Really," he says.

I hide a smile with my hand and then tell Jeremy I'm cold, and we turn to go back inside.

Dad isn't in the hospital room when I get back. Mom doesn't explain but tells me we're leaving. We drive home and when we return, Dad is already there. They tiptoe around each other as if they're strangers. I head straight for my room.

We all sleep for a few hours and then pile back in the car and return to the hospital in the morning. I don't even ask about going to school.

Kristina is awake when we get to her room.

"We have a meeting with the doctor tomorrow at ten thirty," Mom says, and smoothes her hand across Kristina's bald head.

"I want Tess here," Kristina says.

I nod, but all I can think about is that I'll be missing an important lecture in science. Our midterm exam is going to be based on the lecture. There goes my GPA.

She wins hands down, but a part of me longs for the right to mourn my own losses too.

No matter how insignificant they are compared to cancer.

• • •

The next day, I skip another class to get to the hospital on time. Dad is supposed to pick me up on his way from the university, but at the last minute he calls to say he's still rushing around and asks me to hop a cab to the hospital and he'll pay me back.

I hang up on him without saying good-bye.

I end up making it to the hospital before both of them and sit in the room with my sister, not really knowing what to say. Minutes after Mom and Dad rush into the room, clearly angry with each other, the doctor from the clinic walks in. Dr. Turner. She looks different in the hospital setting. More formal somehow. She has a file folder tucked under her arm. She greets us all by name and then clears her throat. The expression on her face drains all the blood out of my body. I look at Kristina who is sitting up on the bed, hugging her knees.

"I'm afraid the tumor didn't respond to the chemo treatment," the doctor says.

My head starts spinning in dizzy circles. The room is moving; everyone is completely still. "Actually, the tumor enlarged during the initial treatment." She opens the file and consults her notes but doesn't look up at any of us. "At this point, limb-saving surgery is impossible. We'll have to do above-knee amputation."

I hear shuffling feet from the hallway behind us. There's a low mumbling of voices, people going on with their lives, but the words are indistinguishable. The doctor keeps talking. I hear words but don't register what she's saying. I stare at my feet. My two feet. Two legs and two feet, both planted firmly on the floor. I can't look at my sister's face. I can't bear to see her expression.

The doctor is still speaking and when I hear her say Tuesday, I tune in. "The surgery will be this Tuesday."

Today is Thursday. My mind slowly does the math as if I'm in first grade and have to count by ticking off the days on my fingers.

Five days.

In five days they'll chop off Kristina's leg.

Kristina moans and it's not a sound I've heard before. The anguish in her vocal cords crushes me. My mom goes to her and squeezes her tight, but she's crying too and their noises meld together in stereo.

Dad is in the corner. Expressionless. He isn't looking at Kristina.

I can't bear to think. I don't want to make myself imagine what her leg will look like when the operation is done.

It's worst-case scenario. I swallow and imagine a revving chain saw coming down on her knee. Bone flying in the air. The stump that she'll have instead of a calf and a foot. But then it gets even worse.

"It's unfortunate there wasn't time for a fertility treatment to save some of your eggs. It would have safeguarded your chances of having children in the future."

I'd like to hand her an award for bad timing, but I guess she's emotionally distanced herself and is doing her job, covering all the bases. Kristina and Mom cling to each other as Dr. Turner mumbles more meaningless words about the surgery, but I'm too stunned to speak and from the looks of it the rest of my family is shell-shocked as well. After a moment the doctor stands. She hands Kristina a brochure about the operation and Kristina grips it in her hand, crumples it.

The doctor walks to the door and then turns, staring at us, her hand on the door.

She reaches into her pocket and hands me a card. I presume it's because I'm standing closest to her.

"This is the card for the American Cancer Society," she says. She turns to Kristina. "If any questions come up, call me."

She walks out, treading softly; her white sneakers make hardly any noise on the floor. The door clicks behind her.

Kristina sobs louder. Her eyes are frantic, not seeing anything. Kristina pushes my Mom away but Mom holds on tighter. Kristina whines and cries and fights her off, but Mom holds on, wrapping her arms around her. Eventually Kristina falls against her, her face buried in Mom's shirt.

Mom's tears pour down her cheeks, dripping onto Kristina's back. Dad stands next to them. His eyes are glazed. My mom continues to cover Kristina's body with her own. They rock back and forth, not saying a word. Just moving. Crying. I watch my parents, feeling detached, as if I'm watching a bad after-school movie special plagued with overacting.

I want to leave the room, run, but can't make myself move. I want to sneak out, slip outside unseen. I remember being a kid and staring at people who were different until Mom whispered that it was rude. I remember seeing a woman at the swimming pool as Kristina was trying to teach me to dive. Kristina would do a perfect dive, time after time, trying to get me to follow her lead.

The woman had a stump for an arm. I'd stared and stared at the stump, horrified and fascinated, until Mom told me to stop staring and start diving. I kept sneaking peeks though, wondering how it felt to have no arm. How she could swim and what she thought about when she looked at people with two arms.

Did she miss the one that was gone?

chapter thirteen

Dad's still home when I'm getting ready for school, and he waits, telling me he'll drive me. I don't think anyone in the house slept a wink and my body is so tired it hurts to move, so I take him up on his offer. I hope that Kristina slept all right at the hospital and that for once, the exhaustion of cancer and medication offer some relief for her.

Dad is home but Mom's packed up and gone before I even get up. I guess now that dreams about Kristina's Olympic volleyball team future are spent, Mom is finally ready to stop pretending everything is okay. She can't even daydream about the perfect grandkids Kristina will give her one day. All she has a chance for now are my second-rate ones. If that ever happens. It seems pretty unlikely at this point in my life.

On the car ride to school we're mostly silent, but as we approach the street where he'll drop me off, he glances sideways at me.

"How are you doing, sweetie?" he asks. I can't remember the last time he used that term for me. Since I was a little girl.

I lift a shoulder and stare out the window. Cars pass by us, people going on with their lives, unaware that my sister's entire future has been crushed.

He clears his throat and I glance back to him. His face is contorted; he's holding in tears. It twists my insides like the word games we used to play when we were younger would do to my tongue. He spurts and brings up a fist to his mouth, coughing, his other hand tight on the wheel.

"I'm sorry," he sputters.

I reach out and touch his hand, but he takes it from his mouth and re-grips the steering wheel.

"For what, Daddy?" I ask. Now it's my turn to use pet names long discarded.

"For not being stronger. For not handling this better. I want to do better. It's just…" He clears his throat. "It's difficult," he says and his voice hardens, almost angry.

I nod. He pulls up to the curb then, and stares out the window. I wait for a moment, hoping he'll say more but he doesn't, so I open the door.

"I love you, Tess," he says, still focused on something outside the front window. "You and Kristina both."

"I know," I say softly. "Bye, Dad." I close the door and watch as he pulls away, driving quickly as if he can't wait to leave me behind.

Inside the school, I head toward my locker and some people stare at me with wide, curious eyes, but lots smile and say hi. The popular ones are confident enough to walk right up and ask me straight out how Kristina is doing. I mumble and keep going. All this attention is overwhelming and draining, but I force myself to keep it together, smiling and pretending to make sure no one forgets how much they like her. Kristina. Not her stupid infected leg. Maybe I'm more like my mom than I thought, because faking a personality isn't nearly as hard as I'd imagined. It surprises me how I manage small talk and it makes me wonder if it was in me all along.

When I turn the last corner toward my locker, someone is standing in front of it, waiting for me. I hold my breath for a second, thinking it's Melissa coming to apologize, telling me it was all a mistake. But it's not. Melissa's no longer my person. Instead it's Clark Trent who smiles when he spots me and, without thinking, I grin in return.

"Superman," I say to Clark.

He pushes up his glasses and his cheeks turn a cute color of pink. "That's getting old," he says in a voice that says it's okay with him anyway.

He steps out of the way so I can open my locker.

"You've been assigned to protect me?" I ask in a dry tone, but smile.

He laughs. "I guess," he says and then waits while I get my books.

We're both such brilliant conversationalists.

"You ready for our test?" he asks.

I stare up at him and then close my locker door and put on the lock. "Test?"

He lifts an eyebrow. "In English. On soliloquies?"

"Today?"

"You're kidding, right? Mr. Pepson told us to study on Friday."

"I totally forgot." I lean against the lockers. It should be a level-four tragedy but I can't muster up the energy to register it as one. It pales in comparison to my sister's day.

"Well, I mean, you should talk to Mr. Pepson. I'm sure he'd understand. You know. Under the circumstances."

"I'm not going to use my sister's cancer as an excuse to get out of things," I tell him, and my voice is sharper than I intended.

"You know," he says and looks away, "the Honor Society isn't the be-all, end-all."

And just like that it's over.

"I didn't get in?" I say quietly. It's not really a question, but a statement. I swallow a sizeable lump in my throat. My dream of being on the elite team of brainiacs slips right out of my fingers. It's so unfair I want to cry. It should have been easy for me. It should have been a given. Instead Kristina got sick and I got sidetracked and now…

"They posted the members on the board outside Mr. Pepson's classroom. You should talk to him about it. I mean, it's not really fair. There's still time left in the semester for you to get your grades up." A few people trickle past us, but for once they ignore me. Two geeks talking about Honor Society.

"It's more than just grades," I say softly. "I didn't choose a service project and, well, there was the time I had the meltdown in front of Mr. Meekers."

I push off the locker. I've also been trying to focus on my art project, but I don't tell Clark that.

"It's crap," Clark says.

"It doesn't matter."

"Yes, it does. You're being punished."

"For what? For Kristina's cancer? Not likely. No, I haven't met the requirements. They're stated in black and white. Marks. Leadership. Volunteerism."

"But it's circumstantial. They should take it into consideration."

I don't want to go there. My problems don't even compare to my sister's.

"What about Melissa?" I ask instead.

Clark looks away and then shakes his head, a quick no. "I guess she didn't have the right personality or something."

Despite everything, I feel worse for Melissa. She's the one who wanted it so badly. In the end she needs it more than I do now. I've got other things to worry about.

I start walking and Clark easily matches my stride, using his bigger body to protect me from prying eyes again as we head down the hallway toward class. People stare, but I kind of like having him as a personal bodyguard.

Without asking, he starts filling me in on his definitions and theories on soliloquies, trying to prep me for the exam. As he talks, his glance kind of sweeps around as if he's sending warning signals to the kids staring at me. It works, because no one approaches with prying questions.

I look around to see if Melissa is watching me, hiding out, but don't see her anywhere. My heart dips. She really is gone. I focus on Clark and try to listen as he attempts to cram my brain with information for the test.

A few weeks ago I would have had a fit that I didn't study, but I know I'll be okay. Shakespeare is a geek-love of mine and I can pull off a test about soliloquies. It won't be a perfect score but I'll manage. I actually look forward to burying myself inside an exam.

The fact that Clark is helping me out strikes me as kind of funny, since I was supposed to be his competitor for the top freshman. I'm out of the game now.

We walk around a corner and approach a group of seniors, and I duck my head but not fast enough to see Nick standing off to the side, watching me. He smiles and it's sexy and mysterious and I think about him asking what I'm doing after school.

"Tess!"

The entire group of seniors is staring at me. My invisible shield is permanently down. I forget Nick's unasked question.

"How's it going?" I squint and see that Devon made the shout-out. He smiles and lifts his hand in greeting. Like we're buds. "You see the Seekers hockey game on TV last night?"

I shake my head but don't answer.

Unlike the rest of Great Heights, I don't worship the college hockey team. On the nights when they play at home, the stadium spotlights light up the sky. Every game sells out and is treated with the enthusiasm of a championship game.

Devon walks over and even Clark seems to shrink down a little. "Well, even if you don't like the college team, you should at least come out and see the high school team play. Go, Great Heights High, right?"

It's not about me, I remind myself. It's about Kristina. They want me to be her voice. Keep her whole.

"Yeah, maybe," I lie, because that's what they want to hear.

"Kristina loved watching me play hockey," he says. "Almost as much as I loved watching her play volleyball." He laughs. "You know. Those little spankies…" He stops and his face turns bright red.

Yeah. She might not look as cute in her little spankies soon. And he doesn't even know the truth of it yet. An overwhelming desire to start crying consumes me but I shove it down.

"It's okay," I say softly, because he didn't mean anything. He wants to believe she'll be back, just the way she was before. But it's the sort of stupid, insensitive thing that is going to be a part of her life now, and I want to wail for her.

Clark must sense the shift in my mood because he uses his big body to block me and starts talking overly loud about soliloquies and he walks me away. I'm barely managing to not melt into puddles on the floor. I can't do this today. I don't want her friends being nice to me. I don't want to be nice to anyone else. I can't handle it. Today I just want to make it through.

• • •

After school, when I walk inside the house, it's quiet. My guess is Mom is at the hospital with Kristina so I head for the kitchen and start searching the pantry for a snack. I pour milk on a huge bowl of Cap'n Crunch and, as I'm chewing, I feel someone watching and look up.

Mom leans against the wall watching me. She's got a glass in her hand. It tinkles with ice. I look closer and my eyebrows shoot up. Amber. I can smell the peaty stench from where I sit. Scotch on the rocks? I try to remember if I've ever seen her drink except the occasional one she nurses at parties.

"You're eating that horrible cereal again," she says. Her Southern accent is pronounced. She tilts her glass and polishes off the rest.

I look around the kitchen as if someone will miraculously appear to save me from what is happening. My heart beats like humming-bird wings. The mom I know doesn't slink around swilling drinks in the afternoon.

"How's Kristina?" I ask.

"Fine. That boy came to her room today. Jeremy. She asked me to leave. She isn't my same little girl anymore."

"Well, how could she be?" I ask.

She takes a step toward me, but loses her balance and giggles. She reaches for the wall with her free hand, but misses it and stumbles.

I put the spoon down as quietly as I can. "Mom? Are you okay? You want me to call Dad?"

"Your dad. Why? What's he going to do?" She pouts as if she's going to cry. "When's the last time he bothered to come home to talk? He's too busy working or playing golf."

My mom doesn't talk about Dad behind his back, no matter what. My butt melds to the chair. I don't know this person wearing my mom's body.

"I guess that's the way he's coping?" I say, defending him even though I'm plenty angry with his disappearing act too.

"What about me? When do I get to hide?"

"Uh, Mom?" I say and stop. I want to tell her she has been, but frankly she's scaring me.

She wobbles to the fridge, stands on her tiptoes, and reaches for the cupboard above it, and pulls out a bottle of Scotch. She unscrews the cap and weaves back to the table, sloshing a few ounces in her glass, spilling some on the floor.

"What, Tess?" she snaps. "What do you want?"

I stand up and push back from the table, and reach my hand out to take the glass from her, but she pulls back and lifts the glass to her lips. Then she laughs but it's a hollow sound, and I feel the vapors of desperation in the spittle that lands on my arm.

"Stop it!" I yell. I'm not emotionally equipped to handle this.

"Stop what? Drinking?" She lifts her glass, saluting me, and then finishes it and jiggles around the remaining ice cubes. "All gone." She begins to laugh.

"Stop it," I repeat, shaking my head, but she starts moving, stumbling to get past me. She walks like a zombie.

"Cut it out!" I yell.

"Cut it out?" She stops moving and stares at me. Her eyes are bloodshot and her makeup is smudged.

"Don't you see, Tess," she says and she speaks slowly, over-enunciating her words. "They *are* cutting it out. Your sister's leg. They're cutting out the cancer and taking off your sister's leg."

Tears leak from my eyes. "This is why Dad says you don't drink."

She swings around. Her free hand whacks me on the side of my face. The pain is instant but it's masked by shock. My mom has never laid a hand on me. Not once.

"You're the one who this should be happening to," she says, and her voice slurs, dripping with her visit to the dark side. "You'd rather sit around all day drawing pictures, like a five-year-old. Your sister had a future in volleyball!"

She starts to run away but she trips and falls to the floor. Her head droops to her shoulders and she folds into herself and weeps. My heart feels like it's been forced through a shredder, physically broken. I gasp and turn to leave her, crumpled and crying, a mess on the kitchen floor.

"Tess," she calls, her voice pitiful and repulsive.

Queasy from her words mixing with the smell of Scotch, I tear out of the house as she continues to weep and call my name. Bile rises in my throat.

I run to the garage, jump on my bike, and pedal.

chapter fourteen

I pull up to Nick's place and the nerves in my belly help to block the memory of my mom. One foot hits the pavement. His house is old and small. Green paint chips off in chunks on the house and the fence that surrounds the front yard. The fence is rotting and broken apart in places. It would make a great haunted house for Halloween, but it's not decorated on purpose.

I get off my bike and roll it forward, and my nose wrinkles up at the smell that lingers in the air, a mixture of dog poo and garbage. Inside my head, I hear the disapproving voice of my mother. Except it's me. My voice. And I'm not supposed to care about stuff like that. I don't want to be anything like her.

I drop my bike on brown, weedy grass and take a deep breath. I force myself to walk to the door and ring the doorbell. It sounds sick, like it has a cold. The bell sets off a dog's barks inside the house and a man's deep voice bellows out a curse.

"Someone get the goddamn door," he screeches. The yapping dog gets louder until it's right at the front, separated from me by a flimsy door with a screen in front of it.

There's a bang, and the door opens and a little girl appears behind the screen. She's thin, with dirty-looking brown hair.

She's wearing an unfashionable flowered dress that hangs to knobby knees. The girl has one hand on the dog's head. He's the homeliest dog I have ever seen. Lopsided ears, one sticking up, the other hanging down, long gray wiry fur. Luckily his tail is wagging and he's not snarling like I'm his midafternoon snack. "Yes?" she asks me.

"Uh, is Nick home?"

She stares at me. "Are you Tess?" she says.

I hide my surprise, but nod.

"Nick told me about you." She smiles and her face lights up, and I see the beauty underneath the dirt and old clothes. She has Nick's features, but a smaller, feminine nose.

"Goddamn it, Natalie. Who's at the door?" the voice bellows from inside the house. I imagine the giant from Jack and the Beanstalk. For a moment I'm afraid he's going to appear, come out and find me on his front porch and chase me away, or worse, pull me inside and gobble me up.

"If they're selling something, tell 'em to get lost," the voice shouts.

"It's okay, Dad. It's no one," the girl calls without taking her eyes off me.

"Then get me another beer, would you? And hurry your lazy ass up."

"Wait here," she says softly to me, and then she disappears from the door. The dog sits and stares at me with a low growl.

I stand in front of the door, shifting from foot to foot, embarrassed and not sure where to look or what to do. The dog's penetrating gaze makes me nervous. Just as I'm contemplating turning around to leave, the door bangs again and Nick appears in the doorway. My heart does a little machine gun sequence and my stomach burns.

"Slumming?" he says. He doesn't look very happy to see me. Like the little girl, his hand automatically goes to the dog's head.

"Uh, I was hoping we could talk."

"How'd you even know where I live, Tess?"

I shrug. "I found it on the Internet."

"My address?"

"You wouldn't believe what else I found on there," I joke.

He doesn't smile, just stares at me, then looks behind him in the house. He opens the door and steps outside and the dog joins him and he holds the screen door so it closes quietly behind him.

"Come on," he says. "Let's walk."

"Uh, shouldn't your dog be on a leash?"

"Killer? Nah. She's doesn't need one."

I don't say anything, but glance nervously at the dog. Killer stares at me with alert brown eyes.

"You're not afraid of dogs, are you?"

"No." I step back when Killer starts to pant.

He laughs. "You are so." He scratches the dog behind the ear and her tail thumps back and forth. "Don't worry. Despite the name, she wouldn't hurt a fly."

"You're sure?"

"I trust her more than I'd trust any human being in this world," Nick says. "Go on, let her smell your hand."

I don't want to stick out my hand in case Killer wants to snap it off for a snack. I don't want to look like a chicken either, so I put it out and Killer sniffs and then her long pink tongue darts out and she slurps my palm.

I wipe the slobber on my pants and follow Nick down the sidewalk as he starts to walk. He takes big steps and I hustle to keep up with him and his four-legged friend who trots happily at his side.

We stroll in silence to the end of his street, past equally beat-up houses, but when we turn around the corner the condition of the houses improves here and there. His house is no longer in view and he slows down and the dog matches his pace. His body seems less tense. He looks at me. "You okay?" he asks.

I fight to keep myself from breaking into tears. My nose drips and, mortified, I wipe it with the back of my hand.

"Something happen to your sister?" he asks.

His question sparks some rage, which takes me by surprise but helps keep tears away. "I don't want to talk about my sister." I glare at him. "What about your sister? I didn't even know you had a sister."

He stops moving and stares at me. "There are a lot of things you don't know about me, Tess." He starts walking again past huge poplar trees that line the street.

My cheeks warm. His voice sounds harder than it does at school. I wonder if he's mad at me for coming to his house. A stupid impulse. "Yeah? There are a lot of things you don't know about me too."

We pass a house decorated with hanging skeletons and a row of pumpkins on the porch. The house across the street has a small tree in front covered in fake spider webs. Must be kids in the house, excited for Halloween night.

"Hey. You came to find me. You're the one who wants to talk. So talk."

Killer growls at a squirrel jumping from one tree to another, busy collecting a stash for the winter. Nick reaches down and pats her head and her tail wags.

"Do you want to go out with me?" I blurt.

Nick stops walking and scratches behind Killer's ear, watching me. "You mean, on a date?" he finally asks.

When I see his confused look, I want to disappear through the cracks in the sidewalk, like a long-legged spider. I wish I could pluck my words back from the air. I am such an idiot! I was totally wrong. He obviously never had any intention of asking me out. And now I've made a total ass of myself.

Who was I trying to kid? What was I expecting? He'd be holding the glass slipper I left at the ball? I don't even want to be Cinderella. On principle, I'm supposed to be opposed to the idea of being rescued by a prince or even attending a ball.

I really need some cooperation from God for once and pray to be struck down by a freakish bolt of lightning. I hold in my tears and mortification and study the sidewalk, feeling like I've been picked last for a soccer team. Again.

There's a sudden streak of wetness on the back of my hand and I pull back, surprised. Killer is using me as a licking post.

"Whoa, Killer likes you," Nick says.

At least someone does. I search for words inside my head to deal with this horrible mess I've created.

"She's a good judge of character," he adds in a soft voice.

"What did you want from me?" I ask him.

"Uh, you came to *my* house," Nick answers.

"I'm not talking about now," I say. "What do you want to ask me? You keep saying you have something to ask me and then you never do. I thought…" I stop, too humiliated to go on.

He sighs and his hand reaches up and he pushes back his hair. "I wanted to ask you to help. My sister. Well, she has a hard time in school. I can't afford to get her a tutor and my old man doesn't give a shit. So, I thought about you. I thought you might want to add tutoring to your school resume, you know. I thought you might tutor her, but then when I found out about your sister, well, I couldn't ask."

"Your sister?" I repeat. "The little kid at your house?" No wonder she knew who I was. He told her I would be her friggin' baby-sitter.

"She's small but she's in the seventh grade. I think she has learning disabilities, but we can't afford to get her tested and the school won't do it. Not enough funding. It's always about the money you know. But, I thought maybe you would do it, you know, volunteer hours for your Honor Society."

I don't answer, feeling somehow ashamed of my Dad's over-flowing bank account and six-figure job. Getting his sister help wouldn't be an issue in my family.

"I'm sorry. She looks younger than seventh grade," I say, instead of apologizing for my family's wealth. "But I didn't make it anyway."

"What?"

"The Honor Society."

"How could you not make it?"

"Skipping classes. Missing homework. You know, the usual. Anyhow, I don't think I could help your sister. There's my sister and then this drawing contest." I picture his sister's cute smile and horrible dress and it makes me feel selfish. As if my life is the only thing that matters.

"Drawing contest?" he asks.

It amazes me how much it jazzes me he's asking about it. No one else bothered to ask. "For contemporary drawing. The Oswald Drawing Prize for emerging artists. It's friggin' amazing. There's a Junior Division for grades nine to twelve and a winner from each state gets art listings across the country and the Grand Champion gets a full scholarship to the Academy of Art University in San Francisco in their graduating year." The info rambles from my tongue almost as one run-on sentence.

Nick rubs his chin and his eyes show interest. "Wow. I didn't know you were into art."

"Totally."

He nods.

"The winners also get a free trip to San Francisco."

"Sweet. So, you entered already? For free?"

"No. There's an entry fee, a few hundred dollars, but my problem is more that I can't seem to finish. It's like I've been stalled or something. Ever since Kristina, well, I haven't sent my entry in yet." I laugh bitterly. "I only have a few days. The entries have to be in soon."

He runs his hand through his hair. "That's cool. Really cool."

Killer rubs against me then and almost knocks me over. I try not to freak out. I have no idea why this dog is taking to me. Dogs usually hate me as much as I hate them.

"Anyhow. Sorry about your sister," I say. "I just can't cut it right now."

"Yeah. That's too bad. She would like you. I told her about you."

"Well, maybe I could help," I mumble, but my voice isn't very convincing, even to me. Adding tutoring his sister to my plate is too overwhelming to think about.

He shrugs. On the street, a man gets out of a station wagon that's probably older than my parents and slams the door. He glares at us with distaste and heads up a driveway and then disappears inside the house.

"Don't worry about it. I'll figure something out. You don't have to say yes to everything, you know. It's okay to say no." He puts his arm around my shoulder and squeezes. I want to pretend he's doing it because he wants to but I know he's not. It's patronizing.

"Anyhow. About your question," he says it with a grin but it quickly fades and he stares at me all serious and remorseful.

"No." I squirm out from his arm. "Forget it." My cheeks light up like glow sticks, so I turn away. "I didn't really mean it. I mean, you know. I'm just having a crappy day and needed some comic relief, so I thought humiliating myself would provide that."

He takes my hand, folding my fingers inside his bigger ones. I shiver and practically swoon. My insides celebrate the sensation and I have an overwhelming desire to press my body against his, so the whole thing can feel as alive and as wonderful as my hand. The urge makes my cheeks flare brighter.

He holds on to my hand, smiling his lopsided smile. He takes a step toward me so we're even closer and he leans down so we're nose to nose. His fingers brush against my cheek and he wipes away a tear I didn't even know was there. And then he does the strangest thing. He lifts his finger to his mouth and licks my tear. It should be gross, but it's so sweet that another tear drops from my eyes.

"You taste sad," he says and then groans. "Man, Tess. You're just a kid."

He pulls my body toward his and slides a hand around my waist and it makes me dizzy. His breath on my cheek melts me. I don't dare move. Or breathe. I want. I want so badly for him to kiss me and I might break into pieces and perish if he doesn't.

He leans down and his lips, his soft, gentle lips, press against my cheek. My eyes close as I imagine the feeling on my lips. I want to know that feeling.

"Damn," he whispers and pulls away.

I barely manage to stifle a moan. My eyes are closed and I'm still dizzy. And then I sense him as he leans closer again. I hold my breath. For a brief exquisite moment he presses his lips against mine. Somewhere my brain registers it, but everything is focused on those lips. They're moist and soft and the feel of them is thrilling. A new, yet somehow familiar, sensation travels all the way through my body as my lips respond to his by instinct. I open them just slightly and his open and my head spins with pleasure. He's the most exquisite kisser in the entire world. I practically fall against him, weak and infected. I can't believe this is happening to me. Me!

Then, it happens.

He pulls back.

My eyes open in protest as he takes a step back. I almost cry out. His tongue flicks out as he licks his lips. I lift my fingers to my mouth, jealous.

"Damn," he says again. "I shouldn't have done that. You're just a kid."

"I'm not a kid," I reply, but my body betrays me. I'm jumpy with my longing but also shy and afraid. Inexperienced.

"You're only fifteen," he says.

"And you're only eighteen," I manage to say, sounding much, much braver than I feel.

"Older in more ways than you know, princess. Remember what your sister said. I'm a man-whore."

Ouch. But it's true. She did say that. But not with me. I'm not like the other girls. I'm different. Smarter. I think I understand him. I've seen his softer side, and Lord knows, he's seen mine.

He grins and then growls like a cartoon wolf and his smile widens. He crosses his arms and stares down at me, as if he's challenging me to a duel or something. "So you didn't really want to ask me out?"

I look at my feet, unable to answer.

"What about your boyfriend?"

This gets my attention and I look up. "My boyfriend?"

"That guy who's attached to your side, the tall kid with the glasses. He glares at everyone who looks at you."

"Superman?" A giggle escapes my mouth and I cover it with my hand.

Nick raises his brows in question.

"Clark Trent, I mean. He's not my boyfriend. He's just a friend."

"You sure he knows that?"

Nick stares down at me with an intense look in his blue eyes. I lean forward, trying to give him the hint it's okay to kiss again, but he steps back and runs his hand through his hair. Killer walks around and sits by his feet and begins panting. Loudly.

"Man, Tess. I can't do this to you. You don't know me. I mean, I'm not a good guy when it comes to girls."

Boy fail. I blink quickly and my back straightens. He doesn't like me. Before I can stop it, another tear slips out and slides down my cheek. I let it fall without even bothering to wipe it away. I feel like such an incredible idiot and a horrible loser.

"Don't cry." He shuffles from one foot to the next and his expression says he would rather be sitting in a dentist's chair than dealing with me. "You're a nice kid. You've got a tough deal with your sister. I know what it's like to look for someone to fill up the hole inside you. But I'm not that person. Trust me."

His eyes plead for understanding but I turn to leave. Killer pokes her nose right in my butt and I squeal. Humiliated and insulted, I flap my hand at her head and she moves back to Nick's side.

I'm not just a kid, running away from my sister's cancer. That's just the way he sees me. He grabs my hand and gently spins me around so I face him again, and he doesn't let go.

"You want the truth, Tess? I like you. I do. Probably more than I should. But listen. For one, I don't do relationships. I'm not that kind of guy. And second, I don't want to get involved in someone's life. I have enough problems of my own."

A shock of anger runs through me and my jaws clench. I jerk my hand away. He thinks I'm a bundle of problems? It insults me to the core. Like I'm damaged goods. Not good enough for anyone with my flaws and baggage.

He tries to take my hand again, but I slide it behind my back and move away.

"You can do better than me. You're brilliant and beautiful," he says.

"I'm not beautiful," I say bitterly, not wanting excuses and lies. His words echo. He doesn't need my problems. No one will want me with my problems.

"You don't even see it, Tess. I mean it."

I break away and start to walk as fast as I can, wishing I'd never made the mistake of thinking he was my friend. More.

I want to die. I'm such an idiot. Killer barks and then, with his much longer legs, Nick catches up and is at my side in seconds.

"You have something your sister doesn't even have, Tess. No offense, you know, with everything that's happening to Kristina. She was beautiful…"

My jaw snaps and my mouth opens and I stop, freezing in place.

"I mean, *she is* beautiful."

I shake my head, insulted now on Kristina's behalf as well as my own.

"You've got something special. You're not the typical girl. I mean, you look great, but it's not all you care about. You've also got a kicking brain to keep a guy on his toes. And the fact that you're an artist too. Well, that just rocks."

It's flattering and insulting. And I may suck at physical activities, but he's not exactly an athlete either and my chances of outrunning him are pretty good. It hits me that I'd be faster than Kristina now. For the first time in my life, I'm the sporty sister.

I think about bolting and doubling back later for my bike, but chances are, in this neighborhood, it would get stolen. Even if it is hot pink. Considering it's my only form of transportation, I don't really want that to happen. I walk faster.

"Find a guy your own age," he says. "Someone you have more in common with."

I snort as a car whizzes past us, windows open, rock music blasting. "Jailbait!" the teenager in the passenger seat yells out the window as they speed down the street.

I can't decide if I should laugh or cry.

Nick laughs. "See?"

I give him the finger.

"You think I'm kidding? Okay. So what'd you think of my house?" He spits it out, trying to sound nonchalant, but there's bitterness tainting his voice. "You think your old man wants to shoot a couple of rounds of golf with my old man?"

My pace slows. "I don't care about your house, Nick." But uneasiness slinks around my insides. This neighborhood is nothing like the one I live in. And I don't know what to say about the man who was bellowing from his house. His dad.

"No? Well, I do. I care that I live in an ass shithole and my old man is a drunk. He's mean. I think my sister was fine until he smacked her around when I wasn't home to protect her."

I wince at his acidic voice. He marches on, his legs stiff like a soldier.

"And I'm a jerk, because I still leave her alone with him. That's what you get with me. A jerk. I learned from the best."

We walk past another old house, where a couple is yelling at each other. The windows are open and we hear loud, drunk-sounding voices. Nick grins. "Like my neighbors?"

I speed up, not wanting to hear the argument.

"So, speaking of sisters," he says, his voice still black and twisty. "How's yours?"

"I don't want to talk about her," I say, and press my lips tight, watching another car whizz past. At least this time no one shouts insults.

"No? Well, she's got it bad for sure, but at least your parents can afford to get her the best care. I'm sure she'll beat the cancer thing."

I stare at him, blown away by his insensitivity. "Do you have any idea what's happening?" I ask. But of course he doesn't. "She's going to lose her leg. They're chopping it off. It doesn't matter who her doctor is. How can that possibly be okay? How is she supposed to cope with that?"

Nick's eyes open wider. We eyeball each other and then he drops his gaze first. "Are you serious?"

When I don't answer, he swears softly under his breath. "I'm sorry," he says. "I didn't realize. I mean, I guess I assumed that she would be okay."

"Why? Because we're rich? You think that guarantees anything? It doesn't."

He nods once. "I guess, right? I never thought of it before. It just seems like things would be so much easier."

Killer pokes my hand with her snout and I pet her scraggly head. "It's not. Things are not okay. My best friend hates me and the first boy I ever kissed did it because he pitied me." My cheeks warm as soon as I realize what I said.

"Me?" Nick asks and glances sideways at me.

I don't answer.

"I didn't kiss you because I pity you," he says.

Killer barks. She wants us to start moving again. Some of my anger melts. "Never mind. It doesn't matter." Before he can fumble around trying to make me feel better, I blurt out, "My mom was drunk when I got home from school." I bite my lip. "She told me she wishes I was the one losing my leg. Not Kristina."

Nick blows air through his teeth, but there's no harmony. He looks down at me but keeps moving. "She really said that?"

I nod, struggling to keep my emotions inside.

"She drink a lot?" he asks.

"I've never seen her drunk before."

He laughs, but it's bitter. "Lucky you. I hardly know what it's like to see my dad not drunk. Or hungover." He runs both hands through his hair. "I'm sorry. That's messed up. I'm sure she didn't mean it."

I lift a shoulder. "Kristina had volleyball. My mom thought she was going to go far with it. I'm not the one who uses my legs."

"That's crap, Tess." He gets a weird look on his face, then lunges forward and pulls me into a tight hug. My arms hang stiff, pointing down at my side, but he keeps squeezing hard. It's not in the least romantic. Finally he lets me go. "Drunk people suck," he says as he steps back.

Killer barks at a squirrel, but it sounds like she's agreeing with us. We both laugh as we head toward his house. He picks up my bike and holds it for me. My hand brushes his as I grab it and he pulls away, as if touching me is grotesque or something. He's a weird boy. No wonder I'm crushing on him.

I jump on the bike and start pedaling without saying good-bye. The closer to home, the farther and more surreal my encounter with Nick feels. My first kiss. It was awesome, but it was also…not.

I drag my bike inside the garage and close the door, dreading seeing my mom. When I get inside she's nowhere around, so I check her bedroom and see a big lump under the bedspread. I go forward and poke to make sure she's passed out and sleeping and not dead.

When dinnertime comes, Dad isn't home. I fix myself a peanut butter and banana sandwich and have three glasses of milk and watch the Discovery Channel. When I finally head to bed, Dad is still not home from work.

In the morning, when I'm dressed and go to the kitchen, Mom is already there making freshly squeezed orange juice. She's wearing yoga pants and a tank top and her hair is pulled high in a ponytail. She's got on her full makeup.

"Morning, Tess," she says in a normal tone, but she doesn't look me in the eye. "Have some of your Cap'n Crunch if you want. I didn't make a hot breakfast."

She turns her back to me, wiping down the counter and putting away things. I bite my lip, wondering how to bring last night up. She ignores me, so I get the box of Cap'n Crunch and finish off the last of it while she unloads the dishwasher.

Dad rushes into the kitchen, briefcase in hand. He pecks my mom on the cheek and winks at me. "How's it going, Tess?"

"Fine, Dad. Great. Couldn't be better," I say with as much sarcasm as I can. I want to jump up and down, wave my hands in front of his face, see if he even notices.

"Good. Gotta go." He kisses Mom again and mumbles something to her about Kristina, and then rushes out the door as fast as he swirled in.

Mom stands at the counter watching him go, her back to me, completely still. She stays like that for a moment, and then begins wiping down the counter like it's the most important thing in the world.

"Will you come to the hospital after school?" she says. "Kristina's going to need us." Her voice is tight and quivery, as if she's holding in tears. She doesn't stop scrubbing.

Despite everything, my heart swells for her. "Of course."

"Take a cab," she says. "I'm sure your father is working late again tonight."

"Yeah, I'm sure he is."

She hurries out of the kitchen, and I watch her leave with a heavy heart.

I go to the living room and log on to the computer. There are postings all over my wall on Facebook.

"Tell Tee we love her."

"Get well, Tee."

"Your sister rocks."

I have new friend requests and every single one of them has a note asking about my sister. My fingers pause on the keyboard. I'm tempted to type in the news. Tell the school the horrible truth. My sister is going to lose her leg. It will be big news for a while but I wonder how long it will be before they forget her.

• • •

My first class is English and when I walk in as the bell rings, Clark raises his eyebrows. My cheeks warm and I quickly look away. My body feels beat-up and bruised. It's an effort to breathe. Mr. Pepson assigns some chapters to read from our textbook and then calls me to the front of the class.

"I'm sorry about the Honor Society, Tess," he tells me in a low solemn voice when I sit in the chair opposite his.

I have to keep myself from rolling my eyes. As if it matters now. I lift a shoulder and glance back at the class. Clark is watching me, and doesn't make an effort to pretend he's not. I turn back to Mr. Pepson.

"You're an excellent student with enormous potential. I know that your sister…is…well, having a tough time right now. I would have liked to make exceptions but…we have standards, I suppose. The others voted that we couldn't accept excuses for letting performance slip."

"Really?" I say. "They couldn't?" I stand up. "Well, they're kind of assholes then. Don't you think?"

I turn and go back to my seat. Mr. Pepson does not call me back or reprimand me. I wouldn't care if he did. I think he knows it.

• • •

Clark appears at my side as soon as the bell rings.

"You okay?" he asks. "You look really upset."

I struggle to keep myself together. "No, I'm fine." If you don't count having my mother tell me she wishes I were the one with cancer and throwing myself at the high school man-slut.

"You sure?" he asks.

I can't do it. I can't do it today. I bite my lip and nod. He takes the hint and doesn't say another word, but stays by my side as we navigate the hallway to our next class. My insides are mashing with guilt, as if he somehow must know I kissed Nick. It feels like I betrayed him in some way, which is stupid, but I can't shake it.

"Tess! Tess!" A voice screams over the noise.

Gee comes running for me. She smiles at Clark, used to him being a permanent fixture at my side. "Seriously. I haven't talked to her in ages. She just disappeared. She didn't even call or anything after we sent the flowers. Is she okay? I mean. Well, you know what I mean."

My lip quivers.

"I miss her. My mom says I should just try popping over. Force her to see me. Devon wants to come with me. A surprise attack! My mom says she needs us." Her lips turn up hopefully. "She's got to know we still love her. No matter what."

"No!" I shout. "Don't do that."

She frowns and steps back. "She really doesn't want to see me? I mean, we were best friends." She makes a face. "We are best friends."

"She's going through a lot, Gee. She's not herself." Bubbles float up my lungs and I can't swallow them down. I'm afraid I will drown.

I put my hand over my mouth. "She's going through a lot of changes," I mumble.

Clark puts a hand on my arm. And then Gee surprises me by rushing forward to hug me tight. She squeezes hard and, in a fit of weakness, I squeeze back and close my eyes.

When I open them, Melissa is stopped in the hallway, glaring at me. As if I'm betraying her. Gee spots her and pulls me tighter.

My heart flutters at the gesture and I wish my sister would give Gee a chance. She seems genuine. I open my mouth, about to tell her maybe I'll try slipping her in the house, but then the bell rings. She reaches into her purse and hands me an envelope.

"It's a note. Will you give it to Tee for me?"

I watch as she tears off down the hall toward her class, wondering how she'll deal with the news about Kristina's leg.

• • •

"Kristina wants to talk to you. Alone," Mom says as soon as I walk into the hospital room after school. Her eyes are bloodshot and I'm not sure if it's from exhaustion or a hangover.

I feel her pain. My day sucked too. Mom leaves and I walk over to Kristina's bed. She's tiny and broken-looking in her wrinkly blue gown.

"My operation is tomorrow morning," Kristina says. "Seven a.m."

I bite down on my lip hard to keep from leaking.

"I need something from you," she says.

I pull up a chair to her bed as, in a robotic voice, she explains to me that she's not handling things well. Her voice quivers and her hands shake.

"Who would be handling it well?" I ask.

"I talked to my doctor and she suggested sedating me before the operation. I don't think I can get through without it."

I chew on my thumb and nod.

"I'm barely hanging on. I need you to talk to Mom. So she knows and doesn't freak out when she finds out. I have to do it this way. To cope."

I don't remind her how opposed Mom is to extra medication. We both know what her reaction will be. But what Kristina doesn't know is that Mommy dear has been doing a different kind of medicating all her own.

And I won't let her make it harder for Kristina. I'll fight for her if I have to.

chapter fifteen

Mom makes Dad stay with Kristina at the hospital and asks me to go home with her for a short break. We don't speak in the car, and at home I retreat to my room to go over my artwork, trying not to think about the operation. Mom goes to Kristina's room to pick out some stuff to take to the hospital. After a few minutes, she strolls into my room and sits down on the edge of my bed. She glances around at the heap of clothes on my floor, the dirty dishes on my night table, books lying in a messy stack beside them. Sketch pads are heaped in piles around my bed, and right beside me is my entry. The Volcano. Despite the overwhelming evidence I've been busy drawing, she doesn't ask about it. I could tell her. Right now. About the contest.

"It's messy in here," she says, and my body stiffens, waiting for the lecture about how cleanliness is next to godliness. And how my future husband is going to have a hard time staying married to me if I'm such a slob. I'm pretty sure my chances aren't great with God or a future husband. Not the way the cards are being dealt.

"Tess?" she says.

I wait for the lecture.

"I love you. I don't always understand you, but I love you. You're so different from me, you know. You're your father's daughter. Your brains. I've always been a little envious of that."

She shuts her eyes and breathes out loudly. "I'm very sorry about yesterday."

I pick at the comforter on my bed, not wanting this conversation. My stomach burns and clenches tightly. "It's okay."

I want her to ask about my art. Say something. I want to tell her about the Oswald Prize, tell her how frustrated I am that I can't seem to finish. I want it to be the best piece I've ever done. I want to ask her if she thinks Nick likes me. Or if he thinks I'm just a dumb kid. Do guys kiss girls they don't like?

"No. It's not." She lets out another huge breath. "My mom drank, just like your father's dad," she says. "I hated her for it. It embarrassed me. I never wanted to do that to you girls. I promised myself I wouldn't."

Pick, pick, pick. I grab a thread on the comforter and pull harder. She's never talked about her parents. I want to hear more about them, but also want her to stop talking.

"I know this is hard for you too, Tess. You're handling it better than me." She coughs. "I'm proud of you. For who you are, you know." She inhales deeply. "I don't wish this on you instead of your sister, no matter what I said to you when I was drinking."

I still don't look at her, just shake my head back and forth, shame running through me as if it's somehow my fault that I got the good gene. The non-cancer one. I wonder sometimes if it will come for me too, but for now I'm the lucky one.

"Your father is proud of how smart you are. I am too. I just don't know what to do with it. Kristina's volleyball, I get that, I relate to sports. Or I did. I got it." She pauses for a second, but I still don't look at her. She snorts. "Sports came easy to me. I learned to get by with what I was good at. Having a bubbly personality was easier than remembering where I came from. And when I met your father, it changed my whole life. I tucked the person who I was away and never looked at her again." She laughs, but there's no happiness in the sound, and then she touches the cover of one of my sketchbooks, but doesn't open it. "Your grandma was artistic. Really talented. You get that from her."

I look up, surprised. I open my mouth to tell her about the drawing prize but she continues.

"Your dad is having a tough time. He doesn't know how to deal with this. Neither of us do, I guess. But we're going to have to try harder. Kristina needs us. All of us."

Tears stream down my cheeks. I want to say that I need them too. That I need help too, but it sounds selfish and petty inside my head.

She reaches over and pats my hand. "Thank you," she says. "For stepping up. For being strong for your sister. I know it's not easy for you either."

My tears flow faster then.

"What did Kristina want to talk to you about yesterday?" she asks in a soft voice.

I close my eyes for a moment and breathe, realizing this was her whole purpose. The reason she came to talk to me. Searching for answers. I have an urge to push her away. Tell her nothing. But Kristina asked me to handle it. I have to do it for her.

"Kristina wants sedatives," I tell my mom. I don't meet her eyes. I guess a part of me is still afraid she might try to blame me again. "She didn't want to tell you herself." I sit up straighter. "No. She's afraid to tell you herself because she knows you'll disapprove and she doesn't have the strength to fight you. But she needs them and you need to accept that. No matter how you feel about that kind of medication."

I want sedatives too, handfuls actually, but no one is going to hand any to me. I have to be strong. Talk. Be the voice. Keep all my bones.

"Oh, Tess. I don't think it's a good idea…" Mom starts to say. "I wonder if that's safe. With the anesthetic she's going to get, it might be too risky…"

As if it's her decision to make.

"Mom. She wants freaking sedatives to help her cope with the fact that they're cutting off her leg. Let her have them. Let her have whatever she needs to get through this."

Mom stands, crossing her arms and glaring down at me on the bed.

"You don't have to remind me what the operation is for." Her voice is curt, her tone unapologetic and sure.

"No. Well, let me remind you then that she needs sedatives to deal. She's freaking out. Kristina is having a really hard time and I say she's more than welcome to take whatever she needs to get through it."

Mom shakes her head and opens her mouth, but I hold up my hand, stopping her.

"No offense, Mom, but it's not really your decision. She is

worried about what you will say and you need to let her know it's okay. She's been doing things to please you her whole entire life. Volleyball. Popularity. Being the Beautiful One. And now they're taking it all away. She's looking at a future exactly opposite of the one you painted for her."

She stares into space, her eyes unfocused.

I have an urge to smack her.

"Okay," she agrees. "Okay." She glances at her watch. "We need to get back to the hospital."

I grab my sketch pad on the way out. Maybe doodling will help keep my mind off the looming operation. I have less than forty-eight hours to get my entry in the mail. A ball of anxiety rolls around in the pit of my stomach. It's down to the wire.

chapter sixteen

Hospital. Five a.m. It's Halloween morning. A gruesome day for limb removal.

I wonder if Kristina is aware what day it is and if it will ruin Halloween for her forever. It's always been her favorite holiday, the parties, dressing up. This is the first year since she was a little kid she hasn't gone to at least two Halloween parties.

Dad reaches out to give me a hug. I let him squeeze hard and don't let go. He hasn't hugged me like that since I was a little girl, when it would make me feel one hundred percent safe. It doesn't work like that anymore.

"I love you," he whispers in my ear. Again. I went years without hearing it.

Mom paces the hallway, back and forth, like a caged lioness at the zoo. She strides in the same pattern, over and over.

Dr. Turner comes to the waiting room to talk to us and asks us to come see Kristina before they prep her for the operation. They've sedated her already and she's groggy. I don't say a word. I mean, what do you say?

The three of us return to the waiting room while they operate. Mom paces. Dad plays musical chairs. I have no idea how long we've waited when a nurse comes out and quietly updates us. It's going well, no problems with bleeding or clotting, she says. They've removed the diseased bone and are beginning the second part of the operation, constructing a stump that allows for the use of prostheses.

A few bottles of Coke later, the nurse appears again and lets us know the operation is complete. Kristina has been moved to post-op. When her anesthetic wears off, we can see her.

"You can see her now," a nurse says sometime later.

As we walk down the hallway toward Kristina, Mom's heels click on the floor. Two feet. Click clack. Click clack. I wonder how it will sound when Kristina learns to walk. Click shuffle? For some stupid reason I wonder if she'll be able to wear boots with a prosthetic leg.

We tiptoe inside her room. She's lying on the bed, pale and small. I try not to look at the bottom of the sheets. Where one leg makes a much shorter indent than the other.

She's dozing, but when Mom goes and rubs her shoulder, she opens her eyes and stares vacantly, and then she groans and squeezes them tight.

Her expression blocks air from my lungs. It hurts to breathe. Dad stands a few feet from the bed, not looking at Kristina or her leg. A nurse comes in and whispers for us to let her sleep. We walk out single-file, back to a waiting room. Before long, Kristina is pushed past us, down the hallway on a gurney back to her hospital room.

Mom and Dad are the only two allowed to see her. I sit cross-legged on the uncomfortable chairs and stare at the dirty beige walls in the waiting room. People come and go with various expressions of grief and relief. A little girl sits on her dad's lap, sucking her thumb and holding a worn-out beige teddy bear. Her hair is the same color as Kristina's. As it was. Staring at her, an image pops into my head.

Bending over, I grab my backpack from where it's tucked under the seat and take out my sketch. My entry has been missing the special something that takes a piece from good to great.

In a fit of inspiration, I begin to draw a girl. My fingers fly, my mind transferring the images to the page through my hands. I work, transfixed, shading and contouring, and a girl emerges. Her hands are raised above her head as if she's in flight. She is both brave and fragile, with her features shadowed but her intent clear.

She's diving in. Straight into the erupting volcano.

When it's complete, my body feels drained, but I know it's done. I check my watch. There's still time to postmark the entry before the deadline.

chapter seventeen

Mom and I take turns sitting with Kristina. Dad goes back to work the third day after the amputation. It's probably for the best, since he's acting uncomfortable around Kristina and hasn't said more than a few words to her. I want to smack some sense into him. I know it's hard. But it's hard for all of us.

Jeremy handles it best. He's the one who comes in to visit and sits by her side and talks. He really does have a gift for babbling, but I've discovered it's not a bad thing.

The next few days pass in a haze. I refuse to go to school and no one tries to make me. Who cares about grades? How can they compare to what Kristina's going through? My old obsession with the stupid Honor Society seems so superficial and unimportant.

Thursday afternoon, I'm sitting with Kristina, trying to think of something to say, trying not to stare where her leg used to be. Trying to get used to it. I wait for her to talk. Wait for her to tell me something. Anything. But she stays quiet, her eyes closed.

Mom is off in the cafeteria or talking to someone on the hospital pay phone, I'm not sure. I hear a sound and turn and Jeremy is standing behind me. I glance at my watch. It's after four already. School is out.

"How's she doing?" he asks as he creeps closer.

"I'm awake," Kristina says, and both of us look toward the bed where she's lying. She opens her eyes and turns her head and looks at me for a second and there's a slight reaction in her gaze, but then she focuses on Jeremy.

I feel like I'm failing her again but let him step in front of me.

"Hey, sleepyhead," Jeremy says to her.

"What else do I have to do besides sleep?" she says, and her voice is grumpy but at least she's talking.

"Want to do my calculus homework?" He points to the backpack on his back.

"Ha ha," Kristina says, but a tear slips out of her eye. Jeremy quickly moves to her side and takes her hand.

"Hey. You having a bad day?" he asks.

She nods her head and, even from where I am, I see she's struggling to keep it together, biting her lip and blinking.

"Do you want to talk about it?"

It's such a simple question, but not one I thought to ask.

"Not really," Kristina tells him. "I don't know."

"Okay," he says. "I can't imagine what it's like, but I can imagine how hard this is. I'm here for you. You know that, right? Anything you need, you just ask."

I grab one of the steel chairs and push it up to Jeremy so he can sit with her. He turns when I slide it up. "Thanks," he says.

"No. Thank you," I say and then I quietly leave the room so the two of them have privacy.

I plop myself into a chair in the waiting room and stare at the TV that seems to play twenty-four hours a day. No one else is around and I'm glad I don't have to make phony conversation.

A little while later, Jeremy approaches and sits beside me.

"Thought I'd find you here," he says. "Word has leaked at school. About the amputation," he says.

I inhale deeply and nod. I don't know how, but I suspect that Nick told Gee or Devon. We couldn't expect to keep it hidden for long. I don't want to think about Nick though, or anyone else at school, or what they might be saying. It's so far removed from life in the hospital and the gloom when we're home.

"Clark's asking for you. He's worried about you," Jeremy says.

"How's your mom doing?" I say instead of commenting.

He smiles. "She's back at home."

I'm happy for him but don't say a word about Kristina or ask why he's still spending so much time at the hospital. Kind of obvious.

That night I log on to the computer and see Clark has left a long private note in my Facebook inbox, but I don't read it or write him back. Not yet. My Facebook wall and Kristina's are filled with notes from kids from school. Condolences. Get well soon messages. There are even a couple of anonymous posts making jokes about it. One calls Kristina "Peg." I delete them, but they burn me up inside.

Nick hasn't posted anything on my wall and I pretend it doesn't bother me, but don't dwell on it. He's not stepping up, that much is obvious. When I check voicemail, I hear Gee and Devon's separate messages on my cell phone and on the phone at home, but I don't call them back.

Someone posts pictures of the volleyball tournament on the weekend on my wall. The team dedicated the game to Kristina and had blown-up pictures of action shots of Kristina pasted all over the gym. I think Kristina would hate that, so I don't tell her.

The next morning, Mom and I go back to the hospital. At lunch, we go to the cafeteria, and as Mom and I are eating soggy lettuce and rubbery chicken, I decide to open the discussion.

"Kristina doesn't talk to me," I say between bites of chicken. "I'm kind of worried."

Mom sighs. "Well, Jeremy is here for her. She talks to him."

I hold my fork in the air. "Jeremy is the best thing that happened to her."

She shrugs. "He is. He's the only one she'll talk to. I guess family is not what she wants right now."

We're both grateful for Jeremy, I think, but also a little bit jealous.

After the first week, Mom insists I go back to school. I try to get out of it, but surprisingly she won't give in. I don't announce my return online and all eyes are on me when I show up for my first class. Everyone knows Kristina's leg was amputated, but I'm not capable of talking about it without crying, and thankfully people don't bombard me with questions. They give me space.

A few of the teachers corner me to ask questions about Kristina and ask if there's anything they can do, but I assure them there's not. Kristina doesn't want a rally or gifts or anything at all from the school.

All week I wear hoodies, and pull the hood over my head between classes and wear an iPod with music cranked. It's almost like it used to be before Kristina got sick, with people leaving me alone. Except they stare now and everyone knows my name. But no one tries to penetrate my bubble, not even Clark, who continues to escort me to class despite the fact I'm hooded and plugged. I see Nick once or twice in the hallway, but don't have the energy to worry about what he thinks of me or what I did. Melissa keeps her distance and for that I'm glad too.

And then as if he knows I've been hiding out in the library at lunchtime and senses my desperation and growing isolation, Clark asks me to join him and Jeremy for lunch. I'm actually grateful for human contact and, for reasons I don't even understand, agree and walk with him to the lunchroom. Jeremy joins us at a table, but doesn't mention my sister.

Across the room at their table, the volleyball girls and guys watch with big eyes when I sit down with my healthy packed lunch, but thankfully they don't approach me. I don't imagine they know what to say.

The following week, the doctor gives her okay for Kristina to be discharged from the hospital. Kristina's desperate to leave. Well, according to Mom. She still isn't saying much to me.

Mom's already bought Kristina the best wheelchair money can buy, crutches, and had ramps installed by workmen at the back door to the house. Dad's office has been converted to a main-floor bedroom, and she's moved down Kristina's bedroom furniture.

I volunteer to go with Mom to pick Kristina up in the morning. I'm surprised when Dad meets us at the hospital. I'm used to his absence.

The nurses pop by as we are getting things ready to leave. They offer Mom last-minute advice on changing the wound's dressing and helping to care for Kristina. When Kristina uses the washroom with the help of one of the nurses, another asks about psychological help. Though Dad is present in body, he doesn't say a word, and Mom evades the question.

When Kristina gets back, Mom and I help her into the wheelchair. She doesn't smile or speak as we wheel her down the hallway. She keeps her hands folded in her lap and her eyes down the entire way to the parking lot. Dad walks behind us, silent.

We manage to get her in the passenger seat of Mom's car without much of a problem. I sit in the back, and Dad goes to his own car to head to work. Neither Kristina nor I speak on the ride home, but Mom chirps on and on about the nice weather, the traffic, her plants, and while it's a little unnerving, I have to salute her efforts. Once we get her inside the house, Kristina insists on going to her new room.

I follow her and linger as she hoists herself out of the wheelchair and settles herself into her bed. The nurses told Mom to let her do it herself, but I ache for how clumsy and unsure of her own body she is. But she does it, her mouth set with determination. Wincing as if with pain.

"So?" I say once she's settled, trying to be natural. "Glad to be home?"

She stares at me and I think she's going to continue with the silence, but when she laughs it's a harsh sound. "What do you think, Tess?"

"I know," I say. "But things will get better."

"Yeah? You think I'll be like a salamander and grow a new leg?"

I can't think of a reply to that one.

She reaches down and smoothes out her pants. Her fingers stop at the safety pin holding up her pant leg just above her stump. "It's weird how much it hurts. I know it's phantom pain. How can my leg hurt, when it's not even there, right?"

"I'm sorry," I say, wishing I had more. It's the most she's spoken to me since her operation and I have nothing to give her back.

"No," Kristina says, and breathes out a heavy sigh. "It's my fault. That this happened. I've thought and thought about it. All the running and jumping I did. I should have taken it easier. I pushed myself too hard and brought this on."

A single tear runs down her cheek and drips on her shirt.

"Kristina, you have cancer. You can't bring that on by exercising too hard." My heart swells with pain for her and I don't bother pointing out that no one else on her volleyball team has a limb amputated from pushing themselves too hard.

She shakes her head. "No. It was me. I kept going even when it hurt. I waited a long time before I said anything. Didn't want to upset anyone. Push. Be the best. I wanted to be the best, and look what it cost me."

"It's not your fault," I repeat.

"I kind of hoped I'd die in the surgery. That they'd cut the wrong vein or something. But no such luck."

"Kristina!"

"Well, look at me!" She points at her missing limb.

I glance around her room, searching for hints, for the right thing to say.

"You're still you. And I don't want you to die," I finally say. It's not profound or fancy, but it's how I feel. I search for more. "I love you, Kristina. I do." My cheeks flush, but it's the only thing I can think of to say that means anything. I know it's not enough, but it's everything I've got.

chapter eighteen

E very day the mailbox overflows with cards for Kristina. I didn't know people even used snail mail that much anymore. Mom opens them and puts them on the mantel in the living room. I don't think Kristina even looks at them.

Flowers arrive almost every other day too, and I think we have a year's supply of chocolate, which horrifies Mom. She doesn't like to have it in her house. I open a couple of boxes and sample some of the good stuff, but mostly they taste like pity and I can't finish them. Eventually Dad starts taking unopened boxes to work.

Another week goes by at school and eventually my hood stays down on my shoulders and I stop avoiding everyone. Well, I continue to avoid Nick, but I'm pretty much used to the fact that he's avoiding me too. I try not to think about the delicious horrible pity kiss.

At lunchtime, I eat with Jeremy and Clark. Clark still acts like a bodyguard and we're spending so much time together I'd have to call him my new best friend. Jeremy and I have an understanding. We don't talk about Kristina at lunch or the fact that he's practically a fixture at my house after school. He's Kristina's friend first and I don't want to interfere. I don't ask him what they talk about.

He did tell me his mom is scheduled for reconstructive surgery in a few more weeks. He doesn't even flinch talking to me about it.

Since Clark and Jeremy both have early birthdays, they have driver's licenses, and Clark offers to drive me to school. I turn him down since I actually prefer to bike now. My calves have developed muscle tone. My hamstrings aren't as scrawny. I can bike the whole way to school without getting winded. I know the weather won't hold out forever but it's unusually mild for late November, so I pedal on.

While my physical condition improves, Kristina's deteriorates. She's disappearing further and further into herself. The only person she spends time with is Jeremy. She's weak and not feeling well most of the time, on heavy pain meds and antibiotics. I guess what energy she does have, she saves for Jeremy. Mom takes her to physio appointments twice a day, but tells me Kristina won't push herself and doesn't seem interested in learning how to use the specially designed prosthesis she's been fitted for. She hasn't started using her prosthetic leg at home.

Friday afternoon, when I walk down the hallway to class, I pass the water fountain where Gee and the volleyball girls hang out. They wave at me and I paste on my fake smile.

"How's Tee?" Gee calls. The other girls study their nails or gaze into their BlackBerries or iPhones.

I shrug. "You know. Okay."

Gee steps closer and lowers her voice so our conversation is private. "Man, I wish she would talk to me. She won't answer my calls or emails or anything. My mom told me to be patient."

I nod back. "She's struggling," I tell her. So am I.

"Yeah."

From the corner of my eye, I see Devon slide up beside us. I flash my teeth in a smile again, for Kristina's sake.

"Hey, Tessie. We're having a party this weekend. At Cee's. Some sophomores and a few freshmen are invited. You should come," he says.

"Me? No. No."

"Seriously. You should," Gee adds. "It would be great. Almost like having Kristina around. You remind us of her." She smiles and I wonder what the hell she could possibly see in me that reminds her of my sister.

"I heard there's a certain guy who has the hots for you and he's going to be there," Gee says in a singsong voice.

The other girls around her giggle and nod. The popularity thing is trying to lure me in so I play along, pretending some guy is actually into me.

"You should come. I can drive you. I've been wanting to chat with you about something." I turn around. It's Nick. He's grinning down at me like it hasn't been weeks since we spoke. And he's daring me to turn him down in front of everyone.

"Nick, don't you dare lay a finger on this girl," Gee tells him. "Or I will kick your butt."

"It's okay, Tess and I are friends, right?" He grins down at me and I frown slightly, wondering why he's offering to drive me. "Besides, she seems pretty hooked on that Superman kid." He winks.

"Superman is awesome," Gee says. "You stay away from Nick. He's bad news." Gee flicks his shoulder with her fingers.

Nick grabs at his heart and takes my hand in his. "Me? I have nothing but deep respect for Tess. She's safe with me. Tell them you'll let me drive you, Tess. Redeem my bad reputation for me. Let me demonstrate that I am nothing but a gentleman."

The girls start oohing and aahing and egging me on, telling me to come to the party, to get a ride with Nick, and let him walk the talk, show off his gentlemanly side. They all assure him if he lays a hand on me, they will beat him. I think of the kiss, and my cheeks turn pinker.

"Okay, fine, fine." I can't believe I've been peer pressured. Me!

"Good. I'll pick you up at eight. I'll get your address off the Internet." Nick grins and spins around and walks away before I can give him an excuse, leaving me with my mouth hanging open.

Gee taps my arm. "Don't worry, Tess, he's not into freshman girls. For obvious reasons. He's just being nice. But I'll keep my eye on him. Kristina will kill him if he messes with you." She pauses. "Well, I'll kill him for her now."

The mention of my sister takes away some of my excited buzz and I wave and head off to meet Clark and Jeremy for lunch, tempted to tell them I've been invited to the cool kids' party. And I'm getting a ride with a senior. A boy. The first boy I've kissed. I want to ask their advice. If they think it's a date or just a ride.

Of course, I keep it to myself.

After lunch, when we're throwing out our trash, Clark asks what I'm doing on the weekend. For some reason, I lie and tell him nothing and hurry off to my next class alone.

chapter nineteen

On Friday, Mom asks me to be home from school early so she can go to her doctor. Jeremy is taking his mom somewhere and won't be around until after dinner. I don't know which doctor Mom is going to but suspect it's her shrink. With her and Dad barely talking, and him still hiding at work, I'd go to a shrink too if I were her.

I peek into Kristina's makeshift room to see if she wants to talk or anything but when I stick my head in the door, she's lying down resting, so I leave her and head to the living room for mind-numbing television.

Halfway into a show about the red list of animals facing extinction, the front doorbell rings. I glance up from the TV, startled. No one comes to our house anymore except Jeremy and he's not due for a couple hours. I drag my butt from the couch and when I open the door, my mouth drops open. Devon is standing there, holding a single red rose. His face looks blotchy and sweaty and I'm afraid he'll faint right there on the porch.

"Yeah?" I say instead of hello.

"I'm here to see Kristina." His voice shakes. He holds the flower higher as if I missed it or something. As if it's his ticket to get inside.

"Uh, she's sleeping." I take the flower from him. "I can put this in a vase."

"Tess," he says. "Can you tell her I'm here? I'd really like to see her."

I shift from foot to foot and look behind me inside the house.

"Please," he says.

"I can't make the decision for her," I tell him, but I open the door and let him come inside and point to the living room. "Go sit in there. I'll see if she's up for a visitor." I wave toward the sofa.

He takes off his shoes, and I leave him to walk down the hallway to Kristina's room. I knock on the door but she doesn't answer. When I push it open, she's lying on the bed, staring up at the ceiling, awake. Her room is obviously temporary. There are no pictures on the wall, nothing to personalize it as her space. I want to grab some of her posters from upstairs, bring them down, and put them up for her.

"What?" she says without looking at me.

"Devon is here." I hold up the flower.

She glances over. "What?"

"Devon. Is. Here."

"What does he want?"

"He wants to talk to you."

She doesn't say anything, and I'm about to shut the door and go back and tell him she won't see him when she speaks. "Okay, I'll see him," she says quietly. "Might as well get this over with. Can you ask him to come in here?"

I look over my shoulder, surprised. "You sure?"

She nods. "Can you help me sit up?"

I'm not supposed to help her. Mom told me the physio woman wants her to do things alone, but I go to the bed and take her arms, let her lean on me and help her prop herself up.

"Fluff out the covers around my leg, so it's not so noticeable."

I do as she asks, still holding the stupid flower in my hand.

"Okay," she says. "He can come in."

She looks tiny in the bed. Her face looks smaller without hair on it. There's stubble sprouting from her scalp but it's fuzzy and lighter in color. But even like that, even without a stitch of makeup on, she still manages to be more beautiful than anyone I know. I smile at her.

"You look pretty," I say.

"Whatever, Tess." She makes a face. "Can you just get him?"

I go back down the hallway through the kitchen, watching Devon unseen for a moment. He's laughing at something on TV. I move and he hears me and looks up.

I walk closer, into the living room. "She'll see you. You say something to hurt her feelings and I'll kick your ass."

His smile disappears as his expression changes to a more serious one and he nods at me as if he believes me. As if I really will kick his ass. He's smart. I probably would.

He stands slowly and I flick my head, indicating for him to follow me, and we walk toward Kristina's room.

When we reach it, I knock and then open the door, holding it while he goes inside. When it closes behind him, I stomp my feet up and down on the ground, pretending to walk away from the door, but stand still, listening.

"Hey, Tee," he says softly.

Her answer is muted.

"You look good," he says.

I hear her bitter laugh.

"No, I mean it. You'll always look good to me. That doesn't change."

I want to hug him for saying that. It sounds sincere. Nice.

"So why can't you look me in the eye?" Kristina's voice is louder and clear.

Devon mumbles something. If he expected Kristina to make it easy for him, he's getting a reality check.

"How are you feeling?" he says.

She laughs again and I miss her reply.

"I missed you," he says softly. "I didn't talk to you after…well… since that night at my house. When you missed school, I was worried it had something to do with me. Stupid, huh?"

"Yes," she says. "Stupid."

He doesn't answer.

"I had other things to worry about. You know like getting chemo, losing my hair, and getting my leg chopped off."

I barely recognize Kristina's voice.

"I'm sorry," he finally says. "That sounded selfish and stupid. Um, so, are you okay?" He sounds unsure and hurt.

"What do you think?" She clears her voice and laughs harshly. "If you're worried that I expect something from you because we had sex, don't worry. The only reason I did it was because I found out I had cancer and wanted to make sure I didn't die a virgin."

I wince a little on his behalf.

"That's all it was?" Devon sounds upset.

"Weren't you even a little suspicious about why I came running back to you? I mean, you didn't even ask me if something was wrong. You just assumed that I couldn't resist you."

He mumbles something I don't catch, then his voice gets louder. "I'm sorry, Kristina. I didn't know. I was totally into you, I mean, I am, and I assumed we were getting back together. That you wanted to."

"It's okay, Devon. You don't have to pretend you're into me. We broke up because I wouldn't hook up and just because we did doesn't mean we got back together. You didn't even know me. Or try to. Me. Not the perfect Kristina everyone wanted me to be. And trust me, I'm even less perfect than I was before."

"You're still you," Devon says softly. "And I still care about you."

"Well, don't, okay? I mean not more than friends. I never thought we were getting back together. I'm sorry the way I used you. That sucked. But it doesn't mean you have to pretend to want to be my boyfriend."

Devon doesn't say anything.

Kristina laughs again, but it has some spirit in it; it isn't as bitter. "Don't look so guilty, okay? We broke up before all this. So it's not like you're some jerk dumping me after I got my leg cut off. What happened was a mistake. Nobody has to know. And, well, I'm kind of interested in someone else now."

"You are?" Devon sounds as surprised as I feel.

"Yeah, I am."

She is? Jeremy?

"Um, okay." Devon sounds numb. "So, uh, can we still be friends? I care about you, you know."

That's my cue to sneak down the hallway and give them privacy. I have no idea whether he's okay being let off the hook or if he's genuinely hurt and is covering up. Either way, I respect that he came to see her, to deal and make sure she's okay. I find a vase in the kitchen cupboard, fill it with water, and stick in the flower. I put the vase on the counter and return to the living room.

After he leaves, I can hear Kristina's sobs from where I sit. It's loud and heartbreaking. I want to go to her but don't know what to say, so I sit with the walls between us, chewing on my thumbnail, wishing I could do something to make things better.

When six thirty comes and goes and Jeremy still hasn't rung on the doorbell, I hear Kristina shuffling about in the room. She's making a lot of noise and I guess it means she's got her crutches out and is moving around.

"Tess!" she yells.

"What?" I call, trying not to sound worried.

"Where's Mom?"

"She texted to say she went shopping with a friend after her doctor's appointment." Her friend the credit card.

Kristina doesn't bother to ask about Dad. Both of us know he won't be home from work for hours. We don't talk about how much we miss him. Or I do. I wonder if she does too.

"Shoot." Her door opens and she limps through the hallway and kitchen toward the living room. Her gait looks better than it did last time I saw her walking with the crutches.

I pick up the remote and turn the TV off. "You want some food?" I ask. "Mom left some chicken casserole thingy to heat in the microwave."

"No." She hobbles into the living room. "Jeremy is never late. And he hasn't called or texted me."

"He probably just had something to do," I say. I don't tell her but I've been wondering where he is too. He never leaves Kristina waiting.

She hops over and sets herself down on the couch beside me. She's wearing a pair of shorts. I try not to stare at the stump that's right beside my leg. It makes my stomach weak.

She grabs the remote from my hand and flicks the TV back on. "You still watch the Discovery Channel?" she asks.

I make a face at her but I'm not insulted. It's kind of nice to have her make fun of me. Like she used to. I want to go and get ready for the party, which is an occasion in itself, but don't want to leave her, and kind of dread telling her about being invited to a party with her friends. As if I'm trying to take her place. If stupid Jeremy were on time, I wouldn't have to even explain, because she wouldn't care where I was going.

"I wish Jeremy would get here already," she says.

I silently agree.

Another half hour goes by and we quietly stare at the dude on *Man vs. Wild* being dropped in some swamp, supposedly all alone with his cameraman. We watch as he wrestles an alligator but I keep an eye on the clock, expecting Jeremy to knock on the door. When it's ten past seven, my annoyance turns to worry. He just doesn't seem like the type to do this.

235

The phone rings, and both of us jump. I rush to go answer it, easily beating Kristina before she can even make a move for her crutches.

"Hello?" I say, waiting for Jeremy's apologetic voice on the other end, prepared to give him some grief for worrying Kristina.

"Kristina?" a voice asks. It's a woman.

I hear her sob.

"What?" My heart pounds and I turn so Kristina can't see my face. "No, uh, this is Tess." In the background, the Discovery Channel commercial plays.

"Tess?" The woman cries harder into my ear.

The commercial is a happy song. Boom de yada, boom de yada.

"Kristina's sister," I tell her and sweat seeps out of my underarms. The crying makes me queasy. "What's wrong?"

I don't want to know.

"It's Jeremy," she sputters. She takes a deep breath. "There's been an accident, he's been in an accident." Her voice builds in hysterics and she chokes on her own sobs. "He died. Oh my God! My baby is dead."

"What?" I keep my back turned to the couch. "I'm so sorry," I manage to mumble through my shock.

She cries harder and starts to ramble. "He dropped me off at home. He said he was on his way to see Kristina. But a few minutes ago, I got a call. There was a car accident. He didn't make it. Oh God! I thought he was safe at her house. But he died." She wails again. "Please tell your sister." She chokes and swallows. "I know they're close. They were close. Oh God! I can't talk now. Please tell her I'll call later." The phone clicks and the dial tone hums in my ear. In slow motion, I place the phone back on the charger, trying to catch my breath.

I turn. "No," Kristina groans. She's shaking her head back and forth, not looking at me. "No," she repeats. She puts her hands over her ears, still shaking her head from side to side. "Don't tell me. I don't want to know."

"Jeremy…" I say. I flick my hand up and accidently catch the glass vase Kristina's flowers are in. It clangs to the floor and shatters on the tile.

"NO!" she screams. She pushes herself up and then abruptly loses her balance and crashes to the floor. I race back into the living room, almost slipping in the spilled water.

She screams hysterically and I rush to her side. "Are you okay?" I yell. When she doesn't answer I flop down on the floor beside her and wrap my arms around her body. It shocks me how thin she is. Bones jut out everywhere, poking into my skin, but I hold on tight. After a while, I pull her so she's sitting up, and she practically crawls right inside my lap. I keep my arms around her and rock.

"What happened?" she moans.

"There was a car accident, Krissie. I'm so sorry."

She wails harder, sobbing so violently I'm afraid she's going to break. "He's dead?"

I hold her tight and rock her and stroke her hair. "You're going to be okay," I whisper over and over. "You're going to be okay. Jeremy would want you to be strong. For him, Kristina." I murmur the same words over and over. There's nothing we can do for Jeremy now.

Kristina holds on and her body purges itself of tears. I cry with her. For Jeremy. For her cancer. For her lost leg.

I keep chanting. Over and over.

• • •

Kristina is curled up in a ball on the couch, finally asleep. I rummaged around in Mom's medicine cabinet for something to give her and found some sleeping pills. So much for au naturel Mommy.

Kristina didn't resist the pill but refused to go to her room, wanting me to sit with her on the couch while she faded in and out, looking close to death herself.

When she's sleeping, I go to the kitchen, clean up the mess the broken vase made, then pick up the phone to call Nick. It rings once and goes straight to voice mail.

"I can't make the party tonight," I say in a tight voice. "Don't come to my house, okay?" I hang up abruptly, wishing I'd said something more.

I dial Mom's cell number for the fifth time in the last half hour, but her voice mail is picking up too, and like me, I suspect, she's forgotten to turn her cell phone on. In desperation, I dial Dad's number, expecting he's got his head in the books and his voice mail will pick up, but a laughing female voice answers, taking me by surprise.

"Hello? Mr. Smith's phone," the woman says. Her voice is low and all sexy.

"Gabbie, that's not funny, give me the damn phone," Dad calls in the background.

I click the phone off and throw it down on the floor, staring at it in horror. Why is a giggling woman answering my Dad's phone at work?

Oh God. I don't have the time, patience, or stomach to even think about it.

I glance at the couch, but Kristina's eyes are closed and her breathing is slow and even. I chew my thumbnail, staring into space, wishing for someone to save me.

There's a thunk at the front door and then the sound of the key turning in the keyhole. Mom bursts in with a handful of shopping bags. When she looks at my face and Kristina curled up on the couch beside me, she drops all the bags on the floor and rushes forward.

"What's going on? What's wrong with Kristina?"

"While you were out spending Dad's money, Jeremy died." My voice is robotic. I want to be mean. I want her to hurt.

Her face goes completely white. I don't mention Dad's lady friend or the visit from Devon. Neither seems important under the circumstances. Mom hurries to the couch and lays her hand on Kristina's forehead. "What happened?"

"His mom called. A car accident. On the way here." Both of us stare at Kristina as her chest moves up and down.

"I found some sleeping pills in your room," I tell her. "I gave Kristina one."

Mom's lips tighten but she doesn't say anything, just nods her head. Sorrow etches into her skin. I look closer and see how much she's aged in the last few months. Wrinkles around her eyes. I guess trying to keep it all inside doesn't work either.

"I'm so sorry I wasn't here," she says, and plunks down across from us in the love seat she handpicked to match her couch.

"No one is ever here."

Mom rests her head in her hands and stares at the carpet.

I don't offer her forgiveness. Neither of us speak. An image of Nick sitting beside me on the curb pops into my mind. Suddenly it seems imperative to see him. As if he is the one person in this world who can make me feel better.

If Jeremy can die, anyone can.

"I need to go somewhere."

Mom looks up as if she forgot me being in the room with her. "What? Where?"

"I was invited to a party."

"A party? Now? No, Tess. Under the circumstances…" Even as she shakes her head, I stand. I need to see him. Have to.

"I need to see someone. A friend who was supposed to take me. I need to explain why I didn't come. In person."

She stares at me, as if she can't understand what I'm saying to her.

"I'll bike over and be back in an hour. It's at Gee's house. It's not far. Kristina won't even know I'm gone. It's important."

I can't explain to her my overwhelming desire to see Nick. I need to talk to him. Teenagers get sick. Teenagers die. There isn't time to wait.

She lifts her shoulders up and stares at me like she doesn't recognize me. Me. Going to a party. To talk to a boy. But it doesn't matter now. Things have changed around the Smith house. Finally, she nods her head. No questions about who the boy is. Or what I need to talk to him about. "Don't be long, okay?"

I dash upstairs and change into the black jeans Mom bought me, staring into the mirror above my dresser. For a second I actually consider putting on some of Kristina's makeup or something, and then frown at myself. Vanity is wrong. Jeremy is dead.

I grab a warm hoodie from the floor, pull it on, and hurry downstairs. Mom's sitting on the couch now at Kristina's side, holding her limp hand. My heart cracks more and I consider sitting with the two of them to cry and forget the rest of the world, but I force myself outside to deal with my life.

I hop on my bike and pedal as fast as I can to Gee's house. Thank God it's only a few blocks from ours. The air is cold and my thoughts are dark. When I reach her street, it's easy to see her party is a big one. The street is lined with cars and, as I get closer, I can hear the faint whoops and the thump of loud bass emanating from her house.

I ride to her driveway and throw my bike down, ignoring a group of kids on the front lawn spraying each other with water guns. In this weather. I hope they all get sick with colds.

They ignore me as I tread up the sidewalk, open the front door, and step inside Gee's house. Music blasts me in the front landing and the beat from it vibrates my hair. I smell pot and perfume and see a slight haze of smoke covering the house. With my shoes still on, I sneak past a couple pushed up against the wall making out, and peer inside the living room. The first person I spot is Clark. He's sitting alone on a couch at the far side of the room. People stand in groups around him, holding beer bottles and coolers, dancing, mingling, and laughing. A group of girls are huddled on the couch across from him gossiping about something or someone. None of them know yet.

Jeremy is dead.

Clark looks lonely and I remember sitting on a similar couch at a similar party not so long ago, before we knew about Kristina. When Jeremy was still alive.

My heart kerplunks and I close my eyes, wishing it would all change back to the way it was. When I open them, Clark is still sitting on the couch. I am still the one who has to go over and tell him about his best friend. Taking deep breaths, staring at him, I try to think of the right words. In one instant, my information will change his whole life.

A loud giggle pops my consciousness, followed by a drunken whoop from the staircase down the other hallway. I glance over and see Nick stumble as he grabs at Bree. She's giggling as he paws at the front of her shirt. He touches her boob and then presses his face in the middle of her shirt and makes a loud raspberry sound. She pulls him up, and she's laughing as they exchange a loud wet kiss, and then he glances over and sees me watching.

Weariness overcomes me and I turn away and focus on Clark and walk slowly over to him. Nick is just a boy. Another boy needs me right now.

Clark's face lights up when he sees me and it's embarrassing. And sad. Because he is my friend. And because I'm about to tell him horrible, awful news.

Clark stands and points at the seat beside him. "Hey. Gee said you were going to be here. I'm glad you came."

He smiles but it fades when he sees my frown.

"Gee is my cousin," he says, misinterpreting my mood.

Understanding dawns on me, but there are much bigger things to worry about. Bigger things than unrequited love and false kisses.

"We have to talk," I tell him, and sit and take his hand and squeeze it hard.

"What?" he asks.

He sounds nervous, as if he's picked up my vibe. As I'm searching for the right way to break the news, there's a loud bang beside us and then a body crashes against my knees.

"Well…lookee here." Nick stumbles and plops down on the couch beside me. Bree giggles beside him and hangs on, trying to pull him up, but he abruptly shakes her off his arm. "It's Tesh," he slurs. "Holding hands with her boyfriend. Thought you said you couldn't make this party, little Tessie." He snorts drunkenly and leans closer. "Didn't want anyone at your house to see your friend Nick? Bet you also didn't tell your boyfriend you were supposed to be my date tonight? This why you blew me off?"

"What are you talking about, Nicky?" Bree whines.

I glare at both of them and then punch Nick on the arm to get him away from me. "You offered me a ride, that's it. Go away, Nick. You're drunk. Just go away." I punch him again, harder, hating him for being drunk, for being with Bree. For a moment, I wish he were dead and then my heart stops, remembering the reality. Jeremy. This is stupid. A boy is dead. Nick is drunk. Just drunk and stupid.

I jump off the couch, glaring at him, and put a hand out to Clark. "Come on, Clark."

"No. I want to talk, Tess." Nick flashes an intoxicated grin at Clark. "Remember when you came to my house when you wanted to talk. Remember when you kissed me."

"I don't frickin' believe you," I shout.

People stare at me but there's too much going on to worry about this.

I pull on Clark's arm. "Come on."

Clark stands and blocks me from Nick, back in bodyguard mode.

Nick slurs a swear word and attempts to get up, but Bree straddles his lap and starts kissing his neck. She makes disgusting slurping sounds and it takes concentration to ignore them. I grab Clark's hand and pull him quickly toward the front door of Gee's house.

"Was he supposed to be your date tonight?" he asks, and we slip past more partyers and step outside into the cool night air.

"No. Never mind him. Really." It's irrelevant and stupid. So is Nick.

The kids with the water guns are gone. I shiver and sit down on the top stair on the front porch. Clark sits down beside me.

"I'm so sorry, Clark," I say, and look into his eyes. "It's about Jeremy."

• • •

When I get home from the party, Kristina's already woken from her medicated sleep. Mom is snuggled up beside her on the couch, holding her hand. I plunk down on the other side of Kristina and put my head on her shoulder.

A short time later, Dad walks in the door and finds the three of us on the couch. He stares at us but I can't even look at him without wanting to vomit. In an uncertain voice, he asks what's wrong.

"Kristina's friend Jeremy was in a car accident tonight," Mom tells him. "He died."

Dad doesn't move. And then suddenly, he just crumples. He collapses into the chair beside the couch, puts his head in his hands, and his shoulders shake. For the second time in my life, I see my Dad cry. He sits like that for a while and Kristina starts to cry again. I wish there was something I could do, some way of helping cope with the grief. And then I have an idea and stand.

Dad looks up at me, questions in his eyes. I have to pretend that I never called him. And I think he pretends our home number never came up on his call display. We say nothing.

I grab the laptop from the dining room table where Dad has set up a temporary office and bring it to the couch.

"Do you want to do a memorial page for Jeremy?" I ask Kristina in a soft voice.

She trembles a little and then nods.

And so I sit beside her and together we design a Facebook page for Jeremy. We find pictures of him on his page and post them to his memorial site. A tear slips from my eye when I see the picture of Kristina and me from the party where we met Jeremy.

We add links to the page and within the next hour there are over three hundred signatures and wall posts on the page. Technology spreads the word fast. Jeremy is already being remembered.

chapter twenty

A crowd gathers for the funeral. The church walls seem to strain to accommodate the bodies, but there isn't enough space for everyone. People cram together, squished thigh to thigh in the pews, shoulder to shoulder in aisles. The back is standing room only. Not surprisingly, I don't hear anyone complain. I hardly hear any sound at all except the occasional whisper, cough, or sniffle. Everyone wears dark colors, even kids who don't usually follow rules or social customs. I guess it's like that when someone young is snatched from the earth. It's wrong on so many levels that thinking about it makes my already sad heart ache even harder.

Kristina is perched in her wheelchair at the end of the front row where Mrs. Jones asked her to sit with some of Jeremy's family. Aunts and uncles, cousins, and a grandmother. Kristina and Mrs. Jones don't know each other very well but, bonded by loss and a shared sickness, they grip hands. From Kristina's wrist dangles the charm bracelet. I imagine the sound of the dancer clanging against the other charms she loved so much when she was a girl.

Mom and Dad sit on either side of me a couple of rows behind them. We got to the church early to get Kristina in without fuss. Mom took one look at the open casket and her face went white.

Dad refused to look at it. I think it drove home how lucky we are, in the whole scheme of things. We didn't have to say good-bye to Kristina. We just had to adjust to a new way of life.

At the front of the church, Kristina doesn't search out any of her friends. Her eyes stay focused on the black casket. She's wearing a black blouse and a now-baggy pair of black pants with one pant leg pinned up.

Clark Trent sits down the row from me with his parents. He's wearing a suit that looks like he borrowed it from his dad. His dad wears a similar pair of dark glasses. Both of them absently push their glasses up on their nose from time to time. Clark's eyes are red and when he spots me, he lifts his hand, but doesn't smile.

Nick stands at the back of the church. His eyes meet mine when I crane my neck around and see him. We stare at each other for a moment, but he drops his gaze first. I want to hate him. For drinking. For not being who I thought he was, but it's not the time or the place to mourn Nick.

Almost the whole high school shows up, but when the minister takes his place at the front of the church there's silence while people wait for him to speak; only a few sniffles can be heard. I think we're waiting for him to explain how something like this could happen to someone as good and young as Jeremy. But I already know bad things happen to people who don't deserve it.

I hardly knew Jeremy, really. He was my sister's friend, but I miss him too. I miss what he was to Kristina and how unfair it is that he was taken so early. I can't believe we'll never see him again.

chapter twenty-one

Kristina and I sit on an overstuffed, expensive couch. Across from us is the city's top psychologist. When Mom suggested help, Kristina agreed to go see the doctor, but only if I would come to the first few sessions with her. They agreed on the unusual treatment plan, even the doctor.

It's weird, but it feels almost good, to be the one asked to help even though I haven't done much but sit with her. It's our second session with him and we're back in his office. It's huge and smells faintly like strawberry room freshener and male cologne. There's a gigantic bookcase against one wall filled with books about psychology. I avoid staring at titles that feel close to home. Like the *Social Anxiety Workbook*.

To the right of the book shelf is a huge dark wooden desk with a laptop and printer sitting on top of it. The designated patient area is separated by an office chair and a love seat and the couch where we are seated. On the glass coffee table beside the couch there's a box of Kleenex and a clock. As if to say, you can cry, but you're on a time budget.

The doctor sits in the chair, facing us. One leg is crossed over the other and he's leaning back, chewing on his pen cap, watching my sister, a notepad in front of him that he occasionally jots things down on.

"So," the doctor says. He's been talking to Kristina about the stages of grief. "How are you feeling about Jeremy?" the doctor asks.

Kristina makes a face and studies her fingernails. "I miss him."

The clock ticks in the silence. I wonder if it's on purpose that it's so loud. To keep patients talking.

"Of course you do. But what else?" The doctor jots down a note.

What I wouldn't give to be able to go through his notebook and read his observations about patients. What would I write about Kristina? She's slouched over and leans a little bit over her amputated leg, as if trying to cover it. She looks uneasy in her own skin, as if she's not familiar with her own body. The doctor wouldn't know it, but it's a completely different body language than Kristina had months before, when she was unaware of the cancer eating at her bones.

"I'm angry at him, and I don't know why and it makes me mad."

"Because he left you?" the doctor asks.

Her expression is almost petulant and she shifts around as if she's trying to get comfortable. And can't. "He was the only one who saw me as a whole person and now he's gone."

"Why aren't you a whole person anymore?"

It's a stupid question. I want to say something, but the doctor must sense it and subtly shakes his head at me.

"Because I'm not. I have one leg." She points down to her pant leg and her face goes red.

The doctor nods, but doesn't say anything else. The silence kills me but I don't break it.

Finally Kristina continues. "I kind of gave up after the operation. I couldn't talk about it to my friends. All we had in common was sports. And makeup. Boys. Clothes. We never talked about things that really matter. But Jeremy talked about it so matter-of-factly. As if it didn't change me. He helped me. He accepted me for exactly who I was, leg or not. He wasn't afraid to look at me. No one else saw me the way he did."

"What about your sister?" the doctor says, and I want to shake my head at him now. Tell him to leave me out of it. "She's here. That means something, right?"

She glances at me. "Tess has always been…reserved. She's harder to talk to."

My face heats up and she smiles at me, almost apologetically. "But, she's changed too. I mean, we're both different, I guess. I know she's trying."

"You haven't changed that much. You're still kind of self-absorbed," I add, trying to keep it real.

She makes a face at me, but a faint smile cracks through. I glance at the doctor to make sure joking around is acceptable behavior.

"How did her surgery make you feel?" the doctor asks me.

"I don't know," I say automatically. The clock ticks in the background. Timing me. Seeing how long I can go without shouting about how much my life has turned to suckage.

"It's okay," the doctor says, but I shake my head, refusing to elaborate. It's too early. Too hard. I can't tell Kristina how her cancer affected my life too. Losing out on the Honor Society. Losing my best friend. Being made a fool of in front of a boy she warned me about.

In comparison, my problems are insignificant. "I'm just kind of afraid she's going to give up. Because Jeremy isn't around for her." I don't look at Kristina but concentrate on the hem of my jeans.

The doctor stares at me for a moment and then jots down a note. I squirm in my seat with the urge to grab it from his hand. Read what he's saying about me and my amateur evaluations.

The doctor turns his attention back on Kristina. "Are you?" he asks.

"I did." She runs a hand over her stubbly short hair. She reminds me a little of a Chia Pet. But I don't tell her that. "After the operation, I decided I wouldn't use a prosthesis. Like what was the point? Pretending I have a leg when I don't? Pretending to be normal? I knew no one would want to talk to me or hang out with me, so who cared if I could walk? Or wear pants and two shoes."

I squirm but force myself to keep quiet.

"But Jeremy kept coming. Like I wasn't any different. Acting like I was still me. Inside. As if my stump didn't bother him at all. Didn't change who I was."

"You are still you," I start to say but Kristina shakes her head and I close my mouth.

"You have to say that. You're my sister. But Jeremy. He didn't have to keep coming around. He did because he wanted to. He liked me. Me. For me, you know?" She sniffles and wipes under her eyes. "I never had a friend like him before."

I feel guilty for calling Jeremy a stalker and wish for the millionth time we could have him back so I could tell him.

Kristina continues. "Day after day. His mom was sick, and he was busy catching up on school stuff, but he made time to see me. Every day. And it wasn't because I was pretty. Or the captain of the volleyball team. He came to me. He cares about me. I mean, he cared." A tear drops down her cheek, plopping on the fold of her pant leg. "When I couldn't see the point of carrying on, he told me I could. He made me a stupid bet." She stops and sniffles and I reach for the Kleenex, pull one from the box, and hand it to her.

"It was beyond awful, the stupid chemo. Getting sick for nothing. Losing my hair. For no reason. I still lost my leg. For nothing." She blows her nose and breathes in and out, but the doctor and I stay silent.

"I'll never have children," she whispers. "I wanted to. Some day."

Tears stream down her face, but she ignores them. "Jeremy was the best friend I ever had."

"It was a tragedy," the doctor says.

"Yeah. It was." She hesitates, but then keeps talking. "I don't understand why he's the one who ended up dying. It should have been me. Lots of people die from bone cancer. Or from complications of the surgery. But I'm still here. I lost my leg, but I didn't die. I thought I wanted to. I really did. I prayed to die. And then somehow I changed my mind. And because of my selfishness, because I didn't die, he died instead of me. It should have been me. Not Jeremy. It's my fault. He was coming to see me."

Her shoulders shake and her face just crumples and her head drops to her chest as she cries.

I stare at the doctor, angry with him, but he says nothing and makes a note.

"Oh my God, Kristina. It's not your fault." I slide over right next to her and put my arms around her and glare at him.

The doctor clears his throat. He glances at his watch.

"We'll talk more about this our next time. Tess, I'd like you to come back."

The session is up.

There's not always time to say everything.

chapter twenty-two

The principal decides to have a memorial for Jeremy at school in the school gymnasium to "help the student body cope." First Mr. Samson gets on the stage and speaks about Jeremy, but he's overly pompous and condescending and his speech makes me wonder if he even knew who Jeremy was. The guidance counselor takes over the mike and his words ring with genuine emotion. He tells the student body a bit about what kind of person Jeremy was and then talks about death and grief for the survivors.

He mentions the memorial page and I feel stares at the front of the bleachers where Kristina sits in her wheelchair beside me, with Mom flanking her on the other side. Kristina is stiff and expression-free during the entire presentation. She insisted on attending it when she found out. She thought Jeremy would somehow know and would appreciate her being there.

When the ceremony is over, I glance behind and see some kids crying, freshman girls mostly, but others already look bored, as if they need something new to entertain them. It gives me a sore stomach. I want to shout at them. Tell them how wonderful he was at the hospital. How he could babble on and on.

A few people approach us as kids start filing out of the gym. Gee and Devon come together to see Kristina and she manages to smile and say hi to them, but she looks tired and doesn't add anything more. Mom fills her silence with babbling of her own and they get the message and leave.

Everyone else keeps their distance, but if staring could burrow holes in our heads, we'd be more porous than SpongeBob SquarePants. I don't know whether to be angry or relieved when Mom quickly wheels her out of the gym, away from the prying eyes of a student body who once adored her.

I told Kristina and Mom I'd make it home on my own, since I have my bike at school, and return to my locker. As I'm done shuffling books in and out of my backpack and about to close the door, someone taps on my back.

I jump and grab at my chest.

Melissa.

"Whoa. You scared me." For a tiny second I forget that we're not friends anymore and I'm about to smile, but then I remember.

Melissa clears her throat. She probably expects me to say something to make things easier for her. That's how our friendship used to work. But no more following the old script. Things have changed.

"I'm sorry," she says. "About Kristina. About her leg. And Jeremy." She pauses. "I heard they were dating." She looks hopeful, as if I'll give her the dirt on that rumor, deny or confirm it for her.

With a shake of my head, I shift my backpack over my shoulder and fold my arms across my chest. A couple of freshman boys push each other back and forth as they pass by us in the hall. Life goes on at Great Heights High.

"Is she okay?" Melissa asks.

"No. She's not. She has a lot to deal with. One leg and all. And the death of her good friend." I say *good* louder than the other words. The ugly things we've both said hang in the air between us, written in invisible ink.

Melissa opens her eyes wide and then her face reddens. She stares at me, and for the first time I notice how puffy her cheeks are. Her eyes look tiny inside her face. She's put on even more weight over the last couple of months. Without me to share her snacks.

"You hated her too," she says in a soft voice, looking around, but we're the only two in front of the lockers. "Until she got sick."

I stand taller. "I never hated her. Never. She's my sister."

"That doesn't matter. I hate my sister." Her eyes burn brighter, shining with dislike for her stepsister, so skinny and cute. Exactly the child Melissa never was.

"Well, I never hated mine," I tell her and lift my chin higher.

She hesitates. "I didn't mean what I said you know. About her dying. Or only deserving one good leg."

I see two girls walking toward Melissa and me. They're watching both of us with interest.

"That's not for you or me to decide though, is it? Maybe having one leg is part of God's grand scheme of things."

Melissa's mouth opens and she closes it quickly.

"Or maybe God messed up. Maybe it was supposed to be me."

Melissa frowns and her double chin triples.

"Even my mom thought it should have been me. But I didn't want to change places with her. Still don't. Does that make you happy? That I'm a bad sister too?"

It's the truth. I want my leg. It wouldn't change my life as much but in spite of all of that, I don't wish to change places with her. Not really.

I am selfish. And ashamed.

"You don't mean that," Melissa tells me, as if she ever knew me at all.

"How do you know what I mean?" I ask. "You never cared about me. You just hung out with me to have someone to gossip with. Well, I'm done with that. And you."

Tired of the conversation, I turn and walk away from her. She doesn't say a thing or try to stop me, and I head all the way outside. I thought she might fight me. I thought she might care more. The air is fresh but chilly. I pause on the front step to catch my breath. A horn honks. I take a quick look at the street and recognize the car idling in front of the school. A piece of crap with a capital P.

Nick.

I hurry down the stairs and turn left toward the bike rack, not up to dealing with him on top of everything else.

"Hey!" he yells. "Tess."

I ignore him. A car door slams and I hear him chasing after me. I resist the urge to run from him. Barely.

"I'm a jerk," he says when he reaches me.

"I know," I tell him, without looking at his face.

"More than you know." He reaches for my arm, but I push the offensive hand off me.

I curse myself for not getting a ride with Mom and Kristina. "I know enough. I don't need to know more, okay? Are you looking for a freaking Jerk of the Year medal or what?"

"Not really. I mean, I don't want to advertise." He half grins, but it fades when he looks at my face.

"You don't have to. I think everyone already knows." I hurry to the bike rack and bend down to open the combination lock. My hands shake with wanting to get away from him before I lose it completely.

"Tess. Seriously. I'm sorry about that party. I seriously thought you left that message to blow me off. And I was very drunk."

I wrap the chain around my bike seat. "Jeremy died, you jerk. And just so you know, getting drunk is not an excuse for stupid behavior."

"I know. I know." He drops his head and his body collapses into itself a little, but I keep the bulletproof vest strapped around my heart.

"Did you even go to his memorial?" I demand.

He doesn't have to answer. His face shows his guilt.

"It wasn't personal," he says. "I didn't know him that well. He was a freshman. And I had some stuff to deal with."

"Whatever." I throw my leg over the bike.

"It's complicated. I need to talk to you. I wanted to take you to the party. Talk to you about it then. And you blew me off."

"I didn't blow you off," I remind him.

"Sorry. I know." He sighs heavily. "I've been busy dealing with some stuff. I got news."

"Good for you." I don't want to hear it. My insides ferment. I'm just a dumb girl he fooled with false sympathy and disposable kisses.

"I'd like to talk to you. It's important." Nick grabs my handlebar and wraps his fist around it.

"I don't think you even know what's important." I push his hand off. "See ya later, Nick."

He lets go without a struggle and I pedal off toward home.

chapter twenty-three

Kristina and Mom have gone to physio when I get home. Dad walks in while I'm at the table scarfing back peanut butter sandwiches and drinking milk straight from the carton. I glance at the clock on the wall, surprised. It's only four thirty but I don't comment on his arrival time or the fact that he's actually at home before dark. He's holding a thick envelope in his hand and he walks over to the kitchen table and holds it out for me.

"Mail for you," he says.

My heartbeat speeds up. I check the return address. Academy of Art University, San Francisco. I take it from his hand. It's heavy. I smooth my fingers over it.

If I'd won, they would have called. Or at least emailed the news. I try to deal with the unbearable likelihood that I didn't win the contest. I'm not good enough. A loser.

"Peanut butter sandwiches for supper?" he asks.

I ignore him. I don't want to give up hope and cling to the package, rationalizing. They've sent out the winning package by snail mail and it's sitting in my hands. Waiting for me to open it and rejoice. Watch my life change right in front of my eyes. With the slip of paper telling me I'm the Grand Prize winner, I'll go from

Kristina Smith's sister to that incredible artist who won the scholarship to Academy of Art University and, wow, did you see her on TV! She is so cute. Talented. And completely awesome.

"So?" Dad asks. "Is that what I think it is?"

I keep a firm grip on the package, but frown at him and wrinkle up my forehead the way Mom hates. I can barely breathe and certainly can't put together an answer for him. He has no idea what it is or that my entire life is supposed to change.

"Don't worry if you didn't win, Tess. You have many skills besides your art."

My mouth drops open for more reasons than one.

He chuckles. "Don't look so shocked. I knew about you entering that contest. I talked to that kid at the golf course. Nick? You know. That friend of yours from school. Man, that kid can play golf. He caddied for me a couple times."

"You talked to Nick about what?" I demand, not even ready to deal with the fact that Nick actually caddied for my own father.

"The art contest. He told me about it. He thinks you're pretty cool. Smart and creative."

"You *knew* about it?" I have an urge to pitch the envelope at his head. Never open it. Never reveal the answer that terrifies me.

"I do have some idea about what's going on in my own home," he grunts as he opens the pantry and pulls out a loaf of bread.

I stare at him for a moment, amazed he has the gall to say that. "Oh. And how exactly do you do that when you're never here?" I manage to say as I struggle to absorb my shock that he talked to Nick about me. About the contest.

His face pinches up enough that his embarrassment is obvious. "I know I haven't been around much, Tess. I, uh, I've been really busy with work."

His lame excuse adds fire to the pit already burning in my stomach.

"You've been busy avoiding your family and what is going on with Kristina," I snarl. "Never mind Mom and me."

He exhales a loud breath of air. "I'm sorry if it seems that way. I'm just…well, I'm doing the best I can." He opens the loaf of bread and takes a few slices out of the plastic.

I want to tell him his best isn't good enough.

"Hey," Dad says in a softer tone. He slaps a thick layer of peanut butter on the bread and peels a banana and starts cutting up slices on top of the peanut butter. "I'm sorry I didn't mention I knew. I'm sure your art was really good. I saw Nick's entry. He showed it to me before he sent it off."

I place the envelope on my lap, away from his eyes. As if he's tainting it, by being in the same room as it. "What are you talking about?"

"Nick. He told me about a drawing he'd done and how he would have loved to enter, but couldn't. I suspected it was a money thing, so I offered to pay his fee if he'd do some free caddying on the side. We worked out a deal." He carries his plate to the table and sits beside me, reaching over and taking the last crust from my plate and popping it in his mouth before picking up a slice of his own. "He entered too."

My brain feels as though it's been sucked from my head. I can't remember how to take in oxygen. Breathe.

"Nick entered the contest?" I repeat. "And you knew, but didn't tell me?" My fingers stroke the envelope. Dread makes me woozy.

Dad shrugs and manages to look uncomfortable. "I figured he told you. I meant to ask you about it." He taps his fingers on the table as he chews and looks around the kitchen, as if Mom will sweep in any minute and rescue him from this conversation and fix him a chaser for his peanut butter sandwiches. "Mom not around to make supper?"

I could care less if she appeared wearing a Martha Stewart apron and holding a prize-winning chocolate cake. "You sponsored Nick, you saw his entry, and yet you didn't even ask me about mine? You didn't even ask to see what I did?" I swallow tears of anger. I refuse to cry. "Do you have any idea what a big deal this is to me?"

He bites into his sandwich and looks out the patio door. "Well, things have been a little crazy around here, Tess. There hasn't been time to talk about things like art." The defiance in his voice makes me feel crazy.

I stand, gripping the thick envelope in my hand. "Why does no one in this family take my art seriously? Why does no one believe in me? You knew, yet you didn't even ask to see my entry or show some support."

Winning would show them. Winning would redeem me.

But the stupid envelope is heavy in my hand.

"I believe you love art, Tess." He chews and swallows. "And I'm glad you have it as an outlet. Especially now, with your sister. But there's been so much going on around here, there hasn't been time

264

to talk about things like your hobby. Besides, you're meant for bigger things than art. With your brain, you could do anything. Law. Medical school. You could get your doctorate degree and be a professor, like me." He lays his hands on the table as if asking me to understand.

A professor? Who the hell does he think he is? Trying to decide what I want to do with my life?

My self-control is stretched to the limit. I wave the envelope, feeling anger in every cell, every fiber of my being. "Why would I want to be like you? You've deserted your family. You haven't been home since Kristina found out she was sick."

He sits up straighter, his cheeks reddening, but my fury unleashes as if he popped a hole in an angry wasp nest. The anger swarms from me. Hobby? It offends me to my core. Art is a huge part of who I am. It always has been, but no one has bothered to notice. All he cares about is my brains and all Mom cared about was Kristina's sports.

They both got it wrong.

He puts his sandwich down and stands, glaring down at me, his eyes flashing with indignation. "Watch how you're talking to me."

"Why? You think you deserve my respect? You don't even talk to Kristina anymore. You barely look at her since she had her leg removed."

His fist pounds the table and the sound and the action startles me. But I don't stop.

"And who the hell is answering your phone after hours at work? Betty Boop?"

He glares down at me, his lips pressed together, and then he spins and walks out of the kitchen. Walks away. Leaves me standing there.

"Don't walk away from me," I yell, sounding alarmingly like my mom. But it's too late and he doesn't come back.

I'm so furious, so angry, I don't know what to do with it. I run upstairs to my room. Wet tears of anger stream down my cheeks. I throw the thick envelope on my bed. It bounces once and then flops still. Laying there. Taunting me.

I turn and rush back down the stairs, banging the front door, and stomp down the front walk and then pound the pavement on the street, walking fast around the block…fuming as I let the feelings I've been holding in come out, refusing to push them down like I always do.

Anger. For being ignored. For being belittled. For not being good enough. Guilt. For worrying about my stupid problems that pale in comparison to my sister's. More anger for having to compare. Is it so wrong to want what I want? For me? What about me? Don't I count anymore?

I walk and walk, trying to burn off my frustration with physical activity. God! It's becoming a habit. Before I know it I'll be doing runs with Mom. Finally, with nowhere to go, I end up back home.

Inside, the house is quiet. I go to my room and sit on my bed, staring at the envelope that mocks me. Dread floats around and around my body. My hands shake.

I pick it up and rip it open.

My eyes scan the first line. "Thank you for your entry. The jury was very impressed by your obvious talent. Unfortunately the contest was really tight this year. We have decided to go with a different candidate from your state. In addition, your state winner was awarded the Grand Champion." Blah. Blah. Blah.

My heart bleeds green with jealousy, but I read on.

"Your entry has been awarded an honorable mention. Enclosed is an application for a scholarship. We would love to see you apply to Academy of Art University in your graduating year."

There's a knock on my door. "Go away!" I shout.

"Tess?"

It's Mom.

She taps the door lightly again.

"I don't want to talk." I sniff softly so she can't hear.

She opens the door though. Stupid me, not locking it behind me. She hesitates and then walks in and moves to stand at the side of my bed. She looks down at me on the bed. A crumpled-up disaster of a daughter.

"Dad told you we had a fight," I say. It's a statement, not a question.

"I'm sorry, Tess."

"For what?" I can't keep bitterness out of my voice. "For him disappearing from our lives when we need him?"

She presses her lips tight and crosses her arms. "No. I'm sorry about your contest. Your dad told me about it. He said you didn't win."

I chew my bottom lip to keep back the telltale tears of a loser.

"Kristina told us she knew about your drawing. And the contest." Mom uncrosses her arms and perches her tiny perfect butt on the side of my messy bed. "She said you're good."

"I am," I snap, surprising myself.

Mom frowns but quickly wipes the expression away and smiles. "I'm glad you have something you love to do. It's like me and scrapbooking."

I stare at her, horrified. She's comparing my art to her occasional stabs at scrapbooking?

"You know, in the long run, it's probably best you didn't win," she says. "You don't really want to go to an art college, do you? I know you're disappointed you didn't make the Honor Society, but you still have brains. And connections. Your Dad can get you a spot at the university. He's always talked about you working there someday. All you need to do is brush up on your people skills. Maybe join Toastmasters or something." She stands up and walks over to my dresser and starts folding clean clothes heaped on top that she left for me to put away. She starts opening drawers and tucking things where she thinks they belong. Everything has a place. Everything can be shoved into a drawer and forgotten.

"You're a lucky girl, Tess, not having to worry about money. We're all lucky. Even Kristina. Things could be so much worse for her if we couldn't afford the care we've gotten." She rolls up a pair of socks and sticks them in a drawer.

"Lucky?" I ask, staring at this woman who claims to know who I am.

She bends down to pick up a pile of dirty clothes I'd thrown on the floor and takes them to the laundry bin and neatly slides them inside. "Dad gives us everything we need."

I snort. "Except himself."

She doesn't pause as she bends and picks up more clothes scattered across my room. "He's doing the best he can," she says, repeating his sentiments.

How come his best is not enough?

"Anyway," she says, "forget the contest. There's no use having a temper tantrum."

I stare at her as she moves around, frantically trying to put my room into some sort of order. I start to laugh. She can't control things any better than me. She couldn't stop Kristina from getting sick, which ruined her plans for Kristina's future. And she can't decide who I am. Who I get to be.

She bends to pick up my dirty socks and then stops, clutching them close to her chest. "I'm sorry you didn't win," she says in a soft voice. "I really am." And then she starts back into her frenzied movement around my room and I sit up and swing my legs over the side of the bed, watching as she whizzes through my room as if cleaning it can somehow save her. Something's occurred to me.

"How does Dad even know I didn't win?" I ask.

She tosses clothes into my laundry bin and wipes her hands on her pant legs. "There was something on the news. Some boy won. Some boy your dad knows."

No.

She walks toward the door, one hand on the door knob. "It wouldn't kill you to clean up your own room, Tess." As if she won't rush back to do it for me as soon as it gets messy again. "I'm meeting a friend for coffee. I'll be back in a while." She pauses as if she'll say more, but then closes the door behind her.

I blink, staring at the empty space she vacated, almost afraid to breathe.

Nick can't be good at art. He's a man-whore. He drinks too much. He felt up Bree at a stupid party in front of me. He can't be talented.

I'm beyond shocked he learned about the contest from me, but didn't even bother telling me he drew too. Or that he entered it behind my back. With my own dad's money.

No.

Nick doesn't deserve it.

I try not to hear the bellowing of the man in his living room. His dad. I blink away the image of his little sister's dirty face. Her smile. Her learning disability.

He stole the stupid Drawing Prize from me. I hate him. I hate both of them. My dad. Nick. It's not fair.

My life has been crap for fifteen years. I need to win to change my life.

I stand and march down the stairs to the living room. I unplug the laptop and drag it back to my room. When I'm plugged in and logged on, I click on the Oswald Drawing Prize link and stare at the announcement.

The winner for the state of Washington and the Grand Champion: Nick Evonic from Great Heights High School for his piece, "Losing It."

There's a scanned copy of his winning sketch. I stare without blinking.

It's a girl. Crumpled on the sidewalk, a crashed bike off by her side. A car is parked beside her and a boy stands in front of her holding out his hand. Her body is twisted, shrinking away from the boy, in a way that is breathtaking in its complexity of emotion. Without words and with his incredible lines, he's created a story, a rich story each person who views will interpret in their own way.

It's heartbreaking. It's amazing.

It's me.

chapter twenty-four

There's a boy here to see you." Dad knocks at my door and then opens it a tiny bit and pokes his head in. "He seems a little… odd," he adds.

"Odd?"

"See for yourself."

He smiles, unsure, but I don't grin back. I'm not done with him. I'm not going to just drop the conversation he walked out on earlier. We're not going to do things the old way. Pretend nothing happened, pretend everything is fine. I want to finish it.

I get up and slowly leave my room, my heart pattering a little faster. I head down the stairs and stop at the bottom landing, where I see a boy standing in the middle of the living room.

He's wearing a blue T-shirt with a big yellow *S* on the front. And a red cape is tied over his shoulders. He doesn't have his glasses on. The dork. I start to laugh.

"Superman much?" I say and he turns and smiles at me.

The sight of him in the goofy getup makes me laugh harder. He starts to laugh with me as I make my way toward him, wiping under my eyes, wondering if they're as puffy and red as they feel.

"Tess?" my dad says from the hallway behind me. He steps forward and puts a hand on my shoulder.

I shrug his hand off. "It's okay. He's my friend." I stare at him, until he gets the message and nods once and heads back to the kitchen.

Clark takes his glasses from his jeans pocket, puts them on and adjusts them on his nose. "Before he died, Jeremy dared me to do this. To make you laugh," he tells me. "He said you could use a laugh. And now, well, I guess I could too." He stops for a second and bites his bottom lip. "Jeremy lent me this red cape. It's from his old Halloween costume." He pauses. "He liked to make dares."

I move to his side and touch the cape. It's slippery, like polyester. "It is funny," I say quietly. There was more to Jeremy than I chose to see.

"I'm really sorry you lost your best friend." I take my hand off the cape and hold it out toward the couch. He goes to sit and I join him, but far enough away so that it's not uncomfortable and we're not touching.

"He liked you." Clark says. "You might not have known that. But he did."

"He liked my sister more," I joke, trying to keep things light.

"Who wouldn't?" Clark smiles and adjusts his glasses. "Hey, I made you smile again. It was worth walking all the way to your house in this getup after all."

"Really?" For some reason that makes me want to cry.

"Well, to make you smile and to ask if you'd go to the Winter Ball with me?" It comes out in a huge rush and then his cheeks redden and he develops a sudden interest in his feet. "I know it might seem stupid, going to a dance so soon after, well, after Jeremy died. But I think he would have liked this. And I kind of want to do it. For him. If that makes any sense."

"It's tomorrow night. That's not much notice," I point out, but his reasoning makes having a boy on my couch asking me to go to a dance actually make sense.

"I know. I thought about not going, with everything, but then, well, I was thinking about Jeremy and how he dared me to ask you. And I thought I should honor his dare. Do it." His cheeks are flushed and he still hasn't looked up at me.

"And ask a non–Honor Society person like me?" I pretend to be shocked.

He looks up then and laughs. "I can hang with your kind once in a while."

I nod. "As friends?"

"I'll take that," he says. "For now," he adds, but then his tongue flicks out as he licks his lip and it's so nervous and cute that my insides do a little dip. A dip that is not for just a friend.

"My mom will drive us," he says. "She won't let me take the car, afraid I'll get drunk and drive, even though I promised I wouldn't be drinking. Is that okay? Her driving?"

I hide a grin behind my hand and nod.

"We'll pick you up at seven?" He groans and laughs. "Me and my mommy?"

I laugh with him. We sit quietly for a moment.

"You still have a crush on that senior? Nick Evonic?" he blurts out of the blue.

I lower my eyes and develop an interest in my own feet. "No."

"Good," Clark says.

"He's a jerk."

"Yeah. But he won some art contest."

I blink with surprise. "How do you know about it?"

"I saw it on TV."

I punch the pillow on the couch beside me. "He only knew about it because I told him I entered it! And then he entered without even telling me."

"The Oswald Drawing Prize?" he says. "You entered that?"

I feel another blast of sadness. Nick has the fame. The glory. I'm still just Tess. Kristina's little sister.

"Well," Clark says. "You're wicked talented in art. You're the best freshman by far. You'll beat him another year."

"Thanks." I smile then. Damn straight I'm talented. I'm not giving up on my art. I'll work harder. Get better. Something digs inside me and spreads like a good rumor. Determination. I have it in me to fight for what I want. I won't give anyone the satisfaction of keeping me down or getting the last word.

Clark and I chat for a while longer and then when he says he has to get home, I walk him to the front door.

"You flying home?" I ask, grinning at his cape.

He fluffs it behind him. "You bet your ass," he says and grins.

When he's gone, I head down the hallway toward the kitchen. Dad is sitting in the living room, watching me.

"Everything okay?" he calls out. "Any reason that kid was wearing a costume?"

"Yeah. There was. A good one." I cross my arms and glare at him. "How about you, Dad?"

"Me?" He glances around as if I'm talking to some other dad.

"Any reason you are having an affair?" I ask.

"What?" He shakes his head. "No," he answers. "I mean…No."

"It was me," I say. "Who called. When that woman answered."

"I know." He gets to his feet and then sits down again. His face looks pale. "She's just a work friend, Tess. She was in my office when you called. It was nothing. I love your mom," he tells me.

"Well, maybe you should tell her that," I say. "And quit working and golfing all the time."

"I'm sorry I let you down," he says. "All of you. You're all my girls. I'd do anything in the world for you."

"Then start showing up for this family." I turn around and head into the kitchen, not willing to go any deeper. I don't want to know their secrets. There's only so far I can go.

I hear a throat clear. It's Kristina, standing at the kitchen counter, perched on her crutches, a glass of water in her hand.

"Holy shit, you gave it to him, Tess," she says. She rolls her eyes. "You know what? He actually came into my room tonight. Asked me how I was doing. I told him I felt like someone cut off my leg." And then she actually grins. It's the first time I've seen a real one in a while. "So. You have a date for the Winter Dance?"

"Were you eavesdropping on me?" I ask, but I'm not really mad.

"Totally," she says. "Tess?"

I raise my eyebrows. "When I was in the hospital, Jeremy made me a bet. That you would go to the Winter Ball with Clark."

"Really?" I smile. "We're just friends," I tell her.

She nods. "They're the best kind."

chapter twenty-five

I'm wearing a friggin' dress. It's white and frilly with halter straps and it kind of makes me want to vomit. Kristina picked it out from her own closet and I promised to wear it. It's shorter on me of course, and doesn't even cover my knees, but she said she wanted me to show off my great legs. Under the circumstances, how can I argue with that?

She actually giggles when I stroll down the stairs, and I honestly can't tell if she's making fun of me or proud. Either way, it's the first time I've heard her laugh in ages, so it's worth it.

"Tess, you look amazing!" Kristina says, and she sounds like a proud mama.

"I look like an idiot," I mumble.

Mom has her camera out even though she's already seen the outfit and dragged me to the mall for an emergency accessory trip for shoes and jewelry. I gave in and actually let her do my hair and it's surprisingly cute. She managed to make ringlets out of my red mess with a flat iron. She even brushed on a little eye makeup and lip gloss. I swear I thought she was going to start to cry when she was doing it. God! The things that make my mother happy.

I let her have her stupid moment playing dress-up Barbie with me. Not like it's going to happen again for a long, long time. She's snapping so many pictures when I enter the living room, I feel like I'm staring into a strobe light. It's embarrassing and annoying but kind of…well, not exactly nice, but okay.

Clark is in a dark blue suit, standing beside Dad, both of them shifting from foot to foot and it's hard to decide who is more uncomfortable. A woman stands on Clark's other side. She's petite and cute, and he introduces me to his mom, who volunteered/insisted on driving us to the dance. She's much more reserved than my mother and doesn't insist on a million posed pictures.

As soon as we can manage, we hurry out of my house to the car. Clark opens the door for me and tucks me in the backseat. We don't talk much on the ride over, but he turns and grins at me from the passenger seat every once in a while. It's not awkward; it's cute.

The school gym looks like a sad snow globe that wasn't shaken properly. White snowflakes dangle from the rafters. Fake snow is scattered around in clumps and a couple of big blow-up snowmen people put on their lawns at Christmas time are in one corner. Tinny music is being piped out of giant speakers. A top-forty song from the radio plays. Kids hang around in clusters trying not to look self-conscious in their party duds. A few girls are on the dance floor, dancing like they're amateur strippers while boys ogle them from the sidelines.

So this is what a school dance looks like.

I spot Nick standing by a blow-up of two penguins wearing Santa hats. Nick is holding hands with Bree and standing with a group of Kristina's friends. My stomach does a little dip when I see him. Bree is giggling like she checked her brain at the coat check, but looks completely stunning in a low-cut slinky black dress. Nick spots me. He quickly drops Bree's hand and whispers something in her ear. They both look over at me. I glance away but Nick is already heading toward Clark and me.

Clark steps in front of me, but I put a hand on his shoulder. "It's okay," I tell him. "I have to deal with it."

"You sure you're okay?" Clark asks. He obviously saw the exchange too.

I nod. "I have to face him. Prize-stealing jerk."

Clark nods. "I'll go and get you a drink." He steps back and waits until Nick almost reaches us and then discretely slips away.

"Can you make it a Scotch?" I call to him and he laughs. I smile as he leaves me standing by the bleachers.

"You look great," Nick says from behind me.

My smile fades and I turn, checking out Nick in his black suit. It looks expensive and he looks handsome. I wonder if Bree bought it for him. "You don't," I say.

He lifts a shoulder. There's a bunch of girls sitting in their party dresses on the bleachers and they watch us with apparent interest. Kristina's sister and the senior.

"Besides, my boobs aren't as enormous as your girlfriend's."

He doesn't deny that Bree is his girlfriend. It stings a little, but not as much as it would have a few days ago.

"So," he says. "You heard the news?"

"You drew a picture of me," I say in answer. "And you used my dad for financing. You have any idea how much that pisses me off?"

He lifts a shoulder again and brushes his hand over his head. Then he takes a big breath and looks me in the eye. "I drew the picture before I found out about the contest. I knew it was good, and when you told me about it and your dad offered me the entrance fee money, well, it seemed like it was supposed to happen. I'm sorry I didn't tell you. That I entered. I didn't think I would win. I just wanted a chance. You know. Like everyone else."

I swallow. Me too, but my freeze thaws a little. A pop song blasts in the background.

"It feels like you stole from me," I tell him. "Like you used me. In more ways than one."

Nick plays with the collar of his dress shirt. His neck is a little red. I hope it itches.

"I didn't mean to. I drew the picture because you got to me." He glances at me. "You still do."

"Don't feed me crap lines," I snap.

He surprises me by laughing. "You're going to be fine, Tess. You know that. You're going to kick some serious butt when you get older."

"Actually, I wanted to kick your butt now. Well, I would have. If I'd even known you entered." I force a smile. "I never would have guessed you were that good. You should have told me. That you draw."

He tugs at the sleeves of his suit jacket. "It would have sounded lame. You know. Hey, baby, let me take you to my place so I can sketch you." He wiggles his eyebrows up and down. "I don't talk about my art. My dad says it's for 'faggots.' I didn't know you were into it too. Not at first."

"I hate that you beat me," I tell him.

He grins. "I know. You kind of remind me of my sister," he says, as if we'd been discussing family similarities.

My face turns bright red and I curse my fair skin and easily heated cheeks. "I remind you of a twelve-year-old girl?"

He puts out his hand and touches my bare shoulder. I flinch and pull away.

"I didn't mean it as an insult. She hates to lose. And she's got lots of grit. But she also thinks I'm fabulous." He grins and his hand kind of hangs in the air as if he's going to pet me like a puppy dog or something, and then he puts it back at his side and tucks it in his pants pocket.

"I never meant to hurt you, Tess. By uh, you know, kissing you."

I glance up to make sure the girls in the bleachers can't hear, but they're too far away.

"If you were older," he grins. "And I was nicer."

"You were my first kiss, you know," I say, and then my cheeks overheat.

"I know."

I lift my chin. "But I'm totally over it."

He laughs. "Well, good. I was never the right kind of guy for you."

"Yeah," I say. No matter how much I try to tell my head that crushing on this guy was stupid, my hormones have trouble listening. "You are totally not the right guy. You're a man-whore."

He rolls his eyes and his glance goes over to Bree. She wiggles her fingers at him and gives me a pity look and I groan a little inside.

"Clark seems like a nice kid," he says.

"He's taller than you," I helpfully point out.

"But not older. And not as good-looking."

I scoff.

"Congratulations," I say. "On the scholarship. Are you going to San Francisco after graduation?"

"Yeah," he says and smiles. "But only because I worked it out so I can take my sister with me. My aunt lives there. My mom's sister. When I got the news, I called her. She was actually really happy to hear from me. My dad cut her off from us when my mom died. She seems okay. She's taking both of us in. She's registered my sister for school in her neighborhood."

The music pauses and the DJ yells something about ladies' choice.

"That's really cool," I say. "I guess sometimes things happen for a reason, right?"

"Sometimes," he says.

I don't look on the dance floor or around me, but from the corner of my eye I see the girls on the bleachers stand up and start toward a group of boys hanging nearby.

"I wouldn't have this. If it weren't for you, you know," he says.

I shrug. "Well, glad I had a purpose."

"More than you know. You're awesome. And stronger than you think you are. And God, you talk a lot now." He grins.

I see Clark heading back toward us and watch his long legs as they stride closer.

"I got an honorable mention in the Oswald."

"With a scholarship?"

"Maybe. I doubt I'll use it. My dad can afford the tuition, remember?"

I have three years to convince my parents what my true destiny is.

"Well, I'll look for you on campus," he says. "In three years you'll be legal."

Clark steps beside me, holding out a white Styrofoam cup, and Nick steps back away from me as I take it from Clark.

"See you around, kid." Nick turns and walks back toward Bree. She's boogying in place, shaking her hips and huge boobs, having fun. He probably needs a girl like her right now. Someone fun. With big boobs.

"Everything okay?" Clark asks.

"I really wanted to win." I take a sip of the punch and make a face. "Ew." It's warm and flat and awful. I glance around to see if there's a trash can nearby.

"He's a prize-stealing jerk all right." Clark is watching Nick. "And not nearly good enough for you." He puts an arm around my shoulder and takes the cup from my hand.

I don't argue and I don't wiggle away. Instead I leave his hand there, to see how it feels. I'm pretty sure it feels good.

acknowledgments

First of all, I want to thank Sally Young for graciously answering intrusive questions about her battle with osteosarcoma. Although *I'm Not Her* is fictional, Sally helped immensely with medical and emotional questions about the disease and the surgery. I am especially warmed by her courage and the wonderful miracle baby she had against the odds.

To all the wonderful people at Sourcebooks for believing in my book and agreeing to publish it, including Leah Hultenschmidt, Kelly Barrales-Saylor, Kristin Zelazko, Aubrey Poole, and Todd Stocke.

I also want to thank my agent, Jill Corcoran, who is the perfect combination of tough and awesome. And to Daniel Ehrenhaft for saying yes—our paths keep crossing and one day I hope we will work together.

Thank you to writer friends who helped with early drafts, Shana Silver, Denise Jaden, Jennifer Laberty, and C. Lee McKenzie. And special thanks for wonderful and thorough insights from always zen-like author, Cheryl Renée Herbsman.

To the Debs, who still have a connection and help each other on the emo roller coaster that is writing books. A Feast of Awesome.

Thanks to my family for their patience while I worked on this book in the middle of cottage building country. My husband, Larry, who would probably have preferred me to pick up a hammer and pound in nails. My favorite son, Max, who took me on snake and snail hunts between revisions.

Thanks to my parents, Heather and Blair MacLeod, both avid readers, who encouraged my love of reading and writing. My brother Ian, who is weird but in a good way, my brother Kyle, with his gentle support, and my sister Tracey, who has the difficult job of being the oldest child and acts as my PR person just because I'm her sister. I forgive you for being taller and thinner and younger looking because you gave me the best nieces in the world.

Last but not least, this book is for everyone who has a sister. And everyone who always wanted one.

I inhaled a deep breath as I made my way into the café. "Cherry, Cherry" by Neil Diamond piped in over the speakers, one of Grandpa Joe's favorite songs. At the thought of him, I forced my shoulders back.

Tell the truth, he'd have said. Always tell the truth.

Even if it meant breaking someone's world apart? The last thing in the world I'd wanted was intimate involvement in my mom's personal life, but I had front row seats. With binoculars.

Around the room, couples chatted at small, intimate tables. A group of girls giggled together, chairs and tables pushed up to each other. I stared at my mom as I approached her. She looked like a model from the pages of *Today's Business Woman*. A low-cut tank top peeked out from under her blazer. She liked to emphasize her amazing cleavage.

Another check on the long list of things I didn't inherit from her. Boobs. Nope. Blond straight hair. Nope. Coloring. Nope. I'm more a muddy mix of black and white. Mixing colors is pretty basic stuff for artists, but it's trickier with people.

"You look nice," I said as I sat. "You came straight from work?"

Her eyes widened in surprise. Oops. Normally I'd be more careful about pouring it on too thick, but she'd need it after what I had to tell her. And she did look nice.

She nodded. "Thanks." She lifted her mug and sipped her coffee. "I swear I'd almost prefer to wear a uniform like yours. So much easier."

I glanced at my smeared black pants and dingy white T-shirt, the lame Grinds uniform. "This?"

"Well. It's not expensive. And easy to coordinate. Besides you're so tall and slim, and with your coloring, you look good in anything you wear."

"My coloring makes me look cheap and easy?" I tucked my long legs under the table. Being around my glamorous and petite mom made me feel like a clumsy giraffe.

"I said 'not expensive and easy to coordinate.' You're listening with marshmallows in your ears. You're beautiful." She grinned. "You're not having anything to drink?"

"I'm not thirsty."

"Lacey's not working?" Mom asked.

I glanced away. "No. A new guy is." I looked behind the coffee counter at Jackson. He was making a latte for a girl. She twirled blond hair around her finger and giggled as she chatted with him. She obviously had no problems with flirting.

"That's too bad," Mom said, and I focused back on her. Her forehead wrinkled with disappointment. The three-year age difference between Lacey and me didn't bother her. I think she was just glad I'd finally found a friend.

Mom didn't understand how I could go to school with the same kids for years and not have a gaggle of girls to gossip with. She'd had oodles of friends and dated the hottest football player at my age. But look what that got her.

Me.

I'd never told her the truth.

"I thought Lacey might want to shop with us," Mom said. "The sales at the mall are supposed to be amazing. And she's so good at picking out bargains."

My underarms leaked sweat. I sat up straighter. "Lacey is not coming." I didn't think we'd be shopping anyhow, but I didn't say that. Not yet.

Her expression softened. "No big deal. Just you and me is good." She leaned back, studying me. "Hey, I know what looks different about you. You don't have your guitar. You know, you look almost naked without it slung over your shoulder. "

"Why would I bring it shopping?" At the same time, I wished I'd brought it so I could clutch it to my chest like a kid with a teddy bear. My guitar was my most prized possession, and holding it gave me more comfort than I'd even realized until that very moment.

Mom took another sip of her decaf, frowning at me over the top of her mug. "Is everything okay? You seem kind of…off."

I shrugged and stared at her coffee cup.

"How's Grandma?" she asked.

"Grandma?" I frowned and glanced up at her. "The same. Busy."

"Busy saving the world?" She sipped her coffee again and then placed it down on the table. "You're happy with Grandma, aren't you, Jaz?"

My stomach did a backflip.

"No. No. Don't look so worried. I'm not going to ask you to move in with me and Simon again."

My stomach did a double flip then and I swallowed hard, trying to block out an image of Simon. When Mom and Simon first moved in together years before, Mom asked me to move in with them but Grandma and Grandpa fought her. I'd been glad no one made me choose then. I certainly didn't want to live with Mom and Simon now.

"Grandma would have a fit if I tried to take you away from her, especially with Grandpa gone."

I slumped down in my chair, wondering how she managed to read my mind so well sometimes. And other times, not at all. I looked at her perfectly manicured fingers wrapped around her coffee cup, still tan from weekends at the beach. Even sun kissed, they were so much lighter than my own skin.

"I guess I'm just feeling kind of guilty." The corner of her lip quivered. "I was so young when I had you. The same age you are now." She glanced around the coffee shop and then back at me. "It was okay? Growing up the way you did?"

"It works for us." I lifted a shoulder, wondering why she was bringing this up now. Did she sense I was about to rip apart her world?

"I love you just as much as if I'd raised you myself," she said.

I frowned. "Probably more. Grandma says I'm a pain in the ass." Anxiety bubbled around my already troubled belly.

"I have to talk to you about something important," she said just as I opened my mouth to speak.

I shut my trap and rubbed my guitar charm, swallowing the

growing lump of dread in my throat. Had she found out? I closed my eyes for a second, bracing myself for a tough conversation.

"I'm pregnant," she said.

I opened my eyes. "What?"

She giggled. "Pregnant."

Glass tinkled in the background. A shout of laughter erupted from the group of girls at the joined tables. I blinked, thrown completely off guard.

"What do you mean?" I wished I could be teleported to an alternate universe where none of this was happening.

"I think you know what I mean." Her smile wobbled. "You okay? You look like you've seen a ghost."

Pregnant? I coughed. This made things worse. Much, much worse. She frowned. Waiting for me to say something. Anything.

"No. It's…um, you don't look pregnant," I managed.

She wiggled in her chair. "Actually I do." She stood up and turned sideways, thrusting out her belly, placing her hand on it. Two older men at the table beside us studied her belly too. It did stick out. A small bulge where months before it had been perfectly flat in a bikini.

I shot death rays at the men, who quickly looked away.

She sat down. "I'm almost five months already. Look at me. I should have known, but I'm so irregular. And my sex drive is fine."

She smiled apologetically as my cheeks reddened and I glanced at the table beside us, knowing the men could hear.

"Sorry," she said. "Too much info, right?"

"Way too much." Images flashed in my head. "Simon's sex drive seems fine too," I mumbled.

"What?" Her smile vanished, and I saw how her lipstick was bleeding over her top lip. She didn't look so perfect anymore.

I thought about shoving my fist down my throat. "I'm just shocked. You know?" My attempt at a laugh rang feeble and insincere. "You're kind of old to be pregnant." It sounded mean even to my ears, but I couldn't take it back. There was so much that couldn't be taken back.

She forced a smile. "I'm not that old. And hey, you'll be a big sister. It'll be fun."

"Yeah. Fun." I choked on a bitter laugh. "At least the baby will be half black. People might believe I'm actually related to someone in the family now."

I glanced around the café, wishing someone would come and interrupt us, wishing Jackson would accidentally start a fire behind the counter, anything to get me away from this conversation with my mom. When my gaze returned to her face, I winced at the need in her eyes. As if she wanted my approval. Needed it. "When did you find out?" I asked, my voice weak and crackling as I tried to sound like I was happy for her.

"Yesterday. At my physical. When I couldn't remember when I'd had my last period, my doctor insisted on a test. Voilà! Pregnant."

"How's Simon taking it?" I asked, chewing on my lip. I already had a pretty good idea.

Mom played with her hair, a hint of a giggle back on her lips. "I think it kind of freaked him out. That's what I get for dating a younger man." She lifted her shoulder and took a quick sip of her decaf and then put the mug down.

"He went out last night with his brother. To celebrate." She made air quote marks with her fingers. "He was hung over and snoring in bed when I went to work this morning." She looked down, tracing a finger along the rim of her mug. "He hasn't gotten drunk in a long time. I guess he just needed to deal with the news."

"I guess he did." My voice cracked again at the end of the sentence.

She glanced up. "It's no big deal. He's not usually a big drinker."

Which was a good thing, apparently.

She folded a hand across her belly, oblivious to the thoughts bouncing around my head.

"Anyhow, he'll be a great dad. I know he will. Once he's used to the idea. He likes kids."

Yeah. I've seen that too.

She crossed her legs and leaned back, and I noticed the men watching her with matching expressions of disappointment, openly eavesdropping on our conversation now.

"I'm already past the worst part of pregnancy, and I didn't even know it. How funny is that?"

"Hilarious. Hey, I know. Maybe I'll get pregnant too. You could be a pregnant grandma. Now that would be funny."

"Jaz." She uncrossed her leg and then glared at the men, not as unaware of them as she'd pretended to be. They quickly concentrated on their coffee.

"I thought you'd be a little happier, you know? You and Simon are friends. He'll be like a stepdad now."

A wave of nausea gnawed at my stomach. "He's not my stepdad." I pushed myself away from the table. I couldn't be the one to ruin everything for her. Not now. But I also couldn't make it through another minute with her.

"Listen. I meant to tell you right away that I have an English project to finish. I forgot about it, but it's pretty important and I have to get it done this weekend. Can we go shopping another day?" I stood up.

"Really?" She blinked quickly. "I mean, sure. I was hoping you'd help me pick out some maternity clothes, but yeah, I guess we can do it another time."

"I really do have to go," I said, feeling worse.

"You sure you're okay?" she asked. "You're not upset about me and Simon?"

"I'm fine. Just, you know, swamped with work." My toe tapped up and down, wanting to run.

"You like Simon, right?" Her eyes widened. Her bottom lip quivered a tiny bit. "I thought you'd be excited about a baby."

"I'll see you soon." Instead of answering, I turned from the table and bolted.

The truth was that I had liked her boyfriend. Cougar Bait I called him as a joke because of his age. Too young to be my dad. He was one of the few black people I knew, and we'd gotten along great.

Until last night.

Because last night at Marnie Loewen's party, my life had suddenly morphed into a bad imitation of *The Jerry Springer Show*.

It was Simon. Simon with his tongue down the throat of Lacey Stevens. My mom's boyfriend with my best friend. And how could I possibly tell my mom that now?

about the author

An avid reader and chronic journal writer as a teen, Janet Gurtler now lives near the Canadian Rockies with her husband and son and a little dog named Meeko. She does not live in an igloo or play hockey, but she does love maple syrup and says "eh" a lot.

She can be found online at www.janetgurtler.com and welcomes visits from all readers, especially teens!